Baijayanti Mishra's
'ABIBAHITA'
The Nameless Brook

Baijayanti Mishra's 'ABIBAHITA'
The Nameless Brook

Translated by

Jagannath Dash

BLACK EAGLE BOOKS
Dublin, USA | Bhubaneswar, India

Black Eagle Books
USA address:
7464 Wisdom Lane
Dublin, OH 43016

India address:
E/312, Trident Galaxy, Kalinga Nagar,
Bhubaneswar-751003, Odisha, India

E-mail: info@blackeaglebooks.org
Website: www.blackeaglebooks.org

First International Edition Published by
Black Eagle Books, 2025

Baijayanti Mishra's 'ABIBAHITA'
THE NAMELESS BROOK
Translated by **Jagannath Dash**

Cover & Interior Design: Ezy's Publication

ISBN- 978-1-64560-711-3 (Paperback)

Printed in the United States of America

To
The countless nurses like Jhara—
Who serve with quiet strength,
Love without conditions,
And carry the weight of the world with a smile.
Those who walk hospital corridors like warriors in white,
offering comfort in the darkest hours,
singing softly,
"Men may come, men may go, but I go on forever"

O Brook!
"What is thy dwelling?" I asked.
"Where'er thine eyes do find me,"
laughed the brook, in gleaming glee.

-Anonymous

1

Memory of childhood!
What a fragrant flower it is!
Its scent never fades, nor do its colours pale.

Forever fresh and vivid, it lingers along the chatter of kashtandi by the autumn-kissed riverbank—sometimes gleaming like a rainbow in a rain-washed sky, other times blushing like the dancing of a red rose in the cradle of a playful breeze. It comforts like the tender embrace of a spring tide, filling the heart with unspoken warmth. Ah, how it stirs—like a whirlpool spinning through the stream of consciousness, drawing us back to the waters of wonder and innocence!

It was a time when dreams soared high, reaching out to grasp the drifting clouds. A time when treasuring hailstones from an untimely downpour felt like capturing tiny miracles. My mind was like a wild brook, rushing forward without knowing its beginning or end—gliding, giggling, simply reveling in its own joy.

I was the youngest in our happy, contented family. Without questioning who loved me most, I simply believed

I was everyone's favourite. My siblings often said the house would lose its liveliness without me, and I took their words to heart. I laughed a lot—perhaps too much. Grandma would tease me, saying, "Do you know how you came into this family after two sons and two daughters? You were a flood child! We found you stuck in the backyard after a heavy downpour. I was the one who lifted you and placed you on your mother's lap." But I was not one to be easily silenced. I argued with conviction, pointing out that I was the exact replica of my father, even down to the mole beneath my lower lip. "And my hair! Thick and curly, just like Mother's," I would add triumphantly. Grandma would smile, lifting her feet and saying, "Then tell me, whose feet do yours resemble?" I would rest my head on her lap and say, "They look like my father's—but don't his feet resemble yours?"

Grandma often kept me busy with little tasks—fetching her betel case, finding her missing glasses, plucking flowers for *puja*, dusting grandpa's photograph, changing the tablecloth. She had an endless list of chores, and she assigned them to me more than to Biny Apa and Sony Apa. They dodged their share under the excuse of studies, but I found joy in household work. While others were engrossed in their books, I delighted in organizing their study tables, packing their tiffin boxes, and searching for misplaced items.

Father called me *Jhara*, meaning a brook. It was my pet name. Every evening, I eagerly awaited his return from the office. I would rush to take his bag, hand him a glass of water, put away his shoes, and neatly place the things he had brought home. Then, I would fetch his *lungi* and towel. As soon as he emerged from the washroom, I would be ready with his tea—sometimes made by Mother, sometimes by me. Perhaps this is why I became so adept at household work from an early age.

My school was just adjacent to our house, separated only by a boundary wall. From the classroom window, I could see Grandma reading the newspaper on the veranda, hear Father's scooter arriving and leaving, and even smell the spices wafting from Mother's kitchen. That scent—of fish curry in the making—was enough to stir my longing for home. I would often leave school on the pretext of a headache or stomachache, my teacher too kind to refuse me.

The only sound I could not ignore was the clanking of the gate when my eldest brother, Akash Bhai, returned from college. I knew he would insist on eating with me. "How will you eat with me if you go to a faraway school?" he would tease. "I finish my classes by 2 o'clock, but you'll return much later." Without thinking, I would reply, "Then I won't study beyond Class Three." But luck had other plans—I completed my entire schooling in that very institution.

Vikas Bhai, the second brother, was mischievous. He would pull my hair for no reason and never listened to anyone when angry. He fought often with Biny Apa and Sony Apa, especially when they reported his quarrels with other boys. Vikas Bhai, the youngest among the boys, was obsessed with cricket. So much so that he cleared his Matriculation only on his third attempt. It became my duty to look after his sports gear—his jersey, bat, ball, shoes, and socks. He needed lemon water the moment he returned home. At first, Mother prepared it for him, but later, I took up the task with pleasure.

Biny Apa and Sony Apa, though two years Apart, were inseparable. People often mistook them for twins.

They sought help from Akash Bhai in their studies but rarely confided in me. I, on the other hand, spoke to everyone about everything—except academics. My happiness lay in managing household chores rather than poring over books.

Mother sometimes worried about my lack of interest in studies. She idolized Akash Bhai, her pride and joy, and held him as an example in all matters. Truth be told, none of us matched his intelligence. He was calm, composed, and faultless. When he left for Rourkela to pursue engineering, the house lost its rhythm. Mother's eyes were swollen from crying. Father praised his achievements, and Grandma wailed for her favourite grandchild.

The evening before his departure, we all sat together for dinner. Akash Bhai counseled us—urging us to study hard, not waste Father's hard-earned money, help Mother with household work, and take care of Grandma. That day, I realised just how special he was.

After he left, an emptiness settled over our home. Mother lost interest in cooking; she no longer prepared Akash Bhai's favourite dishes. No one came up from behind to ruffle my hair or slip me a chocolate. Once, while playing in the park, I had asked him, "Will you always take me to the swings like this?" Laughing, he had promised, "Sure!" I had pointed to an old woman passing by and asked, "Even when I'm her age?" He had laughed even harder. But I had stubbornly insisted on a 'yes.'

His absence pained me. But I consoled myself and prayed for his success.

Meanwhile, something changed in Biny Apa. She became irritable, secretive, and lost in thought. She skipped meals, argued in whispers with Sony Apa, and often stayed out late. One evening, she returned home unusually late, claiming she had attended a friend's birthday party.

But Mother wasn't convinced. Her sharp eyes had been observing everything.

The atmosphere in our house shifted. Father, too, learned something from Sony Apa, and an eerie silence took over. The next day, Biny Apa did not attend college. No one told me what was happening, though I pleaded with them. In frustration, I wrote a letter to Akash Bhai.

Two days later, he returned. He attended the family meeting but remained silent about it with me. When I demanded answers, he simply said, "Nothing." I sulked, but no one paid heed.

Then, one day, Biny Apa confided in me. She had chosen someone—Chinmay Rath—as her life partner. But in our conservative family, such a choice was unacceptable. Love without parental consent was unheard of.

I met Chinmay Rath soon after. He was charming, generous, and kind. He showered me with chocolates, dolls, and storybooks. I became a willing accomplice, helping Biny Apa meet him in secret.

But secrets never remain hidden for long. One day, Sana Bhai caught us and raised an uproar. Chaos erupted. Father was furious, Mother was devastated, and I was reprimanded.

I often think about how different times are now. Today, boys and girls sit together in cafés for hours. Love is openly celebrated. But in our time, even an innocent bond was seen as a transgression.

And so, the world changed. But our past, like a fragrant flower, remains—its scent never fading, its colours never dimming.

2

The day Father decided to bring the matter to Chinmay's father, Srijay Rath, everything took a devastating turn. That day, Father returned home humiliated, his dignity crushed under the weight of another man's arrogance. It was the first time I saw the cruel pages of an incomprehensible dictionary open before me—words I had never known, emotions I had never felt, all clad in macabre features.

Outside, the sky, once rumbling and weeping, had turned eerily silent, as if Biny Apa had drained every last tear in a desperate attempt to wash away her dreams. Though I was still too young, something in me refused to stand idly by. I took an adventurous step—I went to meet Chinmay Rath.

I had always known that a garden changes with the seasons. But that day, I learned that people like Chinmay Rath were far more deceptive. Their colours shift not with time, but with convenience.

Not long ago, I had seen in him the shadow of my eldest brother. He had swung me on the cradle, handed me chocolates and ice creams, and filled my world with warmth. But now, as I stood before him, derision and disgust made it impossible for me to meet his gaze. This was the man I had connected to Biny Apa, the one I had imagined as the hero of her story. And yet, his words left indelible scratches on my heart.

He sneered. "Love doesn't mean marriage. Spending time with a girl, watching movies, chatting in quiet corners—none of it is a promise. Tell your sister she could have enjoyed it longer if she hadn't foolishly dreamt of marrying me."

A monster. That's what he became to me in that moment. My fingers itched to slap him, to strike him with my slippers until my anger was spent. But I couldn't. I turned and walked away, not knowing how I even found my way home.

There, a different storm raged. Father sat in silence, his face a mask of cold disappointment. Mother's eyes were swollen, her cheeks tear-streaked. Grandma's dim gaze held sorrow deeper than words. And Sony Apa stood mute, as if the weight of the situation had stolen her voice.

And Biny Apa—she was a shadow of herself. She moved like a ghost, unable to meet anyone's eyes. I couldn't bring myself to tell her what Chinmay had said.

A year passed, each day dragging like a sharp pebble underfoot. Father busied himself seeking a match for Biny Apa. She, in turn, barely existed. She had lost all joy, all drive—her spirit like a charred garden, lifeless and grey. She sat, ate, and slept out of necessity, not desire. She was not herself anymore. She could neither stand before Father nor muster the confidence to speak her mind.

Then, after what felt like an eternity, spring returned to her desolate garden.

New seedlings took root, new blossoms opened, and colors slowly returned. Sony Apa and I encouraged her, whispering hope into her weary heart. "Bury the dead yesterdays, Biny Apa," we told her. "The black night will end, and a new dawn will rise."

And then, it did.

Father arranged her marriage to a kind and respectable man—Professor Srikant Patnaik, a gentle and courteous teacher of Economics at a government college. Our home, once heavy with sorrow, suddenly came alive. The past was momentarily forgotten in the flurry of wedding preparations.

Bada Bhai returned from Rourkela, his presence filling the house with energy. The ring ceremony took place, and Sripanchami was set as the wedding day. Around the same time, Bada Bhai secured a job in Hyderabad—a prestigious position with a good salary. It was a time of new beginnings.

For months, heavy clouds of expectation had loomed over us during those cruel summer days of hardship. But now, they scattered, and the sky seemed brighter. I let myself dream again, plucking red and blue lilies of fancy, imagining a life ahead.

Bada Bhai smiled. "This time, you will stay with me and continue your studies," he said.

His name suited him—Akash, the vast sky. Steady and unshaken, unaffected by the storms of life. He worked tirelessly for Biny Apa's wedding, overseeing everything from decorations and catering to invitations and music.

Then came the sacred day of Sripanchami.

Our home overflowed with guests, laughter, and the fragrance of flowers. The haldi ceremony was completed, and Biny Apa sat draped in boula pata, her face glowing under the turmeric's golden hue. The shehnai played a soft, melodious tune. Aunts, neighbours, and young girls accompanied Satia ma, the barber woman, to the temple to fetch holy water.

But amidst the celebration, Biny Apa sat silent.

Her eyes, wide and fearful, carried a question she dared not ask aloud.

Was she thinking of Chinmay Rath?

Did memories of their stolen moments still haunt her?

I sat beside her and took her hand. "Biny Apa, what are you thinking? Forget that rascal," I whispered. "Listen to the shehnai—it sings of happiness. Look at Father's face—he is smiling! See Grandma, Mother, Bada Bhai—everyone is happy for you. Don't let the past steal this moment from you."

She hesitated before murmuring, "Will he come back? If someone tells him something… will he misunderstand?"

A shadow passed over her face, her turmeric-stained hands trembling in her lap.

Even now, even after all he had done, she feared his return.

I clenched my fists. "Nothing will happen, Biny Apa. Akash Bhai and I will take care of everything. I'm going to the square now to watch for the groom's arrival. I'll make sure no one says anything. Trust me."

For the first time, she leaned on me, resting her head against my shoulder. And in that moment, I knew—her strength was returning.

The groom arrived in a grand procession, his presence commanding admiration. The wedding proceeded smoothly. Srikant Bhai was as composed and kind as ever, insisting on a no-dowry marriage. He left with Biny Apa, taking nothing but his bride. In today's world, such men were rare. My head bowed in silent respect.

As Biny Apa stepped out of our home, she left behind her past. She left behind her house, her childhood, her family—and the haunting memory of a shattered dream.

Soon after, Sony Apa and I moved to Hyderabad with Bada Bhai.

For someone born in a lower-middle-class family,

stepping into such a vast city felt surreal. Some friends congratulated us, others envied us, and some simply called it luck. But we knew—this new life was possible because of Akash Bhai.

The Apartment was beautiful—a fully furnished 2BHK with a modern kitchen and a cozy living room. I gasped in amazement. "Wah! Who bought all this furniture?"

Bada Bhai chuckled. "You foolish girl, this is a furnished flat. The next tenants will use it too."

For the first time, I tasted the modern lifestyle. But beneath the glamour, I struggled.

I had pursued Science against my will, drowning in voluminous books, suffocating in competition. The professors' accents were unfamiliar, their lessons incomprehensible. Coming from an Odia-medium school, I felt like a misfit. Loneliness crept in, and an inferiority complex took root.

I missed home. I missed Grandma's betel-stained lips, Father's affectionate pat, Mother's gentle scolding, and Vikas Bhai's annoying antics.

Should I go back?

Was this struggle worth it?

Bhai was sacrificing so much for us. But was I even capable of meeting his expectations?

The full moon shone bright as we sat together, chatting. But whenever Bhai asked about my studies, the light dimmed.

My heart pounded. I concocted an excuse, a small lie to slip away.

"Everything is going well," I murmured. And with that, I vanished into the night, leaving the truth unspoken.

3

A year slipped by in deception and self-doubt, each day a struggle between guilt and survival. When the time came for the results to be published, dread settled in my bones.

Sony Apa had secured a first-class score in her semester exams. She beamed with pride, eagerly presenting her mark-sheet to Bhai, expecting his words of praise. Meanwhile, I did my best to hide my own shortcomings.

Then, out of nowhere, I declared, "I won't study anymore. I want to go back home. Mother needs help with her work, and Grandma is growing older day by day. I will take care of her and Father. Science is not for me."

Sony Apa, surprisingly, agreed. "You're right. Science is tough. If you're not comfortable, there's no point forcing it," she said, sensing my distress. She dropped a few hints to Bhai, and I remained hopeful. Perhaps he would understand. Maybe he would ask me to pursue a different course instead, at least for a year. After all, Sony Apa had one more year left in Hyderabad, and I hated the thought of leaving her alone.

But Bhai was unyielding. His voice was firm, his decision absolute.

"You will study science. You will become a doctor."

Sony Apa burst into laughter. But I stood frozen. Me? A doctor? The thought was so absurd, so far removed from reality, that it left me dizzy. I felt feverish without a fever, restless without reason.

This vast city, this intimidating college, the classmates who neither spoke my language nor understood my fears—everything blended into one overwhelming experience. I was suffocating under the weight of expectations. And worst of all, for the first time in my life, a wall had risen between my brother and me. The bond we shared—the love I held dearer than life itself—stood on the other side of this impenetrable barrier.

And so, I cursed my fate. I cursed God.

Then came a sliver of relief—summer vacation. Just like in Odisha, Hyderabad also had its break. This year, the exams had been internal, and failing a subject or two wouldn't prevent my promotion to the next year. Bhai didn't know this. I had lied, telling him I hadn't received my marksheet.

Sony Apa's vacation lasted only a month, but the mere thought of returning home filled me with excitement. We packed our bags with giddy anticipation—everything except my books. I had made up my mind. I wasn't coming back.

Let my education end here. Enough was enough.

Bhai himself had mentioned a two-month training out of town. It was the perfect opportunity. Before leaving, I wandered through Hyderabad, visiting Charminar, Dolardani, and Snow World, savouring every moment as if bidding farewell to the city. We feasted on delicious meals, and for once, I forgot my burdens. Bhai had never deprived us of anything. He had given us everything—except the freedom to choose our own paths.

That evening, as Bhai returned from work, we eagerly announced our plans. "Bhai, book our tickets to Odisha," we said.

His expression darkened.

Two days ago, he had agreed. But now, his voice held a new firmness, a finality I had never encountered before.

"No," he said.

The single word sent shivers down my spine. He handed me the mark sheet he had collected from my college.

I stood there trembling, like a criminal caught red-handed.

Our plans were ruined. There would be no trip to Odisha. Instead, Bhai arranged for a private tutor, taking my education into his own hands. No matter how exhausted he was after work, he sat with me every evening, ensuring I studied under his watchful eye. His dedication astounded me. He wasn't just determined to educate me—he was determined to make me self-reliant.

Perhaps he sensed our disappointment because, shortly after, he did something unexpected.

He called Mother and Grandma to Hyderabad.

The moment they arrived, our small rented house overflowed with warmth and joy. It was their first visit to a big city, and their excitement was infectious. Mother and Grandma marvelled at the towering buildings, the dazzling shopping centres, the endless sea of people. Their laughter filled every corner of our home.

We three siblings cherished every moment. Mother's cooking brought back the comfort of home. We spent hours on the terrace, chatting, reminiscing, and watching the city lights flicker like distant stars.

Sometimes, Grandma would doze off mid-conversation, lulled by the cool evening breeze. I would place my head on her lap, gazing up at the moonlit sky.

"Look, Mother," I whispered. "The same moon shines over our home in Odisha. Right now, it must be peeking through the window of Vikas Bhai's hostel, casting silver beams over Biny Apa's courtyard. It watches over us all, storing our thoughts and secrets with quiet tenderness."

Sony Apa chuckled. "You should have studied philosophy instead of science."

As if waiting for the perfect moment, Bhai interjected. "Jhara, you've wasted enough time. Go and study. Your tutor starts tomorrow."

Grandma, half-asleep, muttered in her dreamy voice, "Why spend so much money on their studies? Just get them married instead."

Sony Apa and I gasped in horror. "No! No! No!"

And just like that, laughter burst through the walls of our home, washing away, for a moment, the silent war between duty and desire.

4

One day, Vikas Bhai arrived unexpectedly. He had been selected as a state player and had come to Hyderabad for a tournament. After the event, Bada Bhai had asked him to stay with us for a few days before returning.

A few days later, Father arrived as well, intending to take Mother back home. Bhai, however, insisted that Grandma stay a little longer.

Though we had been in Hyderabad for a year, we had rarely visited our neighbours. Then, one day, a get-together was arranged at our 'Visual Apartment,' bringing all the residents together. Mother and Grandma were reluctant to attend, but Bhai was not the kind of person to take no for an answer. And so, all of us went.

The evening was lively, filled with music and laughter. Grandma, watching the performances with childlike wonder, kept murmuring, "It's only because of Akash that we came here and got to witness such beautiful things. Otherwise, how would we have ever seen all this?"

Seated behind us were a mother and daughter. Hearing us speak, the woman leaned forward and asked, "Are you Odias?"

I nodded.

A spark of familiarity lit up her face, and soon, Grandma and she were deep in conversation. It was there, in that very hall, that we learned six Odia families lived nearby. Grandma wasted no time in collecting their contact numbers.

As the feast and entertainment came to an end, we bid our newfound Odia friends farewell, wishing each other the best. I noticed how unusually cheerful Grandma was.

Before we could even visit the mother and daughter's home, they arrived at ours. The daughter, Gouri, was strikingly beautiful. She had recently joined an insurance company and was eager to know more about Hyderabad, since we had been here longer. Her mother, a warm and sociable woman, had no one but Gouri. She had chosen to stay with her daughter, unable to bear the thought of her living alone in a distant city.

In no time, our families grew close.

Vikas Bhai, too, seemed to enjoy himself so much that he cancelled his return ticket, deciding to stay longer. Mother, however, returned home with Father, leaving just the four of us behind.

Then, one day, out of the blue, Vikas Bhai announced that he had landed a job through a walk-in interview. It should have been a joyous moment—but that night, he returned home reeking of alcohol.

Perhaps he had celebrated a little too much.

Disgust settled in the pit of my stomach as the sharp stench of liquor clung to the air around him. He stumbled to bed without a word, falling into a deep, oblivious sleep.

Bhai noticed, but said nothing. He merely turned away, choosing to let the matter rest for the night.

Lying in bed, I found myself comparing the two brothers—one as vast and composed as the open sky, the other stubborn and tempestuous. Vikas Bhai's presence at home felt like an impending storm.

Man proposes, God disposes.

Vikas Bhai joined the company, but the salary was modest. Renting a separate house was out of the question, so he continued staying with us. During holidays, he was still drawn to the cricket field, spending hours playing matches. After office hours, he lingered with friends, chatting late into the night.

And sometimes, he returned home drunk.

If that weren't enough, he had picked up a gutkha habit. His pockets were always stuffed with pouches of it, and no amount of persuasion could make him quit. He never listened to anyone. Instead, he expected everything to be done for him—his clothes washed, his meals prepared exactly to his liking.

The slightest deviation from his expectations would stir up an argument.

At times, life with him was unbearably difficult.

Some nights, he would bring his friends home after dinner and demand that food be served. We had no choice but to cook while fighting off sleep, our exhausted hands moving over the stove in the dead of night.

It was as if a storm had been trapped within the walls of our home—a quiet, relentless turmoil that refused to settle.

5

Grandma's fondness for Akash Bhai was as deep as her disappointment in Vikas Bhai. She often tried to counsel him, but her words fell on deaf ears. Then, one day, Vikas Bhai returned home bearing bad news—he had been retrenched. He hadn't even completed a year in the job. Just as suddenly as he had found it, he had lost it. We were taken aback.

That evening, when Akash Bhai came home from the office, his face was unusually grave. A sum of two lakh rupees had to be deposited in the company's account—Vikas Bhai had been accused of theft. The weight of those words crushed the air from the room. We sat there, stunned, while Vikas Bhai silently walked out.

We assumed he would return after drinking, as he often did. But that night, he didn't. For the first time, we felt the endless stretch of a night, its vast emptiness filled with the echoes of silence. We waited, burning the midnight oil, hoping for the sound of his footsteps, the creak of the door—anything. But he never came back.

The next day, Akash Bhai did everything he could to find him, but his search yielded nothing. A month passed. The once lively home turned into a zone of silence, haunted by the absence of a brother. The matter had reached our parents, and we could only imagine the torment they were enduring.

Grandma, in her unwavering faith, lit a lamp before the deity every evening, shedding silent tears as she fed Akash Bhai with her own hands. Stroking his head gently, she whispered, "He will come back. I can feel it in my heart. Wherever he is, he is safe." The glow of the lamp mirrored the undying hope in her eyes. Though she often scolded Vikas Bhai, calling him a wayward soul, the tenderness in her voice betrayed her annoyance.

As time passed, life at home slowly regained a semblance of normalcy. News of Akash Bhai's promotion and Sony Apa's excellent academic performance lifted our spirits. Yet, the wounds left by Vikas Bhai's disappearance remained unhealed.

Not all dreams come true. I had failed the entrance exam, dashing Akash Bhai's hopes of me pursuing medicine. Still, he wasted no time and enrolled me in a nursing school. Twenty-five days remained before classes began, so we—Grandma, Sony Apa, and I—planned a visit to Odisha. Meanwhile, Biny Apa called, inviting us to Vizag for a short stay.

Akash Bhai was reluctant to let Grandma go, but she seemed anxious to return home. Perhaps she sensed something about Father's deteriorating health. Before we left, Bhai meticulously packed gifts for everyone—Father, Mother, Biny Apa, and Srikant Bhai. Watching him, I felt the depth of his love, an immeasurable force binding us together. In my heart, I prayed to be his sister in every lifetime.

Sony Apa and I exchanged glances as we saw Grandma secretly wiping her tears. No one could truly grasp what it was about Bhai that tethered us so tightly to him. She fussed over him as always, reminding him to eat on time, to take care of himself.

Biny Apa and Srikant Bhai met us at Vizag station. Their happiness was contagious, and the love between them was evident in the way he cared for her. Not just for her, but for all of us. We stepped into Biny Apa's home for the first time, and her impeccable housekeeping left us in awe. Grandma, always playful, teased them both, and in doing so, stumbled upon a delightful secret—soon, there would be a new member in the family.

That night, we sat up chatting for hours. Srikant Bhai insisted on serving us ice cream for the third time. When I refused, he joked, "You had plenty with Biny Apa and Chinmay Rath before. Why not now?"

His words jolted me like an electric shock. I looked at Biny Apa, whose bright eyes held a wealth of unspoken emotions. Srikant Bhai knew about Chinmay Rath. Yet, he never let it taint their relationship. His love for her was unwavering, his heart magnanimous.

Three days passed in a blur of happiness. Could people, who weren't bound by blood, still be so dear, so intimate? As I pondered this, I realised something—Srikant Bhai, in many ways, reminded me of Akash Bhai.

And yet, amidst all the joy, a single shadow loomed over us—Vikas Bhai. Where was he? Did he never think of us—our parents, our siblings, even Grandma? How could he stay away, indifferent, when we spent every waking moment worrying about him?

Back home, we found Mother drained and lifeless, and Father looked like he had aged years in mere months. Mother muttered bitterly that Vikas had stolen all their happiness, leaving them to drag out the rest of their lives in silent suffering. She had taken to worshipping and fasting, praying desperately for his return.

Meanwhile, good marriage proposals came for Sony

Apa, but Akash Bhai refused them all. He wanted her to secure a job first. Father, on the other hand, longed to see her settled before his health worsened.

Our parents, weary of a rented life, decided to return to the village after Father's retirement. Their only pillar of strength was Akash Bhai. They consulted him in everything.

Grandma, however, refused to leave this time. Perhaps she, too, wanted to stay by Father's side as his health declined.

As the holiday drew to an end, my heart grew heavy. I had to return to Hyderabad to begin my nursing course—another daunting challenge. Nervous, I confided in Mother. She reassured me with quiet conviction, "Your brother has chosen this for you, which means it must be good. Besides, nursing is a noble service. Think of it as God's blessing."

Her words settled in my heart. If I couldn't be a doctor, I could still serve the sick. That, too, was a purpose worth embracing.

Two days before our departure, a surprise shook us all—Vikas Bhai returned, and with him, Gouri. He had married her in a temple.

Father remained silent, his pride wounded by the disregard for tradition. Mother wept quietly. Only Grandma voiced her discontent, delivering a sharp but loving rebuke.

We couldn't arrange a formal reception. Gouri, however, humbly touched the feet of the elders, seeking their blessings. Despite the whispers and gossip of the neighbourhood, our house buzzed with visitors eager to meet the new bride. Somehow, amidst the murmurs of criticism, Vikas Bhai's disgrace—his job loss, the theft accusation—was momentarily forgotten.

He knew well enough that the family's faith lay entirely in Akash Bhai. And yet, he conveniently omitted the fact that it was Akash Bhai who had helped clear his name. It didn't surprise us. Bhai never spoke of his deeds, never sought recognition.

Only Gouri and her mother knew the truth. Watching Gouri, I wondered—what was it about Vikas Bhai that had drawn her to him?

Before long, we—Biny Apa, Sony Apa, and I—returned to Hyderabad as scheduled. Vikas Bhai and Gouri stayed behind a little longer.

I joined my nursing course, and though it was a new field, my science background proved useful. Sony Apa became engrossed in her new project, which required frequent travel. Meanwhile, the family's focus shifted to Akash Bhai's marriage. But he, ever selfless, refused to settle down until Sony Apa was married.

We kept in touch with home through phone calls. Mother, in a rare moment of contentment, spoke highly of Gouri. Jokingly, I said, "She's on a one-month trial. Let's see if she stays this good." But Mother was all praise for her.

Her mother would come to our house in the evening hours with her hand-made cakes and curries. Could Gouri Bhauja be assessed from her mother's behaviour?

But deep down, I wondered—was Gouri truly different? Only time would tell.

6

How swiftly time's chariot moves! Days and months slipped by, carrying with them the ebb and flow of life. Then came the joyous news—Biny Apa had given birth to a baby boy. A new life, a new joy! A new bond!

I could stay with her for only two days, as my exams loomed ahead. Yet, in those fleeting moments, I marvelled at the tiny miracle before me—his delicate hands and feet, his soft, rosy skin, the hairless head with its throbbing crown, the small fingers that curled around mine. Holding him in my lap was unlike anything I had ever felt before. It was as if I cradled the world's most precious doll, but this one breathed, squirmed, and filled our hearts with an indescribable warmth.

Biny Apa and Srikant Bhai were radiant with happiness. Biny Apa, especially, couldn't take her eyes off her son. It reminded us of our childhood, of the times we fought over a doll. But this doll was hers alone. I had no right to claim him, though for those two days, I exercised my privilege as an aunt. I ran my cheek against his soft hands and feet, and when my lap was warmed by his tiny accident, I felt strangely elated.

"Jhara, you must come after your exams," Biny Apa urged, her voice tender with affection. "Your nephew will miss you."

Feigning annoyance, I replied, "Don't think you have

all the rights over him just because you gave birth to him. He's not just my nephew—he's my son!"

Srikant Bhai chuckled as we playfully argued over the baby, the room filled with laughter and love.

Two days passed too quickly. I left, but his adorable face followed me everywhere. Whenever I had a holiday, I didn't go to my parents—I went to Vizag, drawn irresistibly to that little soul.

Akash Bhai, the ever guardian of our futures, never forgot to remind me, "This is the age of competition. If you don't score well, you won't get a good posting."

But I was caught in a tug-of-war between my studies and my attachment to Biny Apa's home. My visits to my parents became infrequent. Mother sulked, her voice laced with longing whenever she spoke on the phone.

"Jhara, have you forgotten us?" she asked, her tone carrying both affection and reproach.

Back in Hyderabad, life had taken its own course. Gouri Bhauja had rejoined her job but visited us occasionally. She mostly stayed with her mother, which Grandma didn't mind. Grandma herself refused to come to Hyderabad anymore—she didn't want to become a burden at this age.

Gouri Bhauja, however, insisted that our parents move to Hyderabad, pleading with them with all sincerity. But they always postponed the decision, saying they would come later. Still, it was evident that they were deeply pleased with Gouri Bhauja. She had won everyone over with her warmth and humility. Even Vikas Bhai seemed to be changing under her influence.

Then, like a sudden storm, news arrived—Sony Apa's marriage had been fixed. One of Father's friends had helped arrange the match. Initially, she resisted, but Father had already given his word, and she eventually relented.

Akash Bhai, as always, had done his research. The groom was an IT engineer based in Chennai. Fortunately, he, like Srikant Bhai, had no demand for dowry. He wanted Sony Apa to continue working in Chennai once her project was completed.

The preparations began in full swing. Akash Bhai, along with Vikas Bhai and Gouri Bhauja, took charge of everything. The wedding happened swiftly, almost in the blink of an eye.

After the ceremony, Sony Apa stayed with us in Hyderabad for three to four months. But marriage didn't seem to change her. She remained as she was—practical, composed, and focused. No sentimentality, no dreamy glances at the past. She was always busy with her laptop, lost in work.

If Praveer Bhai called, she would keep the conversation brief before returning to her tasks. One day, I teased her.

"Sony Apa, you're not romantic at all! You just got married, stayed with your husband for only fifteen days, and now you barely speak to him. If I were you, I would have left everything and run away with my husband."

She smiled, shaking her head. "Oh really? Could you leave your studies behind? Listen, foolish girl, in today's world, sentimentality has no place. Without a career, there's no progress."

I found myself comparing my two sisters—one, completely immersed in the joys of her home and child; the other, determined to carve out her own space in the world.

Biny Apa was a devoted homemaker, content with her family. Sony Apa was ambitious, striving for success and independence.

Time slipped away like water held in cupped palms.

Finally, I completed my nursing course. My studies

were over, but Akash Bhai kept reminding me, "You must keep practicing. Skill is everything."

I devoted myself to my work, pouring my heart and soul into it. I nursed patients of all ages, from tiny infants to frail elders. And in doing so, I learned a profound truth—human beings are utterly helpless in the face of illness.

The wealthy can afford the best treatments, clinging to science and medicine. The poor, however, place their faith entirely in God, waiting for either recovery or the inevitable.

Draped in my white uniform, I felt myself growing stronger each day. The timid girl who once feared pulling out a thorn with a safety pin was now assisting surgeons in the operation theatre.

But the greatest realisation was this—I wasn't just a nurse. I was a source of comfort. Patients valued my patience, my care, and my gentle words. My duty didn't end at the hospital doors. At home, too, I became a quiet pillar of support.

With an open heart and a spirit of giving, I loved and cared for everyone around me. And in that love, I found my own strength.

7

Bhai's wedding was fast approaching. He was the backbone of our family, and we all knew it. Gouri Bhauja had also become an integral part of our lives. The way she managed the household made us realise she was far more capable than Vikas Bhai. But it wasn't just about running the house—she had a deep respect for Father, Mother, Brother, Biny Apa, and Sony Apa. Her mother had raised her well.

With quiet determination, she was trying to bring a change in Vikas Bhai, handling his whims with incredible patience. He never stayed in one job for long—sometimes he quit, feeling slighted by his boss, other times he left because the work was too demanding. But Gouri Bhauja never complained. Instead, she managed every situation with such composure that no issues arose.

Then came the marriage proposal for Akash Bhai, brought by our uncle—Mother's brother. Father and Mother went to meet the girl, and she was to their liking. Akash Bhai, well-established, qualified, and handsome, never once questioned their choice. In fact, anyone would have chosen Jaya Bhauja without hesitation. Bhai wasn't entirely satisfied with her level of education, but as always, he remained silent, accepting their decision as if he had been born only to make others happy.

And so, Jaya Bhauja entered our family. Everyone who

saw her had nothing but praise—she was calm, courteous, and soft-spoken. Gouri Bhauja, brimming with excitement, took on the role of the elder daughter-in-law, even though she was the younger one. She spent the entire day looking after Jaya Bhauja, ensuring she was comfortable.

I noticed how Akash Bhai, whom I loved more than myself, stole sidelong glances at his new bride. Teasing him, I asked, "So, Bhai, what do you think of Uncle's choice?"

He smiled faintly, then evaded the question. "Looks aren't everything," he said. "What truly matters is how well she wins over all of you. If she does, she'll have me, too."

Grandma, pleased by his words, patted his head and said, "Why wouldn't she be good?"

Her confidence was unwavering.

Father, now relieved that almost all his responsibilities were fulfilled, would often say, "Only one remains—Jhara's marriage. Then, I can finally rest."

Hearing this, Vikas Bhai suddenly appeared, playfully tugging at my braid. "Why don't you charm a doctor, so we can all be at peace?"

From a distance, Gouri Bhauja quipped, "Not everyone is like you."

Bada Bhai smiled. Grandma, chuckling, said to Vikas Bhai, "Whatever you are, you still managed to steal a piece of diamond."

Mother's eyes gleamed with satisfaction as she looked at her two daughters-in-law.

Our days were filled with boundless joy, with the laughter of my sisters, brothers-in-law, and my darling nephew echoing through our home. But soon, we had to return, as Akash Bhai's leave was ending. Gouri Bhauja came back with us.

For reasons unknown, Mother's eyes welled up as

Gouri Bhauja prepared to leave. She had been busy until the very last moment, making sure Grandma's betel case was stocked, Father's medicine was set out with a glass of water, and dinner was prepared in advance. She never stopped. She cleaned the kitchen and storeroom, separated stones from the rice and dal, pressed Grandma's and Father's clothes, and watered the withering plants in the garden.

She was flawless.

Grandma often joked with Vikas Bhai, saying, "A monkey wearing a garland of pearls."

I bowed down before Gouri Bhauja in admiration. It was she who ensured gifts and clothes were sent to our sisters' homes, relieving Father of such responsibilities. Despite her young age, she carried an immense sense of duty.

Back in Hyderabad, our routine resumed. Gouri Bhauja immersed herself in work, while I returned to my duties at the hospital. But I managed to convince Biny Apa to stay with us for a while, along with my darling nephew. I had become more possessive over the baby than even she was. After returning from my hospital shifts, I would play with him endlessly, delighting in his laughter and cries.

Sometimes, over the phone, I pestered Sony Apa. "Apa, don't you think it's time you had a daughter?"

She responded bluntly, "Why? Get married yourself, and you'll have one."

But I wasn't one to let her off so easily. Laughing, I retorted, "Just wait. Not one or two — I'll have half a dozen!"

Though I said it in jest, in the quiet moments of my solitude, I often wondered — would I, too, get married? Would I leave my brother's house and have a home of my own? Would my brother's heart ache when the time came to bid me farewell? I felt he loved me even more than he loved Biny Apa and Sony Apa.

For now, Akash Bhai left Jaya Bhauja at home with Father and Mother for a month. He believed it was her first opportunity to serve the elders and earn their blessings. "Missing such a chance," he had said, "is like missing a lifetime opportunity."

Jaya Bhauja was different. She hadn't grown up in a city like Gouri Bhauja, nor was she as educated. Gouri Bhauja had lost her father early in life, and her mother had raised her alone, instilling resilience and self-reliance in her. She had been accustomed to responsibilities from a young age. Marrying someone as unpredictable as Vikas Bhai and balancing a job while managing a household—her life had been no less than a test of endurance.

She was a role model. There was so much to learn from her.

A month later, Jaya Bhauja returned to Hyderabad. I called home to check on her, but while Father and Mother remained silent, Grandma sighed, "Not like Gouri."

The words stung.

I recalled Akash Bhai's remark: *She can win me if she wins over all of you.*

But then I consoled myself. Most newly married women take time to adjust. Not everyone wins hearts instantly.

When she arrived, everything in Bhai's well-furnished house felt new to her. She had only ever seen Cuttack and Bhubaneswar. Once, at the dining table, Bhai remarked, "Jhara, your Bhauja has a lot to learn. She hasn't picked up much yet. Maybe you could ask Gouri to stay here for a while and teach her."

It sounded reasonable, but I doubted if Gouri Bhauja would leave her mother alone.

Surprisingly, she agreed. Her mother, with her characteristic selflessness, assured us, "I'll manage. Gouri should stay and help."

Gouri Bhauja had one advantage—her office was on the way to her mother's house, so she could check on her daily.

She came, and as expected, she handled everything flawlessly. Whether it was marketing, cooking, or laundry, she did it all—always with a smile, never a complaint. She had mastered the art of suppressing her own troubles for the sake of others.

But Jaya Bhauja remained distant—silent, reserved, emotionless. No interest, no excitement, no inclination to help.

Even after Gouri Bhauja returned home, she continued to send food for us every Sunday, coming with Vikas Bhai and preparing Bhai's favourite dishes. We praised her endlessly, but Vikas Bhai, the miser of words, never acknowledged her efforts. A grumpy fellow—always ordering, always demanding.

And then, news arrived—Akash Bhai had been promoted. We were thrilled. That day, he took Jaya Bhauja to the temple, bought sarees for her, for Gouri Bhauja, and for me. But her reaction was blank, as if it was nothing special.

In her absence, Bhai sighed and said, "Jhara, she's not what I hoped for."

My heart clenched at his words. I had never expected to hear something like that from him. With what grief, he mustn't have said that!

And so, fate took its course.

Jaya Bhauja never seemed to form any real bond with our family. Biny Apa and Sony Apa kept their distance, and even I, living under the same roof, could sense her discomfort with anyone's presence—except for Akash Bhai's. Gouri Bhauja had once tried to bridge the gap, hoping to draw her closer to us. But in the end, Jaya Bhauja belonged to no one, nor could she truly accept anyone as her own.

We received a message from home that Baba was unwell. Concerned, Akash Bhai asked Vikas Bhai to bring him to Hyderabad. When he arrived, he looked terribly frail. Bhai immediately admitted him to Apollo Hospital and took charge of every detail—tests, doctors, bills—everything.

Vikas Bhai, Gouri Bhauja, and I visited Baba regularly. Biny Apa and Sony Apa also came to be by his side. But Jaya Bhauja remained untouched by it all. While the rest of us were anxious and emotionally drained, she spent hours chatting with her parents on the phone, as if nothing had happened.

It hurt me deeply. Had this been Vikas Bhai's wife, perhaps I could've dismissed it as expected. But Akash Bhai—the soul of our family, the quiet strength we all leaned on—deserved better. He had always carried the weight of everyone's happiness. Why was he fated to live with such indifference?

I felt a surge of resentment toward the uncle who had reassured our mother years ago, saying, *"Village girls are always better. She's even completed her Plus Three. She'll be obedient. Can a working girl ever manage your household? Will she ever take care of you or Akash?"* How naïve my parents had been. Relying on his words, they had unknowingly handed Akash Bhai a life of silent suffering.

With treatment, Baba's health improved. But his heart—perhaps weary of the emotional coldness around him—grew restless. Though Bhai pleaded with him to stay longer in Hyderabad, Baba remained firm. Maybe he didn't want to let his wounded heart bleed any further in our presence.

He stayed only a day more. Jaya Bhauja showed no tenderness, no concern. Even Gouri Bhauja tried to reason with him, to convince him to stay. But Baba refused to bend. He quietly asked Vikas Bhai to take him back to the village.

Desperate, I pleaded, "Baba, I'm your daughter—a nurse. If I cannot serve you now, what meaning does my profession hold? Let me care for you. I will carry that debt in my heart forever. Please, don't deny me this privilege."

But he had made up his mind. No words could sway him.

I remembered how, in my childhood, he would call out, "Jhara, Jhara!" the moment he returned from the office, wanting me close by to carry out his little errands. And today—he refuses even my help. Have I become a stranger to him so suddenly?

Perhaps he sensed that Jaya Bhauja's cold indifference—watching Gouri Bhauja and me tending to him—might wound Akash Bhai. Maybe that's why he quietly returned to the village, never once looking back. We stood there, eyes brimming with tears.

Jaya Bhauja had said, "Father couldn't build a house in the city despite working here for years. In a critical condition, anything could happen while bringing him to the hospital from this far."

Our suppressed emotions began to stir and spill over. By then, Bhai had already left for the station with our father.

I didn't like staying with Jaya Bhauja, but I had no choice. Bhai didn't allow me to stay in the nursing hostel, even though I often lingered there under the guise of duty.

My days passed in the hospital—among friends, among patients. While caring for them, I saw glimpses of my grandmother, my parents, my siblings. I ached for them. Often, I longed to return to their world.

Memory is tethered tightly to tears. They fall on their own, needing no reason. That day, I had dozed off in the Duty Room. Two streaks of tears had washed away my collyrium, leaving dark trails down my cheeks. I startled awake to the voice of Dr. Ayush calling my name.

He needed the patient file from Cabin Number 9. I quickly handed it to him and followed him to the bedside, noting down his prescriptions as he spoke.

On our way back, he asked, "Sister, may I ask you something—if you don't mind?"

"Oh, not at all, sir. Please go ahead."

"I've noticed most nurses rush back to their rooms the moment duty ends. But you… you stay back. Why is that?"

I didn't know what to say. It didn't feel right to speak of family troubles. So, I simply replied, "Sir, in our profession, duty never really ends. I only leave when there's real urgency."

He seemed surprised. That day, we spoke for a while. Somewhere in the middle of our conversation, he remarked that I looked unhappy.

He wasn't wrong. But I smiled, brushing it aside with a practiced look—pretending everything was fine.

8

Mother informed us over the phone that Father's condition had worsened. Vikas Bhai was away on an official tour. Without a second thought, Bhai, Gouri Bhauja, and I decided to leave for the village immediately. Jaya Bhauja showed no interest, but on Bhai's insistence, she reluctantly prepared to join us. Bhai's face was pale, his worry evident in his silence. I could understand his turmoil—poor fellow! He swallowed his despair like Nilakantha, the God of gods, who consumed poison to save the world.

But we were too late. By the time we reached home, Father was gone. The house was already filling with mourners, and the sight of Mother and Grandma was unbearable. Their grief was beyond control.

Father's face was almost unrecognisable. I couldn't comprehend how it had all happened so suddenly. No one had warned us about the severity of his condition. What is the use of having so many children if, in the end, a father must leave this world unseen, unattended? He had done everything for us with his meager income. Yet, Mother told us that he had forbidden her from informing us earlier. The same old words—"Why trouble the children?"

Was this why he had avoided looking back even once while leaving Hyderabad? At the very least, he shouldn't have been indifferent to Akash Bhai. Why had he severed ties with him, just as he had with Bhauja?

Father's frail body seemed to have merged with the mattress. Mother and Grandma, too, looked emaciated, as if they had been ailing alongside him. The entire family—my sisters, brothers-in-law—sat around him, motionless and speechless, like trees uprooted by a storm.

The house was full of people, yet it felt emptier than ever.

All the rituals were completed. Just a few days ago, this very house had witnessed celebrations. The wedding decorations of Akash Bhai and Jaya Bhauja still adorned the walls—the painted banana tree with its hanging cluster, the earthen pot, the kalasa, and the marriage altar. And now, the same house had become the site of funeral rites. The principal figure who had orchestrated our lives had now left us forever. We were his family, his children—yet, how unfortunate we were! We couldn't do anything for him. He had never neglected us, whether it was our education, our health, or our financial needs. But what had we given him in return?

Was he lying there, silent, meditating on the bed, preparing to leave this world alone?

Grandma had become a shadow of herself. She had lost her husband, and now her son—the only solace in her old age—was gone. She had shared her love with us, but how would she survive without him? Her lips trembled, her frail body shook as she whispered something incoherent. But one thing was clear—she was preparing to fade away. The one who should have carried her to her funeral pyre had left before her. She had lived to see this cruel reversal of fate.

How swiftly life changes! In just one day, our world

had turned upside down. The bright vermillion mark on Mother's forehead disappeared. The bangles that once adorned her hands were gone. She had never worn gold—only glass bangles. If she ever had a costly saree, she would save it for her daughters. Her only joy had been in our happiness. Food and clothing had never interested her.

With tears in her eyes, Gouri Bhauja performed all the necessary rituals. The funeral rites were completed with everyone's cooperation.

We often recalled Father—his sacrifices, his sincerity, the values he instilled in us. Once, we had relied on him for everything, following his decisions with humility. But as children grow up, they fly away, like fledglings leaving the nest. Parents spend their entire lives carrying the weight of their children, yet when they grow old, their children have little patience to bear their burdens.

Bhai couldn't bear the thought of leaving Mother and Grandma alone in the village. But, like Father, Mother refused to come to Hyderabad. When we pleaded with her, Bhauja remained silent. Not once did she offer a word of comfort. I often wondered—what kind of person was she?

In the end, it was Gouri Bhauja who made the decision. She packed up their belongings, and despite their resistance, they had to yield.

Mother's world collapsed. She was too numb to comprehend the changes around her. Handing the house keys to our neighbour, Meera Bhauja, we left for Hyderabad. For some reason, it felt as if we had abandoned the house forever, as if it no longer belonged to us. Father, the house, the garden—everything was now just a memory. As we drove past the village deity's shrine, a strange feeling gripped me—as though we had left Father behind in that closed house.

Time passed, bringing many changes. Mother and Grandma stayed with Gouri Bhauja. I was helpless, left in Bhai's house, where Jaya Bhauja ruled. And as time went on, her reign became unbearable. She became irritable over trivial matters, dissatisfied no matter how hard I worked. I felt like a burden to her. I had read about such women in books, seen them in films—women who could "make or break a family."

I couldn't leave Bhai, but I also couldn't confide in Mother, not wanting to add to her grief. So, I suffered in silence.

Bhai was searching for a suitable match for me. If someone could be finalised before Father's anniversary, my marriage would take place within a year. He often invited friends and acquaintances home, but Bhauja disliked it. She would conveniently leave the house. She wouldn't even exchange a few courteous words with them. If I was such a burden, then it was better that I got married and left the house.

She couldn't tolerate Bhai's affection for us. He would visit Mother and Grandma often, buy them medicines, sit and talk with them. But each time he returned home, he faced a storm—silent at first, then explosive. The door would slam. Her voice would rise, drowning out his.

Some nights, I would go to bed with nothing but a glass of water, leaving my untouched dinner in the refrigerator. Lying in bed, I would think about my god-like brother. Who could I share my pain with? Not Mother— she was already drowning in grief.

Sometimes, I thought of calling Biny Apa. But from the other end, I would hear her cheerful voice:

"The baby keeps troubling me! He's going to be as

smart as his father. Your Bhai got me diamond earrings for our anniversary!"

How could I burden her with my sorrows?

I tried Sony Apa. A sleepy voice answered:

"Jhara, haven't you slept yet? I have a presentation tomorrow. I'll call you later, okay?"

My throat tightened. Who else could I talk to?

I longed to pour my heart out to Mother, but how could I? How could someone drowning in the rain shelter me with an umbrella?

When I heard Mother say, "Gouri is such a good girl. She takes such care of us," my heart found a little relief. At least, let her remaining days be peaceful.

But I had to return—to Bhauja's pinching remarks, to her storms over the smallest things. She hated Gouri Bhauja, hated even the smallest kindness I showed Bhai. If I cooked his favourite dish, she would make a scene. I couldn't do anything without her permission.

And Bhai—he had become a shadow of himself. The brother I had once been so close to now felt distant, unreachable.

I buried myself in work to escape.

Then, one night at the hospital, I forgot to bring my dinner. I was looking toward the canteen when a voice startled me:

"Hey, Jharana, forgot your dinner?"

I turned to see Dr. Ayush.

A bit shrunken, I murmured, "Yes, sir, I forgot in my haste."

Without a word, he turned and left abruptly. A wave of unease swept over me. Hadn't he gone to the canteen? Why should he trouble himself for me? Moments later, he returned, placing a tiffin box on my table.

"Eat," he said firmly.

"But sir, what about you?"

"Don't worry. Mother packed plenty. I've already finished one container."

Out of shame and gratitude, I lowered my gaze. By the time I looked up, he had already left. With no choice, I ate. Afterward, I washed the tiffin box and went to return it, struggling to find the right words to thank him.

He gestured for me to sit beside him. His generosity overwhelmed me. Then, with a teasing smile, he said, "Jharana, you know it's a custom not to return a tiffin box empty."

I hesitated, unsure whether to take his words seriously, but he laughed and waved it off. As the conversation deepened, he asked about my family—the people I lived with, our struggles.

It was then I realised he hadn't known about my father's passing. He had been out of the headquarters for two months. When I told him, his face darkened with sympathy. "Jharana," he said gently, "prosperity and adversity, like day and night, are two sides of the same coin. After the darkest night, morning always comes. We have to endure."

His words struck a chord deep within me. He was the first person, after Akash Bhai, who could read my face, sense my burdens without my saying a word. Dr. Ayush was known as a compassionate doctor—wise beyond his years, selfless, and untainted by greed. Patients revered him as a living god.

Being around him gave me comfort. His kind words filled the hollowness in my heart. He understood me in a way no one else did.

One day, he took me to his house, introducing me to

his mother. She was as warm and affectionate as he was. Our bond deepened. Later, I invited him to Gouri Bhauja's house, introducing him to my family—my brothers, my mother, my grandmother.

Life is strange. It brings together souls from different worlds, binding them in ways beyond comprehension. How does someone, unrelated by blood, become more than family? I often wondered how I would have endured my silent sufferings without him.

Yes, I was a nurse, and assisting him was my duty. But his presence, his care—it was an elixir to my parched soul. With him, I momentarily forgot my loneliness, my struggles. Perhaps, this was the reason fate had placed me here.

It wasn't just me—my entire family had come to admire him. He became our guiding light. My sisters, brothers-in-law, and relatives turned to him for medical care, trusting him implicitly. He was not just a doctor; he was our guardian.

His parents' care and kindness pulled me to their home time and again. In him, I saw the father I had lost. Comparing the shattered state of my own family with his well-disciplined, happy one, an ache settled deep in my chest.

Then, one night, the phone rang.

At the other end, Gouri Bhauja's trembling voice called out, "Jhara, do something immediately. Mother isn't responding!"

Panic surged through me. I called an ambulance and rushed her to the hospital. She was admitted to the ICU, her face pale, eyes shut, her heartbeat irregular.

Dr. Ayush worked tirelessly, treating her as if she were his own. But despite his best efforts, mother took her final breath.

Outside the ICU, my brothers and Gouri Bhauja clung to the last shred of hope. Hope that crumbled in silence.

Before I could fully comprehend, they asked me to step out.

Time blurred. We returned home—without her.

The rituals were carried out as per custom. Sony Apa and Srikant Bhai arrived later. Through it all, Dr. Ayush stood like a pillar, arranging everything as if he were mother's eldest son.

Akash Bhai performed the last rites with his help, his patience a testament to his grief.

Father had left us only months ago. Now, mother followed.

Gouri Bhauja wept inconsolably, whispering through her sobs, "Mother longed to see her son's happy family… to see Jharana married… and now…."

But desires lie in the hands of fate.

She left this world with her dreams unfulfilled.

Grandma, unable to bear the loss, became bedridden. She stopped eating, stopped speaking. Perhaps, she was waiting for her own call to join her son and daughter-in-law.

The pain of losing mother was unbearable. Death is inevitable, yet when it arrives, it feels cruel, unjust. Mother had endured a life of sorrow, and in the end, she left with burdens still weighing on her heart.

I remembered a question she had asked me a week before she passed.

"Jhara… do his family members approve?"

I had been startled. Never had such a thought crossed my mind. Though there was an unspoken bond between Dr. Ayush and me, I never imagined it as anything more.

"No, Mother," I had answered firmly. "We've never

thought that way. He is only my well-wisher, my guide, my strength."

She had looked defeated. "May it not turn into a mirage," she had murmured.

To reassure her, I had said, "Dr. Ayush is a person to be revered. He is a living god. Unlike stone gods who remain unmoved, he comes to people's rescue. Having found such a god, what more could I ask for in this life?"

But my words had only deepened the shadows in her eyes.

In a voice heavy with unspoken pain, she had asked, "What about your marriage? Will I never see it?"

I had no answer. And after that day, she never spoke again.

Perhaps, I was the thorn in her heart. Perhaps, she carried another wound—the cruelty of Jaya Bhauja.

Losing her shattered us. But in the depth of our grief, there was one solace—she was finally free. Free from suffering, from selfishness, from unfulfilled dreams.

After her passing, Akash Bhai changed. He grew more withdrawn, more weary. His wife's cold indifference only added to his burdens.

One day, unexpectedly, he visited me at the hospital.

"I want to fulfill all my responsibilities, Jhara," he said. "Now, I worry only about you."

I looked at him—my beloved brother, who had aged beyond his years. Lines of sorrow etched his face, his hair graying. He had been burning in silent agony.

I wanted to tell him, *If my marriage could bring you peace, I would marry in an instant. But Bhai, marriage is a gamble—some win, some lose. Look at your own life.*

Before I could speak, he interrupted, "Yours won't be like mine. If you agree, I can speak to Dr. Ayush."

His words echoed mother's.

But Ayush and I were worlds Apart—like the sky and the earth. The sky never descends; the earth never rises. The earth only gazes up, longing, while the sky sends down fleeting drops of rain.

Before I could respond, Dr. Ayush appeared.

"Hi, Akash Bhai! I was hoping to meet you. One of my relatives works in a bank. If you don't mind, we could propose Jhara's hand to him."

I left the room.

Had he sensed what Bhai wanted to ask? Was this his way of preventing an awkward situation?

They talked for a long time. In the end, Bhai left with the address of the prospective groom.

I should have been indifferent. But a strange sadness settled in me.

Before my heart could take root in a towering tree, the roots were severed.

Ayush remained unchanged—his speech, his manner, all the same. But something inside me had shifted.

He tried to lift my spirits, showing me sarees, speaking of the bank employee with enthusiasm.

But my heart, like a stubborn child reaching for the moon, ached with an irrational longing.

The untimely rain had abated, but the sky remained heavy with clouds. Out of nowhere, Ayush arrived at our house, accompanied by a handsome young man. Bhai seemed prepared, though he had never explicitly mentioned it. I had sensed that Ayush would visit that evening. Bhai had arranged refreshments, and for the first time, Jaya Bhauja stepped into the drawing room to join them.

After a while, Bhai called me out from my solitude. It

was as if he was about to ask me to serve the tiffin tray. Just as I reached for it, Ayush and Bhai stopped me.

Ayush grinned. "We're here for that. Or do you plan to welcome your would-be husband like the girls of yore—shy, head bowed, carrying a tray?"

To my surprise, the renowned Dr. Ayush took the tiffin tray himself, while I walked in empty-handed. Bhai gestured for me to sit across from the gentleman.

Ayush spoke at length, playing the role of a seasoned matchmaker. He praised my dedication, discipline, and service-mindedness. Instead of feeling flattered, I grew restless. The young man said nothing, nor did I lift my gaze to look at him. Somewhere along the way, my own interest had faded without my realising it. Bhai, however, looked satisfied after they left.

Jaya Bhauja spoke, her voice sharp. "Reject the proposal outright if they ask for dowry. Jhara earns her own money—why should we pay? Besides, Gouri should bear the wedding expenses. She has a job, doesn't she?"

Her words stung more than their meaning. Her once-beautiful face now seemed harsh, her features distorted by something deeper. In that moment, I understood—true beauty lies in the heart. A bitter mind can make even the fairest face look repulsive.

Tragedy shadowed our family.

After Mother's passing, Grandma, bedridden and frail, seemed to be waiting for the icy hands of death. One by one, three members of our family left us within a year. When Grandma finally passed, I told myself she was relieved from her suffering. She had never known life without Mother, her constant support. How could she have endured it?

Gouri Bhauja and her mother had cared for her with

devotion. Grandma adored Gouri Bhauja, but this only fueled Jaya Bhauja's jealousy. She refused to accompany Bhai when he went to visit Gouri Bhauja's house, leaving him to grieve alone. Poor Grandma—she had loved Bhai deeply. But because of his wife, he couldn't keep her with him. None of us had affection left for Jaya Bhauja. How could we love a woman who had driven a wedge between Bhai and his family?

On the other hand, Gouri Bhauja had become a source of warmth for all of us. I admired her unwavering kindness, her quiet strength. Akash Bhai and Vikas Bhai performed all the rites with quiet diligence, following every custom to the letter. Through it all, Gouri Bhauja stayed beside me, a constant presence—comforting, steady.

At one point, I whispered, "Bhauja, you've fulfilled all your duties. You don't need to do anything more."

She gently pinched my cheek and smiled, "And what about my dearest sister-in-law's wedding? Isn't that my duty too?"

Her words, so full of warmth, always touched something deep in me. Over time, even Vikas Bhai—once distant and withdrawn—began to soften. Her presence had a way of melting walls.

Sometimes, I would tease Gouri Bhauja's mother, saying, "Aunty, you've truly raised a gem. Look at how daughters-in-law often pull their husbands away from the family—but your daughter? She's the one who binds us closer."

I returned to duty after my leave, and a new presence immediately caught my attention—a calm, composed face that somehow overwhelmed me with its warmth.

Dr. Ayush introduced her, "Jhara, meet Dr. Renuka. She's just been transferred from Kerala."

To my surprise, Dr. Renuka and I connected almost instantly. We began working together, and I found her to be remarkably polite—gracious, even. There was a quiet strength in her, and a broadness of heart that made everyone feel seen. She became close not just to me, but to many of us in a very short time.

She already knew a bit about me—thanks to Dr. Ayush, I later learned—and treated me with a kindness that felt deeply personal, as if we had known each other much longer. Like him, she wasn't one to keep her emotions hidden. She shared her joys and sorrows freely, and listened to mine with the same ease.

Every time she visited Kerala, she would return with thoughtful gifts—for me, for the others. Her bond with Dr. Ayush also grew stronger over time. They often dined out together, and would always include me in their plans. Their invitations felt genuine, but it didn't go unnoticed—some of the other nurses began to look at me differently, a quiet envy blooming in their eyes.

One evening, as I sat reminiscing about the past, Sony Apa called. She had completed her Ph.D., but we barely spoke nowadays. Still, I kept in touch with her and Biny Apa, eager to hear updates. I longed to see Biny Apa's little son, to hold him. But where would they stay if they visited? Jaya Bhauja's hostility had already distanced our relatives. Bhai shared my longing and encouraged me to invite Sony Apa.

"She might not want to stay here," I admitted. "Maybe she could stay with Gouri Bhauja. We can visit her there."

So, Biny Apa came for a month. Her arrival was met with silent disapproval from Jaya Bhauja, who demanded that Bhai not step foot in Gouri Bhauja's house while Sony Apa was there. But Bhai, ever devoted to family, defied her wishes. The more she tried to isolate him, the tighter he clung to us.

I worked tirelessly to appease Jaya Bhauja, hoping—foolishly—that I could earn even a sliver of affection. But no matter how much I toiled, I remained no more than an unpaid servant in her eyes. In contrast, she lavished attention on her own family, ensuring their every comfort.

Gouri Bhauja, on the other hand, welcomed Biny Apa with open arms. Her home overflowed with laughter, love, and the innocent giggles of a baby. I found myself drawn to the warmth of her house, where even Bhai found solace.

One evening, as Biny Apa played with her son, she casually turned to Bhai. "What about Jhara's marriage?"

Bhai sighed. "They're coming next month. If the boy's family agrees, we'll finalise it."

Something inside me twisted. Was I really going to leave everything behind?

Biny Apa smiled, trying to lighten the mood. "At least tell me—how does he look?"

I smirked. "A blackberry-complexioned man."

Vikas Bhai chuckled. "Not at all! He's quite handsome—more than our brothers-in-law."

Biny Apa sighed, running her fingers through my hair. "Jhara has endured so much. May God bless her with all the happiness in the world."

Childhood memories surfaced. Thoughts of Grandma, Ma, and Father filled the room like invisible guests. And yet, there was no place for Jaya Bhauja in these recollections.

Jaya Bhauja, with her ever-watchful eyes and quiet jealousy, had a way of keeping herself distant. No matter how long she stayed under the same roof, she never managed to claim even a sliver of space in anyone's heart.

A month slipped by. During that time, Dr. Ayush

visited Gouri Bhauja, even before Biny Apa's return. Though he wasn't tied to us by blood, his presence had begun to feel familial—natural, comforting. When Biny Apa met him, she was taken aback by his humility, his effortless warmth.

Then came the blow. Ayush arrived one evening with a heaviness in his voice—the marriage proposal had collapsed. The dowry demands were far beyond our means. The suitor, charming as he seemed, declared with pride that he was an obedient son and could never marry against his parents' wishes.

I couldn't help but think, *If more men like him exist, at least the legend of Shravan Kumar won't fade into myth.*

I wasn't shattered—but Bhai… he looked crushed. Since our parents' passing, he had taken my future upon his shoulders like a quiet burden, and every rejection carved into him a little deeper. Ayush, as always, stepped in—not with loud promises, but with the quiet assurance of someone who truly cared.

I would be lying if I said I had never dreamed of Ayush. He was everything a woman could wish for— handsome, kind, reliable. But dreams are just that—dreams. And while mine remained half-seen, his materialised. He had found his match in Dr. Renuka. Their friendship had blossomed into love, and soon they were making plans for a future together.

I tried to be happy for them, but jealousy gnawed at the edges of my heart. My mind felt like a torn book—pages missing, its title erased. What meaning does a flower have without petals? A book without words?

But I could never bring myself to resent Renuka. She enveloped me in a kind of warmth I hadn't known in years—showering me with affection, treating me not as a colleague but as family. When she went shopping for her bridal saree and kitchenware, she made sure to pick up a few things for me too, as if I were her younger sister.

And yet, beneath their gestures, I sometimes wondered—was it love, or pity? Perhaps, in their hearts, I was just a love-starved, unmarried orphan girl they had taken under their wing. At times, I felt like someone rescued from an orphanage—grateful, but never fully belonging.

Still, their kindness never wavered. "We won't marry until you do," they would say with unshakable sincerity. And they meant it. Together, they searched for a suitable match for me, combing through possibilities with hope and persistence. But two years passed, and nothing came of it— only time, slipping quietly through our fingers.

Then came a moment of joy—Gouri Bhauja was blessed with a baby girl. Everyone said the child was the very image of Grandma. And I saw it too—in her delicate hands, her tiny feet, even the warm tone of her skin. Of course she resembled Grandma. From the moment they met, Grandma had adored Gouri Bhauja, perhaps even more than she did Vikas Bhai. And that love was returned, unwaveringly. Gouri Bhauja had done more for Grandma than anyone could have expected—her care was both dutiful and full of affection.

For three months after the baby was born, I stayed with her, doing whatever I could—changing nappies, cooking simple meals, sitting beside her through sleepless nights. It felt like the tiniest repayment for the immense love she had given me over the years. Those three months passed like three fleeting weeks.

Family and neighbors came to see the newborn, their faces lit with joy. But Jaya Bhauja never came—not even once. We heard she was upset, though no one knew the exact reason. Still, Bhai kept going to her, hoping to bridge the growing distance, though each time he returned, his face carried the weight of silent sorrow.

Perhaps, seeing Biny Apa's son and Gouri Bhauja's daughter, he was reminded of his own barren world. More than once, I pleaded with him to see a doctor. It wasn't that he hadn't tried, but Bhauja... she refused to cooperate.

One day, Bhai confided in me. "I don't even go to gatherings anymore, Jhara. Jaya never invites anyone, and she never wants to visit anyone either."

I realised then how lonely his world had become. Living with an unsocial, unyielding woman—how unbearable it must be.

I was beginning to realise how unbearably difficult it must have been for Bhai to live with someone as distant and unfeeling as Jaya Bhauja—like sharing a home with a stranger, an unsocial animal.

Gouri Bhauja had returned to her duties, and I immersed myself in mine. Then one day, she called out of the blue. "Jhara, please come in the evening without fail," she said, her tone unusually urgent. "I have something important to talk about. Please don't miss it."

I knew immediately—it had to be about a marriage proposal. I could sense it in her voice. Strangely, that very thought dimmed my eagerness. I would have looked forward to the evening more had it not carried the weight of that unspoken "urgent matter."

That same evening, Dr. Ayush and Renuka Madam had invited me for a small birthday celebration. Dr. Ayush was hosting it for Renuka Madam. I informed Gouri Bhauja, hoping she'd understand. She did—but she also hinted there was a special arrangement. Apparently, Dr. Ayush had invited not just me but Gouri Bhauja and her guest as well—a distant cousin of hers who worked in the same company.

We all arrived on time. Gouri Bhauja introduced the guest—Vinit. He was well-spoken, warm, and carried himself with a certain quiet charm. But what struck me most was how naturally he mingled. Ayush and Renuka Madam spoke to him with an ease and warmth that surprised me. At one point, I even felt like it was Vinit's birthday, not Renuka Madam's.

As we chatted, he casually expressed respect for my profession. I could sense, from the flow of conversation and the knowing glances between Dr. Ayush and Renuka Madam, that this meeting had their full blessing. Vinit had, without doubt, left an impression on them.

Later, when he left, there was a faint gleam in his eyes—something unspoken, but deeply sincere.

Akash Bhai was away in Delhi on an official tour. Still, Dr. Ayush called him immediately to share the "good news." Gouri Bhauja looked both relieved and delighted. After the passing of Ma, Baba, and Grandma, she had become my closest companion. Closer even than Sony Apa or Biny Apa. I realised then—family isn't just about blood. Sometimes, it's about presence, about the way someone stays and chooses you over and over again. Gouri Bhauja had done just that.

Two days later, Vinit called. His mother was seriously ill, and he wanted her admitted to our hospital. I reached early the next morning. He was visibly anxious but grew more composed on seeing me—and more so when Dr. Ayush and Renuka Madam arrived. When someone from the medical staff is familiar, treatment feels less daunting. That helped Vinit's mother receive proper care in time.

His father, a stern, serious man, visited briefly and left.

But Vinit stayed through the nights. Though unnecessary, his unwavering attention to his mother moved me. His dedication, his sense of duty—it all left a deep impression.

My bond with Vinit grew stronger by the day. I noticed something else too—Dr. Ayush's affection for Vinit deepening, as though he was gently passing a torch. Once, I jokingly told him, "You're trying to transfer me like a burden to Vinit."

He burst into laughter. "Why, Jhara?" he said. "Have you ever asked Akash Bhai, Vikas Bhai, or Gouri Bhauja such a thing? Don't you consider me your own?"

I went silent. How could I tell him that deep down, I had burned with quiet jealousy the day he chose Renuka Madam?

But I was trying to rise above it.

Vinit's mother began to recover. He introduced me to her warmly, praising my care. But truth be told, I had done nothing more than my duty. Still, her repeated requests for me to visit their home lingered in my heart.

Meanwhile, the closeness among the four of us— Ayush, Renuka Madam, Vinit, and me—grew. We often sat together, talking for hours.

On the day Vinit's mother was discharged, he looked at me with grave eyes and said, "No one in good health stays here. This place belongs to patients, doctors, and nurses." Then, lowering his voice, "You know I've become a patient too—and only you can heal me."

His words struck a chord so deep, I didn't know how to respond.

That night, I thought about what he had said. I had never heard anything like it from Ayush. He had only listened to my troubles with the kindness of a brother. He wanted to see me settled—not for love, but for peace of mind. I bowed to his generosity, but I couldn't deny the ache inside me. And now, a new worry stirred—what if Vinit's father rejected me for dowry, like the others?

Memories of Ma, Grandma, and Baba surged through me. All gone, never to witness my marriage. Baba had once said, "I'll rest in peace only after Jhara is married." But he never got that chance.

The next day, Vinit's mother left the hospital. Vinit kept in touch constantly—sometimes about her health, sometimes just to chat, to break the monotony. He was drawing closer to me, and I was beginning to feel it too.

Dr. Ayush called Akash Bhai to discuss the proposal. Gouri Bhauja was visibly pleased. Her mother even selected an auspicious date from the almanac for our first visit to Vinit's home. When I told Vinit, he said with quiet conviction, "God has already tied us together. The date will be perfect."

I was stunned by his faith—and moved.

But then, suddenly, everything shifted. Renuka Madam got transferred to Ahmedabad. Her father—concerned for his ailing wife—had called her back. Being his only daughter, she agreed without hesitation. That's when I understood Dr. Ayush's urgency about marriage. He was planning to move to Ahmedabad with her.

Everything was changing. I could only watch.

As their departure neared, I felt unsteady—our closeness was unraveling. Renuka Madam was cheerful, excited to reunite with her parents. But she and Ayush insisted that my engagement with Vinit happen before they left.

One day, Dr. Ayush and Akash Bhai visited Vinit's house to speak with his father. Vinit, in his excitement, did what likely annoyed his father—he brought them in his own car and treated them as though the match was already sealed.

It hurt his father's pride. Though he agreed in principle, he insisted the marriage not happen immediately—he wanted a year's time. After much back and forth, it was decided: an engagement now, marriage a year later.

Dr. Ayush and Akash Bhai returned, conflicted. But what hurt me most wasn't their dilemma—it was Vinit's voice on the phone. It trembled. I saw his dejected face in my mind, and for the first time, I admitted it to myself—I had a soft corner for him.

Why did he love someone like me—an ordinary nurse, not especially beautiful, without a prestigious family name? There must have been countless better proposals. And yet, it was me he chose.

His love humbled me. And somewhere deep inside, it also healed something long left unattended.

Vinit dismissed the necessity of formal engagement. To him, the true union was not in rituals but in the meeting of minds.

Dr. Ayush and Renuka madam left the city and the hospital with hopes of a new beginning. Their departure left a void, especially when I passed by Dr. Ayush's cabin—it always stirred nostalgia. He had been more than a colleague; he was family. He would walk into my room unhesitatingly, chat for hours, and uplift my spirits when I was down. I could confide in him about everything—my joys, my sorrows, even my family conflicts. He listened with patience, consoled me when needed, and sometimes laughed things away just to lighten my burden.

I had always considered him as one of my own. And though Renuka madam had taken him away from us, I held no resentment. Her kindness had won me over. Perhaps the world is still filled with enough good people to keep it going.

Even after leaving, Ayush remained in constant touch. He called daily, asking after my well-being, reminding me to take care of myself. But his new responsibilities—both in his career and his impending marriage—kept him occupied. Yet, he never forgot us.

The mind, like a house, never remains empty. Someone or another always occupies it. Ayush's absence left a void, but in time, Vinit found his place in my heart. Unlike before, there were no family objections, no external pressures—only our growing bond. Had Vinit not come into my life, I might have broken under the weight of Ayush's absence.

We met after my shifts—sometimes at a restaurant, sometimes in a quiet park. Our conversations stretched for hours, yet never seemed to reach an end. There was always more to say, more to feel, more to share. Whether in person or over the phone, our talks flowed endlessly. Gouri Bhauja, Vikas Bhai, and Jaya Bhauja were all aware of our relationship. While no one openly opposed it, Jaya Bhauja's disapproval was evident. But I no longer let it wound me. If there were any scars, Vinit's love was enough to heal them.

Sarika was another presence in our lives—linguistically different, professionally distinct, yet a kindred spirit. Newly settled in her own family life, she welcomed us into her home with warmth. She cared for us, invited us over, and stood by us. Jaya Bhauja's bitter remarks about this never fazed me anymore. Vinit, too, saw through them.

But there was a hurdle we could not ignore—Vinit's father. He had made it clear: he would never accept a nurse as his daughter-in-law. His prejudice weighed heavily on Vinit, who bore his father's disapproval with silent suffering. Sarika and Gouri Bhauja even visited his house, hoping to change his mind. But they returned with heavy hearts. His father's words, kept hidden from Dr. Ayush and Akash Bhai, were spoken to them with brutal honesty—he simply didn't want his son to marry someone from my profession.

I took it as a final verdict. Our marriage would never happen. Sarika suggested a court marriage, but Vinit refused. He was just as firm as his father—but for a different reason. He wanted to marry me, to bring me home with full honour, as per our traditions.

"Forget me, Vinit," I told him one day, my voice steady despite the ache in my heart. "Marry someone else—someone your father approves of."

His sharp, incredulous voice shattered the silence. "I never thought I'd hear such filmy dialogue from you, Jhara. Don't say such cheap things again."

Yet, that day, for the first time, I felt ashamed of my profession—not for what it was, but for how the world viewed it. Nursing is not just a job; it is a calling, a service. It demands dedication, sacrifice, and immense strength. How could I respect someone who belittled it?

Despite everything, Vinit and I couldn't distance ourselves from each other. But doubt clouded my mind whenever I saw colleagues marrying with their families' blessings. If others could accept nurses as daughters-in-law, why not me? What crime had I committed to be deemed unworthy?

Vinit reassured me. "Time will change everything," he said. "My father will come around. We just have to wait."

But I wasn't patient enough for an uncertain future.

Time passed—three years of waiting, of stolen moments, of fragile hopes. Yet, no auspicious day arrived for us. Instead, a new obstacle emerged—Vinit's transfer to Karnataka. A government job meant inevitable rellocations, but this transfer felt like fate's cruel intervention. We were not yet settled, and now, distance threatened to tear us apart.

At last, with no other recourse, Vinit confronted his father once more. The answer was the same—a thunderous refusal.

Returning to me, exhausted and defeated, he said, "Jhara, there's no way out. Let's make our dream a reality. I'll leave my family for you. You are my life—my everything. If my parents can crush my happiness, I don't need them. We'll live for each other."

I silenced his emotional outburst with a soft laugh. He looked at me, confused.

"Which movie are these dialogues from, Vinit? They sound perfect for a heart-wrenching love story."

He held my gaze. "Then should our story remain incomplete?"

That night, I couldn't sleep. My heart was torn apart by countless yeses and nos.

I sought guidance from Akash Bhai, Gouri Bhauja, Biny Apa, and Sony Apa. Their responses were eerily similar—"Jhara, you're old enough to decide for yourself. Do what you think is right."

I felt utterly abandoned—as if the whole world had stepped away, leaving me stranded in a place where neither forward nor backward was possible. For the first time, I truly felt the weight of my loneliness. Not just mine— everyone's. In moments of crisis, you realise how solitary the human experience really is. No one comes forward to say, *"Leave it to us—we'll handle it."* No one offers the comfort of, *"Even if Vinit's father doesn't agree, we're here for*

you. We'll see you married, we'll bless your path with flowers."
Silence was the only answer.

Only four days remained. After that, everything would change. We'd be living in two different worlds. The thought unsettled even Dr. Ayush. He seemed restless. Renuka Madam, always practical, advised me gently, *"Jhara, resign and go with Vinit. Don't let your indecision dim his spirit."* But I was torn.

Sarika had invited us over for dinner a day before. Her husband was away on an official tour and wouldn't return for a week—too late to meet Vinit before he left for Karnataka. That dinner would likely be our last gathering.

I arrived at her apartment that evening. Sarika, with her usual warmth, had cooked a variety of dishes—all of them Vinit's favourites. She did it out of love, I knew, but I couldn't bring myself to enjoy it. My mind was elsewhere. I wore the baby-pink salwar suit Vinit had once gifted me. Coincidentally, he was in the cream shirt and black trousers I had given him. They suited him so well—it should have made me smile, but I couldn't.

Sarika, ever the optimist, declared it an evening for the three of us to catch up and laugh. But Vinit wasn't himself. He sat there—quiet, withdrawn. His face looked pale, his voice lacked energy. The Vinit I knew, always so full of life and banter, seemed like a shadow of himself. I tried to lift the mood, cracking silly jokes, even though my own heart was sinking. But for the first time in three years, I noticed something new in his eyes—an irritation, a heaviness. My efforts to cheer him up only seemed to agitate him.

Then, without warning, he said it—in front of Sarika. That everything about me, including my love for him, was a façade. Pretence. The words landed like a slap.

But strangely, I didn't feel anger. Instead, I felt a strange elation, a painful joy. I thought to myself, *"Vinit, even if you're angry now—even if you push me away—nothing will ever truly separate us. You live inside me. Always will."* Let the world say I have the *heart of a nurse*—that I'm cold, or distant. They don't understand. Even you, Vinit, couldn't see that what I said wasn't mockery, but the raw tenderness of someone trying not to fall apart.

Perhaps he mistook my words as a jab at his father's rejection. But it was nothing more than sentiment, spilling out the only way it knew how.

It wasn't yet time for dinner. Sarika was setting the table when her phone rang. An emergency call from the hospital. She sighed in frustration but didn't hesitate. Duty calls can't be ignored. *"I'll be back in an hour,"* she said, slipping on her sandals. The hospital was just across the road, but the rain had started. She bolted the door from outside—the wind kept slamming it open otherwise.

And just like that, we were alone.

Something about that moment made me uneasy. The room felt too quiet. I couldn't explain it—but a strange embarrassment settled over me, as if I was intruding into a space too intimate, too fragile. We sat on the sofa, facing each other. The sound of rain pattered against the windows. Vinit's face, under the soft yellow light, looked hauntingly sad. My heart tightened.

He looked like someone carrying the weight of something unspoken—something unbearable. And I didn't know how to reach him.

An awkward silence settled between us. He sat with his head lowered, refusing food.

"Will you have some soup?" I asked gently.

"No," he said, voice heavy. "I don't have an appetite."

"Not even for Sarika's sake? She cooked your favourites."

Turning the pages of a magazine, he muttered, "You've already dissected my mind. Haven't you?"

His sulky words made me smile.

"If our love were a test," he said, "I'd score a hundred. You, maybe ten."

I laughed, but it stung him.

Looking at me, he whispered, "I'm sorry for my father's words. Please forgive me. Let all your pain be mine—I only want to see you happy."

His voice trembled, and in that moment, I surrendered—not just to him, but to the depth of his love.

We held each other, hearts beating in sync, lost in the storm outside and within.

And yet, we knew—our story had already been written, and it was not one with a happy ending.

After a while, we quietly pulled away from each other. I returned to my original spot on the sofa. There was a shift in the air—something tender and wordless passed between us. His eyes held a depth I couldn't name, something distant yet achingly close. I had never seen him like this before, never shared such a fragile, intimate silence with him.

Though our hearts resisted, we stepped back—not out of will, but because the moment demanded it. Something deeper than desire pulled us apart. Conscience, dignity, perhaps the quiet voice of self-respect—we were both held in check by something invisible yet firm.

Then the doorbell rang, breaking the spell. Sarika rushed in, breathless and slightly flustered. *"So sorry for the delay!"* she said quickly, heading to the washbasin to rinse her hands before changing. There was a faint trace of guilt in her voice, as if she sensed something had passed in her absence.

Still lost in the quiet ache of the moment, Vinit and I exchanged a glance. We couldn't look away. The room was filled not with words, but with the lingering presence of something that had almost taken shape—and then dissolved.

At dinner, Vinit barely touched his food, despite Sarika's coaxing and mine. His appetite had vanished, though he said nothing.

When it was time to leave, Sarika handed each of us a small gift, wrapped with care. *"Just a little something,"* she smiled, trying to lift the mood. Vinit accepted it with a quiet *"Thank you."* Then, almost under his breath, he added, *"This evening… I'll never forget it."*

His eyes met mine one last time, and something in that gaze—sharp, searching, unspeakable—struck me deep. It wasn't a look; it was a wound. A message that bypassed language. A chill ran down my spine.

There was a storm in the house the next morning.

Jaya Bhauja made it clear—there was no place for a "characterless girl" like me. Her words hit hard, though I knew the reason behind her outburst. Vinit had dropped me off at the gate late at night. It would've been simpler to lie, to say I had night duty. But the fact that I had gone with him, invited to Sarika's house as a guest, stung her like a thorn. That was the real issue.

She had always hovered, waiting for a crack to appear, some excuse to raise a storm in a teacup. This time, she didn't hold back. "I won't stay in this house if she does," she declared. Her voice was shrill, decisive.

But my brother knew me. He trusted me. He knew I would never do anything to bring shame upon him. Still, despite Bhai's efforts to pacify the situation, the storm only grew louder. Perhaps she had long waited for a moment like this. And now that it had arrived, she seized it without hesitation—twisting my words, flinging utensils in a fit of rage.

I said nothing. Quietly, I gathered a few clothes and daily essentials and stepped out of the house. Bhai didn't stop me. Perhaps he too wished I would escape the sharp edge of her bitterness.

I found a small room in the staff quarters. When Vinit learned what had happened, his face darkened.

"Resign, Jhara," he said firmly. "Come with me. I can give up everything for you. Can't you leave this job for me?"

How could I make him understand? This job wasn't just a means of survival. It was my spine, my wings. It was the one thing that allowed me to dream of touching the sky. It was my foundation—my past, my present, and the thread leading to my future. Through this profession, I had begun to understand life, people, even myself. And had I not walked this path—how would I have met him?

Who knows what tomorrow holds? Tomorrow is never loyal.

That Sunday, Gouri Bhauja had invited Vinit for breakfast—his train was at three. She had also asked me to stay at their place for a few days. I couldn't. Even though I knew Akash Bhai would be disappointed, the staff quarters felt like the right place for me now.

Vinit wanted to take me along. But Gouri Bhauja, rather than offering clear support or objection, simply said, "Why don't you stay in a live-in relationship?"

I felt scorched, as if her words had singed my skin. *Is this our culture?* Marriage is sacred—a union of souls, sanctified by fire and watched over by the ten guardian deities, the *Dash Dikpalas*. I couldn't embrace an arrangement that felt mechanical, that lacked both depth and dignity. If Vinit's family were ever to accept me wholeheartedly, only then could I think of leaving this job and stepping into family life. Until then, I'd rather live alone than build dreams on a foundation of sand.

Human logic, desires, arguments—all get buried under the debris of time. That day, like two parallel lines, Vinit and I parted.

That night, I cried for hours. His tearful eyes at the moment of goodbye haunted me like a photograph that refused to fade. They kept flashing in my mind—those helpless, pleading eyes. And that weak wave of his hand— how powerless it looked!

The memories came rushing in. The pain of losing loved ones held hands with my present sorrow. I missed Ma. I missed Grandma. I missed Baba. I missed my childhood. And I missed Ayush.

I was in a fragile mental state. My life felt like an open book, each page turned by strangers. Nothing about me was hidden—my friends, my colleagues, the doctors— everyone seemed to have a version of me in their minds.

Some praised my strength, calling me bold and independent. Others whispered behind my back— *arrogant*, they said. Some questioned my choices outright. "If you really loved him, why didn't you go with him?" Others said, "You should've accepted his offer—he was willing to go against his father."

And then, the most venomous ones added their fuel to the fire— "He's a man. Who knows how long he'll remember your love from afar? He might choose someone else."

I listened to everyone. I understood bits and pieces of what they said, but most of it remained incomprehensible—distant echoes in a world that had already moved on.

In big cities, such tragedies leave no lasting scars. Life rushes forward, indifferent. Within days, everything returned to normal. The collapse of my dream-house became just another forgotten event, buried beneath the weight of routine. No one spoke about it. Even Sarika, who understood me better than anyone else, never mentioned Vinit. Maybe she knew everything. Maybe she realised that some wounds should not be touched.

She never reminded me of my pain. Instead, she carried on as if nothing had changed, as if I were the same Jhara. She often invited me over, filling my lonely hours with warmth, offering her quiet companionship without demanding explanations.

Her house held a strange comfort for me. That space, that drawing room, that familiar sofa—it became a sanctuary of memories. I never entered her bedroom. I remained on that sofa, lost in thought, reliving that day over and over. The scent of Vinit still lingered in the air, teasing my senses, whispering of a past that refused to fade. His voice echoed through my being, shaking me to the core.

Solitude became my closest companion. I wandered alone to the places where we once sat together—the quiet restaurant, the familiar corner seat. The waiter would approach me with a knowing look.

"Hasn't sir come today? Would you like to order something?"

I would force a smile and ask for a cup of coffee.

Sometimes, I took Sarika along. I ordered Vinit's favourite dishes, letting his absence sit across from me like an uninvited guest. But when the food arrived, my appetite disappeared, swallowed by the storm inside me. Sarika noticed, always. She would gently remind me, "Don't lose yourself in what's gone, Jhara. Time moves forward."

I tried. I truly tried.

I willed myself to change, to find strength in my duty. I buried myself in work, losing my pain amidst friends, patients, medicines, injections, saline drips, and endless hospital beds.

And yet, in the quiet moments, when the world was not watching, the ache remained.

9

All beginnings have their ends. And it felt as though the chapter with Vinit was coming to a close.

Akash Bhai understood my turmoil. The transitions in my life—the shift to the staff quarters, the abrupt end of my engagement—tortured him. But what pained him more was his helplessness. He could do nothing for me. He could neither bring me back home, fearing Jaya Bhauja's disapproval, nor could he console me in any meaningful way. After all, what could he do? A man who couldn't convince his own wife to see a doctor—how could he possibly set my life right?

Jaya Bhauja could not become a mother. I had urged Bhai countless times to take her to a gynecologist, but he was powerless against her stubbornness. Strange were her ways. A woman is often considered incomplete without motherhood, yet she never showed the slightest sense of longing. Beyond her beauty, there was little warmth in her. Her jealousy, sharp tongue, and self-centeredness pushed people away. No one had ever seen her sit beside Akash Bhai for a quiet conversation.

Gouri Bhauja, on the other hand, felt deeply for me. She knew Vinit well—after all, he was her colleague. It was at her house that he had first proposed. Who could have foreseen that my profession would become the stain on his father's pride? That it would stand as a barrier between Vinit and me?

After that, something in me shifted. Any nurse's marriage surprised me. How did her in-laws agree? What made her fate different from mine? Perhaps, it was destiny's cruel joke. I told myself that. I blamed fate.

In the beginning, Vinit and I called each other often. But gradually, his workload increased. He wanted to come to Hyderabad but couldn't; his office demanded too much of him. I, too, was drowning in my work, yet my heart remained restless. The sound of untimely rain—the soft *drip drop drip drop*—sent me spiraling into memories. Lightning struck outside, and instinctively, I looked for someone. With my eyes closed, I relived those fleeting moments, feeling his presence in the silence.

Then, one day, Vinit took me by surprise.

I was more elated than shocked. Never, not even in my dreams, had I imagined that he would come to me without a single call, without warning. But his unexpected arrival came with an ultimatum.

"Jhara, you have to resign and leave with me right now," he said. "I've spoken to your brother. He has no objection. Please, don't refuse."

His words stunned me. Gouri Bhauja, too, insisted, "See, Jhara, how much he wants you! Leave the job and be happy with him. After all, is it even necessary?"

I nodded, agreeing to leave my job here. But Vinit was not satisfied.

"I will resign," I said, "but I will continue working as a nurse after we move."

Gouri Bhauja tried to reason with me. "Jhara, don't be so rigid. Vinit is in a good position. Consider his family's status. Their reputation. Maybe you're thinking of me—

how I couldn't have survived on your brother's earnings alone. But you're not in my situation. You don't need this job. Just go with him."

Her words stung.

Was my profession so beneath them? They were reminding me—again and again—that my work as a nurse did not *match* Vinit's status.

But tell me, could a doctor heal without a nurse? Could a patient recover without our care? Florence Nightingale remains immortal for a reason. And yet, my work was seen as lowly. Unworthy.

Vinit's love for me—so deep, so unwavering—suddenly seemed as fragile as a water bubble.

His voice was heavy. "Jhara, this is my last meeting with you. If you refuse, it means you never truly loved me."

I stared at him, my throat dry. My heart ached to ask—*"What kind of test is this, Vinit? Why must I choose between love and my profession?"*

Once again, I repeated what I had said before. "Okay, I will leave my job here, but I will work as a nurse after moving."

That was all it took.

Vinit left abruptly, without a backward glance. Gouri Bhauja called after him, but he did not turn. Her face darkened, as if I had committed some great sin.

I sat there, swallowed by silence, staring into the growing darkness like a condemned soul.

After that day, Vinit never called me. Nor did he respond to mine.

Was it my mistake or his? Was it his pride or mine?

I had never imagined our bond would shatter so easily. At first, I believed—*he will call after a few days He will come back.* But as time passed, my confidence waned.

Everyone blamed me—Akash Bhai, Gouri Bhauja, Ayush, Renuka Madam, Biny Apa, Sony Apa. They said I was my own banana peel, that I had ruined my own chances. But why? Why did they see *my* profession as lowly while theirs were symbols of prestige?

I never held a grudge against anyone. But Vinit's attitude hurt me.

Why did he love me so deeply if he could not accept all of me?

But time has a way of numbing even the deepest wounds. I adapted. I changed.

But one cannot live without a foundation, without something to hold onto. My profession—my only anchor—became everything to me.

I embraced it with my heart and soul.

10

The tides of time had shifted. I was searching for my identity in the ashes of my past, sifting through the remnants of old feelings and bygone days. I could claim no one as my own. In solitude, I sought refuge in books, immersing myself in their silent companionship.

It was around this time that I stumbled upon an advertisement for a nursing position at a hospital in Sikkim. The thought of leaving the city had been lingering in my mind, and this opportunity seemed like fate extending a hand. I applied, and after six long months, the appointment letter arrived.

I left for Sikkim against the wishes of my brothers and Gouri bhauja. A new life was beginning, one that I had not imagined but was ready to embrace. My friend Sarika was deeply upset, and others bid me farewell with heavy hearts. Strangely, I felt neither regret nor a sense of loss. When memories of my family surfaced—my childhood, my father, my mother, my grandmother—I felt their absence more profoundly than ever. None of them were here anymore.

To my sister and brother-in-law, I was a fool, a madwoman chasing an illusion. Some whispered that I had lost my mind over Vinit, while others speculated that my refusal to marry had made me eccentric. I laughed at their assumptions. I loved my family, but attachment had long faded. I would call only Biny Apa and Gouri bhauja from time to time. Their children—Biny Apa's son and Gouri bhauja's daughter—became my only sources of innocent joy. Their wide, untainted eyes stirred something within me.

I had also heard about Sony Apa's struggles—an ongoing dispute with her husband over moving abroad. At times, I felt deeply for Akash Bhai, but I trained myself to be strong. How unreal and meaningless this world was! We convince ourselves we cannot live without someone, yet life goes on, indifferent to our pain. I prayed for Akash Bhai, but beyond that, I was powerless.

Sikkim welcomed me with open arms. There was an international school nearby, and from my window, I would watch the children playing in the breeze like petals of a garden in bloom. Their laughter often reached my ears. When they fell ill, they were brought to our hospital, which was closely associated with the school. Additionally, the hospital housed a nursing training institute where girls from various places came to learn the art of care giving.

Despite being far from home, I liked the routine and discipline of hospital life. My close friend Sarika and my old colleagues were miles away, yet, strangely, no one here felt like a stranger.

Hyderabad had taught me many lessons. Back then, I was new to the profession—naïve and easily swayed by sweet words. But Sikkim saw a different version of me— seasoned, self-assured, and no longer willing to be deceived.

Among the many remarkable individuals at the hospital, one stood out—Sijal didi. She was sharp, disciplined, and held in high regard. With only two years left until retirement, she commanded both fear and admiration. People spoke of her stern and reserved nature, and initially,

I was apprehensive. She had a grave, unsmiling demeanor, but her efficiency and work ethic were undeniable.

Though unmarried, she was a mother to all the young nursing trainees. Working with her felt like an honour. Her unwavering commitment to service had earned her immense respect. Yet, beneath her hard exterior lay a heart overflowing with compassion.

At first, she hardly spoke to me. When she did, her words carried an unspoken weight:

"I have seen life up close and studied the human mind carefully. No one has ever truly defeated me, though many have tried."

I pondered over her words. If no one had defeated her, then why did she speak of being challenged? It took me a long time to grasp the truth behind her statement. Sijal didi never allowed anyone to break her spirit, but those who failed to understand her, who ignored her wisdom, lost the chance to receive her warmth and guidance.

I longed to learn from her. She was a book with many pages—one that required patience and wisdom to read. She had no family of her own, yet she sought to bring joy to the world. She nursed orphaned children, offered a safe haven to the helpless, and worked tirelessly in the school, hospital, and NGO. Many honours and awards came her way, but she dismissed them with a simple philosophy:

"Serving others is our duty. What need is there for recognition? Helping is as natural as breathing."

She believed that through service, one could attain God. To the abandoned children she rescued from garbage dumps and hospital corridors, she was more than a nurse— she was their mother.

She served others with a rare devotion—an untiring soul moved by love and compassion. Day and night, she cared for countless disabled and differently-abled children, never once showing weariness. She was a sanctuary for the abandoned, a quiet refuge for the broken.

Her gentle words, spoken in a voice as soft as prayer, were like a jug of cool water to the parched. In her presence, I felt renewed—like a morning after a long, dark night. The golden hue of the rising sun ahead seemed to echo her spirit, guiding me like a beacon through my own fog.

Yet, at times, I found myself lost in reflection, wandering through the wilderness of my past and present. Where had I been? And where had I arrived? Like a train racing past trees, stones, and villages, I had moved on—leaving behind the people I once believed were mine.

Ayush rarely called now. His voice, once familiar, came only in rare intervals, like a distant echo from a dream. Just a few words—enough to remind me that he was somewhere out there, yet no longer close. And Vinit—his name had long since faded into silence. No letters. No calls. No traces.

Among all my family members, only Akash Bhai and Gouri Bhauja kept in touch, calling me now and then, mostly to remind me to take care of myself. Akash Bhai's voice always carried a certain weight, a heaviness that betrayed his inner conflict. There was a quiet sorrow in him—most of it stemming from the looming decision about going abroad. The topic stirred unrest in his household more often than not.

Jaya Bhauja was firm in her ambition for him. She wanted him to take the lucrative position with a multinational American firm. But Akash Bhai, rooted in his love for the country and its soil, had no real desire to leave. Still, as always, he had to yield to her will. I knew how much it cost him. Though it pained me to think of him leaving India, I kept my feelings to myself and offered a formal congratulation—just another mask in the gallery of goodbyes.

Sony Apa had already left the country. She was different—an enigma even within the family. She never shared her thoughts, never asked for anyone's opinion. She lived by her own rules. A woman of fierce independence, perhaps too fierce to belong to anyone. Word had it that her husband was deeply unhappy with her, frustrated by her relentless self-will. Once, Sony Apa had said, "My career is my first priority. Family comes next." She had stood by that belief unwaveringly.

Our connection had long since faded. There was no question of meeting her anymore. How could she be someone else's when she couldn't even belong to the man she had married?

Even Biny Apa, once close, had grown distant. Her calls were rare now. Only Gouri Bhauja, ever steady in her sense of duty, continued to stay in touch. She never forgot to send a gift on my birthday, a token of thoughtfulness I quietly treasured.

It was during one of our casual conversations that Gouri Bhauja, almost offhandedly, told me that Vinit had married. The girl, she added with a touch of candor, "wasn't much to look at—but had a good job."

Her words dropped like a stone into still water. I smiled as if unaffected. But inside, something sank.

A sharp, hidden pain resurfaced. I had tried to bury this chapter of my life, but memories clawed their way back. My heart pounded. Had Vinit ever longed for me the way I ached for him?

I became absent-minded for days. Sijal didi noticed. She called me aside and, in her usual direct manner, said:

"Are you mourning lost love? Let me tell you something—no woman who wastes her life pining for the past ever achieves anything. If a lover dies in love, perhaps grief is justified. But to cry over someone who discarded you? That is foolishness. He buried you in a grave and expects you to remain there. Wipe him from your mind."

Her words struck deep. How had she sensed my turmoil? Had she suffered something similar?

To mask my emotions, I feigned concern over Akash Bhai's departure abroad. But Sijal didi saw through me.

"After a brother marries, the love between siblings divides—like inherited property. The sister-in-law's happiness depends on how little the sister demands of her brother. If you can forgo his love completely, she will be the happiest. Accept this truth and stop grieving."

She was right. I had lost Akash Bhai the day Jaya bhauja entered our home.

Sijal didi hugged me and wiped my tears. Love between lovers, between siblings—it was all an illusion, a performance played out on the stage of life.

Sijal Didi's words had fortified me. I found myself recalling what Gouri Bhauja had said—that Vinit's wife was not beautiful. Strangely, those words filled me with an odd sense of victory. Perhaps it's a petty sentiment, but every woman who has ever loved deeply wishes—at some quiet corner of her heart—that the one who came after her would be somehow…less. Less graceful, less radiant, less everything. It becomes a strange kind of consolation, like a small umbrella in the vast desert of life. Not shade enough to save you, but something to hold onto.

I looked into the mirror and, for a fleeting moment, felt proud of my reflection. I murmured to myself, almost defiantly, *"Vinit, your wife may hold a high position, but in some silent way, I've won. The shadow of that comparison will follow her. It will reach you too—perhaps not today, but someday. And in that moment, you'll see the ache of loss on her face, not mine."*

I suddenly laughed out loud, startling even myself. It was sharp, uncontained, echoing strangely in the still room. The laugh drew puzzled glances. Sijal Didi, ever perceptive, came over and gently patted my back, her eyes kind, saying nothing more. Then she left me to my thoughts.

Yes, they heard my laughter. But no one saw the tears I shed later that night, lying alone in the darkness, the silence pressing down like a weight.

I kept wondering—had I really done something wrong? Had my stubbornness about the job wounded Vinit that deeply? I was proud of what I did. Was that pride my sin?

Vinit had known I was a nurse when he first proposed—through Gouri Bhauja, not even directly. He knew my world, my dreams, my devotion to this profession. If someone resents what you are most proud of, how can that be love?

He never even called me before making the final decision. No conversation. No closure. Just silence.

Such was his love.

Self-respect together with hatred reared the wound in my heart. I gazed at the darkness through the window. Everything looked dreadful. The insects surrounded the street lamp but the lamp light was indifferent like a stoic or one with steadfast wisdom. An unknown bird in some distant tree chirped thinking the night to have ended. It was perhaps due to my agonised state of mind the bird's chirp seemed to have a pathetic strain. Pathos was not there only in the bird's voice, the trees under the cover of darkness looked depressed too.

The pains and agonies suffered during the night are soothed by the healing touch of the morning. The morning hubbub steals away the upset feelings. Time rolls on with day and night, with joys and despondencies. I felt as if I, like Sijal didi had seen the dying-life from a very close quarter.

At times, I would think of asking Sijal didi about her past life which resembled mine. But by and by I suppressed that sort of curiosity as I had stopped to be that loquacious since a long time. Sijal didi used to spend a considerable time talking to the nursing students as if she delivered some spiritual discourses. I realised that Sijal didi had been bestowed with some extraordinary power. She could read the mind from the face.

The suppurating wound in my heart was healing up gradually by her affection and consolation that acted like some ointment.

I felt drowsing while on my chair. A sudden ring from the mobile phone awakened me. It was a surprise to get a phone call from Ayush but it was pleasant one as it brought me the good news of his becoming a father. He had been blessed with a daughter. In the meantime, there had been a gap of two years since we had met. His voice seemed a bit distant to me. So, I had blurted out, "In deed, the relatedness is such a feeling, it seems great when we are near and becomes lighter when separated by distance. Isn't it?" The loud laughter from the other end washed away the seriousness.

By the by, Vinit came to my mind while talking with Ayush over phone. One day a similar news from him will also come. I sighed and went to bed but I had to come out as my colleague called me. It was a serious case. I followed her to the Emergency Ward. A small girl in unconscious state was being carried on the stretcher. The treatment began immediately. The role of Sijal did in such cases is very important. Her style of work in handling the situation was remarkable. The child had become unconscious due to high temperature.

She got back her sense after a long time. Her father, depressed and pensive, was sitting beside her. His helpless and pathetic looks seemed as if praying to all the doctors and nurses to cure his daughter. All gave their hearts to him. The girl broke down to see her father's teary eyes whenever she opened her eyes for a few moments. Sijal didi felt the heart of a helplessly impatient father yet she asked him to go out. We were entrusted with the responsibility of taking all possible care of her so that she would come round.

I sat at her bed throughout the entire night administering saline and injections whenever required. She was coming round slowly. I sat caressing her head. She opened her eyes and asked if I was a nurse. She was speaking in Hindi as she was a non-Odia.

I nodded a yes.

: My PApa? Where is my PApa? She looked around with searching glances.

I asked her to sleep without talking while taking the temperature. It was coming down gradually.

Again, she asked for her PApa. I went out and asked her father to go in. Her father looked nervous. On hearing from me he felt relieved and came to his daughter. Faith and confidence had absconded from his eyes.

I stood on the balcony and gave a cursory look at the world outside. A row of wavy hills, small and big! The moon lay with a hill smearing its silky soothing beams on the hill.

I was brooding over my father. I wished he came

back and called me out, "Jhara!" A few birds flapped away from a tree to another, perhaps to make me aware of the reality. I had such fever several times when I was young. I remember how my father applied water-pads on my forehead sitting beside me throughout the night. He just wanted the night to pass smoothly while thinking of calling the doctor in the morning. And my mother was taking the vow of offering *prasad* to different deities if I got round. No one can pay off the debts of love of fathers and mothers. Neither my mother nor my father gave me any chance of serving them. Ah! How soon they got lost! Even now, I search them in the ailing elderly persons. Seeing old men and women struggling for life, I would console myself that my parents did not suffer so much.

Numerous old men and women, children and youth get admitted here. Some of them go back hale and hearty whereas some people's lifeless bodies are taken away from here. Initially I was very upset at these scenes but gradually I adjusted myself.

The girl's name was Rista, a fresh flower. She was a paragon of beauty with a cascade of long silky hair, a pair of large blue eyes, a cute pointed nose and rosy lips. She had to stay for a week as her treatment continued and when she left, the hospital felt emptier.

As I watched her go, I thought of my nieces and nephews. Would I ever hold them in my arms again? Would they remember me, or was I slowly becoming a stranger?

The world was vast, and I was just a passerby, moving forward, yet leaving pieces of my heart behind.

Today, my family consists of just me—a lone soul navigating life's uncertainties. I often recall Akash Bhai's weary, dispirited look, but I hesitate to call him. What would I even say? What could I expect from him anymore?

I recently heard that he is leaving for Germany next month on a five-year assignment for his company. Bhauja is thrilled, eagerly looking forward to this new chapter. But who knows what changes those five years will bring? Life is a constant ebb and flow of hopes, disappointments, and silent sufferings—so many emotions woven into each fleeting moment, yet so few we can truly hold onto.

I was lost in thought when Sijal Didi's voice pulled me back to the present. She stood before me with a small packet of sweets, her usual grave expression softened by a rare smile. Gently placing a sweet into my mouth, she said, "Rista's father sent these for us through his orderly. It's her birthday today. And the most interesting part? He specifically asked me to give you two extra sweets."

I paused, stunned by the unexpected gesture. How could such a little girl hold such deep affection? What had I done to leave such an impression on her young heart?

Just as we were talking about Rista, the phone in the Duty Room rang. I picked up, and to my astonishment, it was Rista herself on the other end.

"I miss you, Aunty!" her tiny voice chirped.

"Really?" I asked, a smile forming on my lips.

"Yes, Aunty. I wanted to meet you today, but PApa said no."

I could hear someone speaking to her in the background, a gentle warning perhaps, before she quickly replaced the receiver.

We talked about her for a while after that. It turned out that she lived just beyond the compound wall of our hospital. Her father, a high-ranking officer, resided in a bungalow on the hilltop across the road, a place clearly visible from our quarters.

Over time, Rista became an integral part of our lives.

She would send us little notes scribbled in her wobbly ABCD handwriting, often accompanied by tiny gifts—a shiny pebble, a candy wrapped carefully in a scrap of paper. Her innocent, affectionate gestures never failed to bring laughter and warmth. Sijal Didi mentioned that Rista had been admitted to the hospital once before, though her condition had not been serious. Her father, overly anxious about her health, preferred to hospitalize her at the slightest sign of illness, as if doing so could somehow keep her safe from all harm.

That day marked my first rain in Sikkim. The showers danced over the rocky hilltops, their rhythm shifting with the wind. Thunder rumbled across the valley, followed by sharp streaks of lightning that illuminated the night sky. A thrill coursed through me. There has always been something about the sound of rain that stirs my soul, that carries me away to distant memories.

I had no night duty, so I lay on my bed, gazing out the window, watching the rain cascade from the heavens. Though I love the rain, it has a way of making me nostalgic. It pulls me back to my childhood, to those carefree days of running barefoot in the rain, to Grandma's stern yet loving voice warning us against getting drenched. "Hey! Don't stay in the rain—you'll catch a cold!" she would scold, but Vikas Bhai was always the rebellious one. He would splash through puddles in the courtyard, dragging us along, while Akash Bhai—forever the responsible one—stood with Grandma, trying to stop us. Yet, he had his own way of enjoying the rain. He would prepare *masala mudhi*, spicy puffed rice, and serve it to all of us in little paper cones, making the moment even more delightful.

But those days are gone forever. In this lifetime, I don't know if we siblings will ever gather like that again.

Perhaps that is why I cling so tightly to my memories, reliving them whenever the rain whispers to me.

The downpour stirred emotions I had long buried. Vinit—his voice, his touch, his once-soothing presence—flashed through my mind. A wave of shame and regret washed over me. Why had I failed to see through him? Why had I been so naive? He had been the one to propose, knowing full well about my job. If he truly loved me, how could he turn against me over something he had always known? If he chose to value his family's pride over my identity, why should I waste another thought on him?

The rain continued its steady rhythm against the window, lulling my restless thoughts into silence. Eventually, sleep came, wrapping me in its comforting embrace.

At dawn, the world awoke with the melodious chirping of birds, as if washing away the sorrow of the past night.

11

The nurses' quarters here were modest yet sufficient, consisting of a small bedroom, an attached washroom, and a compact kitchen with a cupboard near the veranda—just enough space to cook comfortably. Though there was a common dining area, the kitchen proved useful for preparing something whenever needed, especially when guests visited. In the adjacent quarters lived Swati, a fellow nurse, whose mother had stayed with her for a few days.

Sijal Didi had an exceptional talent for management. The orphanage and the girls' hostel were divided into three sections systematically. A separate Apartment was designated for spinsters like her, while another housed working married women, whose quarters were slightly larger, with an extra room to accommodate their families. If any of us got married, we would have to shift to the working women's Apartment. Adjacent to Sijal Didi's room was a seventy-five-seater dormitory for the younger girls.

The institution maintained a high standard of training, and those who excelled received merit certificates and scholarships. Sijal Didi frequently organized feasts and gatherings, where everyone—from the orphanage children to the nursing staff and trainees—participated. These occasions were filled with warmth, laughter, and entertainment programs, all designed to foster a sense of belonging. She wanted us to be happy, and we loved her for her kindness and selfless devotion.

Her compassion extended far beyond mere duty. If any child in the orphanage fell ill, she would stay awake through the night, praying for their recovery. When one of the girls was about to get married, she made sure they felt special, treating them to a good meal, giving them thoughtful gifts, and wishing them a blissful future.

From time to time, people came to the orphanage seeking to adopt children. But Sijal Didi never agreed hastily. She meticulously assessed their psychological outlook, social background, and financial stability. Only after a thorough legal process would she consent to an adoption, though parting with a child was never easy for her.

Sijal Didi's concern for the children she placed in adoption was unwavering. She remained in constant touch with them, always enquiring about their welfare. This deep care is evident in her updated record of all the children, knowing who was doing what. If she noticed any negligence from the adopters, she would not hesitate to take action. This level of concern and care is a testament to the depth of her relationship with the children.

The Nursing School and the hostel for working women at the orphanage ran smoothly, embraced by the serene beauty of the hills. Rows of pine trees and wildflowers of every hue swayed in the gentle breeze, as if whispering secrets to the wind. At times, I found myself pausing, captivated by the celestial beauty around me.

Yet, even in this tranquility, memories surfaced. The one who once seemed a sincere well-wisher has drifted into their world, barely reaching out anymore. And Vinit? There is no news of him. Perhaps he has long forgotten me. But I remember—I remember all of them. I call Sony Apa, Biny Apa, Gouri Bhauja, Vikas Bhai, and Akash Bhai to check in on their well-being, weaving threads of connection across the distance.

And in these moments, laughter escapes me—unexpected, unbidden. Perhaps I have too much time on my hands, and the waves of endless time crash lazily upon the shores of my solitude. Maybe that is why I brood. Yet, even in this laughter, I find my strength, my ability to carve joy from sorrow, to stand unshaken in the face of life's uncertainties.

Ha!

I never quite understood why Rista loved me so much. Even on my days off, I felt compelled to visit her. She would eagerly take me by the hand, leading me around her little garden, showing me every flower and leaf as if they were treasures. When we sat together, she would gather all her toys, placing them in front of me one by one. Then, as if building a tiny world of her own, she would stack everything—her shoes, socks, uniform, even her tiffin box—into a neat pile.

Her caretaker, Seema, was a gentle and kind woman. It was always at Rista's insistence that she brought her to see us. She would check our duty schedules before letting Rista come over, making sure she wasn't disturbing us. Over time, our bond with Rista, who lived in the neighbouring quarters, grew deeper.

But I had never seen her mother. That surprised me. Was she no longer alive? Rista never mentioned her, and I didn't have the heart to ask.

One day, I visited Rista's house. She clasped my hand and took me on a little tour, leading me through every room with childlike excitement. As we passed a certain doorway, I noticed a room locked from the outside. A glimpse through the window revealed an elegant dressing table, its surface neatly arranged with cosmetics. It had an air of quiet abandonment, as if time had frozen there. Was this her mother's room? I lingered near the window, my heart heavy with unspoken thoughts.

Pointing towards the room, Rista said softly in Hindi, *"Yeh meri mummy ka kamra hai."* Then, looking up at me with innocent eyes, she added, *"Aunty, kya aapko pata hai? Meri mummy ab nahi hain."*

Her words struck me like a deep, invisible wound. Such a small girl—so full of life, yet carrying the weight of a love she would never know again.

However, Seema had told me a completely different story—one that Rista herself was unaware of. Her mother had left her father when Rista was only three months old. Since then, Seema had been the one looking after her. As for Rista's PApa—poor man! What hardships he must have endured while raising her alone! Perhaps that was why, as Sijal Didi mentioned, he would rush Rista to the hospital at the slightest sign of illness.

My bond with Rista deepened over time. She would visit with Seema now and then, and when she didn't, I found myself going to her house instead. From my balcony, I could see her home, and my eyes would instinctively search for her. Such was my love for the child. But it wasn't just me—my colleagues adored her too.

Two years slipped by, and Rista became an inseparable part of my heart. Her sweet babbling, those guileless eyes, that innocent face—ah, how endearing! A single day without seeing her felt incomplete, as if our connection transcended time, as if it had been carried over from another life.

She, too, looked for me. Every morning, on her way to school, she would glance up at my balcony. If she spotted me, her face would light up, and she would wave gleefully before getting into the car. In a world where the present is one's truest companion, Rista was my present—my solace amid the monotonous routine of my life.

Just when we were growing closer, a question emerged between us—one that I had never anticipated.

One day, Sijal Didi brought forth a proposal. Rista needed a mother. Someone like me—exactly like me.

I had refused instantly.

There was no parity between us—neither in caste nor in language. The only bond we shared was one of feelings, of emotions. But that did not mean I could give Rista a mother's love by marrying her father, Mr. Suren.

I knew Mr. Suren to be a reserved man, a person of few words. He had barely spoken to me. In fact, I always made sure to visit Rista's home when he wasn't around. If he happened to return while I was there, he would quietly retreat to his room, and I would acknowledge him only out of courtesy. He had never inquired about me or my family. So, who had even suggested such a proposal to Sijal Didi?

After that, I stopped going to Rista's house.

A few days later, she came to see me with Seema. Perhaps, unknowingly, my demeanor had changed, for Seema seemed to notice the gravity in my expression. But Rista, blissfully unaware, clung to my neck and pleaded for me to visit her home.

A little while later, Seema left with Rista, as if she had begun to piece the puzzle together.

As I sat alone in a quiet moment, I couldn't help but laugh to myself. How easily such proposals came! Did Mr.

Suren truly believe that my love for Rista was, in fact, love for him? That my deepening bond with his daughter had stemmed from some hidden affection for him?

Sijal Didi visited me to share my feelings. Her voice was gentle, almost coaxing.

"Seema regrets your distant behaviour," she said. "She feels guilty. Mr. Suren, too, has apologised—he said 'sorry' to you."

I barely reacted. Still, out of courtesy, I responded, "Oh, what is there to be sorry about?"

Perhaps the idea had arisen from his concern for Rista's future. I could understand that much.

Sijal Didi continued, her tone still soft, trying to reason with me in her own way. "It's not as if there's a shortage of unmarried girls willing to marry an established man like Mr. Suren. But Rista loves you. And apart from that, Seema wants to return to her own home—her husband is about to retire."

That last piece of news startled me more than the proposal itself. Seema's husband was retiring? Before he had even turned thirty? It sounded almost absurd.

Then I recalled—Seema's husband was Nepali. He must have wanted to return to Nepal. And Seema, bound by duty or perhaps resignation, would follow him. He was thirty-two years older than her.

The more I thought about it, the more I pitied Seema. Poor girl! She had thrown away her entire life for a fleeting mistake. But it wasn't just her—hundreds of innocent girls like her fell prey to men who took advantage of their naivety.

Seema's husband had once been a mere gatekeeper at the school she attended. He had built a relationship with her through chocolates, ice creams, small gifts, and sugar-coated words. How could she have known the truth behind his masked kindness?

Before she could even grasp the simplest equations of life, he had already claimed her. He had taken her from city to city, working different jobs, always on the move. Finally, they had ended up in Sikkim. When he found work as an office gatekeeper, Seema had secured a job in Mr. Suren's house.

According to Seema, Mr. Suren's wife had always been a difficult woman—sharp-tongued and quick-tempered. She would lash out at him over the smallest matters. Mr. Suren had never imagined that their differences would escalate to such an extent.

Seema had pleaded with her on multiple occasions, urging her not to leave her husband and their three-month-old daughter, Rista. But Mrs. Suren had been unmoved. She wouldn't listen to anyone. Finally, one day, she walked out of Mr. Suren's house, leaving behind not just her husband but also her infant daughter.

Mr. Suren had tried, time and again, to bring her back. But what use was anyone's persuasion when a mother felt nothing for her own child? In the end, he resigned himself to his fate.

It was Seema who raised Rista with all her heart and soul. And Rista, in return, loved her deeply.

When the time came for Seema to leave, she struggled. She had tried to convince her husband that she couldn't abandon Rista. Mr. Suren had even offered him a job to keep them in Sikkim. But Seema's husband was unyielding—his mind was set on returning to Nepal. Nothing could deter him.

Rista was the centre of Seema's world, an irreplaceable part of her life. Leaving her behind felt unbearable. But what choice did she have?

Seema did not trust her husband. Every month, like clockwork, he would appear—never to spend time with her, never to ask about her well-being, but simply to collect her salary. And once the money was in his hands, she ceased to exist for him.

Love had come to Seema like a raging flood—sweeping her off her feet, only to leave her drowning in its aftermath. It had destroyed her trust forever.

I had once asked her, "Seema, what will you do in Nepal?"

A dry smile flickered across her face—there for a fleeting moment before vanishing.

"What am I doing here?" she replied bitterly. "He'll arrange something for me there, just as he did here. And if he doesn't? Well, where will the money come from? His earnings barely cover his daily liquor. If I don't give him money, how will he survive?"

One morning, I made an attempt to reason with him. I promised him a job at our nursing home. If both of them worked, they would never have to struggle for money again.

But he didn't understand.

I felt a deep, growing resentment toward Saka, Seema's husband. He was that kind of man—unyielding, unwilling to listen, rigid in his ways.

Meanwhile, Mr. Suren was searching for a caretaker for Rista. Seema's absence, even for a day, would be unbearable for the child. After much effort, a woman was finally found. Seema began preparing to leave for Nepal with Saka.

Circumstances shape a person. Some truths don't need to be spoken in detail—they reveal themselves naturally. This was true for Rista. Life had matured her beyond her years. To the world, she appeared unaffected, but deep within, she buried her pain. Her father was her everything, so she pretended to be fine, suppressing her emotions in silence.

My bond with Seema had only deepened because of Rista. And now, Seema's departure weighed heavily on my heart.

Relationships…

A sandcastle on the shore—built only to be washed away by the relentless tides of time.

Seema was such a relationship. Once she left, I might never see her again.

She came to bid us farewell. Her long plait hung below her waist, swaying gently as she walked with her usual unhurried steps. Her face, solemn and subdued, looked like a rain-washed morning—fresh, yet burdened. She must have wept through the night, trying to drain away all the emotions, all the love, before stepping into her new reality.

She would have to start over. She would bear the weight of Saka. She would work under someone else's authority. Who knew what compromises awaited her?

Like my colleagues, I felt an overwhelming sympathy for her. Though she was just an ordinary woman, the frail story of her life had left an indelible mark on our hearts.

With the blessings of our seniors and the love of the younger ones, she took her leave.

What gift could I give her?

When I placed a small envelope—my one month's salary—into her hands, she pulled me into a tight embrace. Her voice trembled, thick with unspoken words, but in that quivering tone, she pleaded with me to look after Rista. It felt as if she was entrusting her daughter to me rather than to the newly appointed caretaker.

With Sijal Didi's permission, I went to see her off. Rista stood beside me, silent and watchful.

Seema loaded her bags onto the auto-rickshaw. Saka, grumpy and indifferent, was already seated inside, waiting.

Dona, the new caretaker, spoke up, "Didi, check once more—have you left anything behind?"

Seema turned to Rista and pulled her close, pressing her daughter against her chest.

"This is my only wealth," she whispered. "And I'm leaving her behind."

Rista buried her face in Seema's body, clinging to her, both of them trembling with silent sobs.

Tears blurred my vision.

How sacred is love! A bond that transcends lifetimes.

12

Seema left, leaving Rista behind.

It felt as if Rista had changed in just a matter of days. The once lively, talkative girl had turned silent. She hadn't visited us for a week. Worried, Sijal Didi took some time out of her day to go see her.

When she returned, her face was grave.

"Rista was so quiet... unnaturally so," she told us. "It's as if Seema took away all her happiness with her."

Mr. Suren had been at home that day. He confided in Sijal Didi that he couldn't fully trust the new caretaker. And Rista... her face looked dry, her usual glow gone.

Hearing this, my heart ached for the child. But what could I do?

Sijal Didi, on the other hand, was seething with anger at Rista's mother. We all shared the same resentment.

Mr. Suren, his voice heavy with concern, had said, "If things are this difficult now, what will happen when Rista grows older? If I can't give her enough time, won't she become like a river that's lost its course?"

Those words struck a chord in Sijal Didi. She knew what he meant. Rista needed a mother's love—someone who could guide her, nurture her, and keep her from feeling abandoned. It was clear to her: Mr. Suren needed to remarry.

If not a mother in the truest sense, at least a caretaker like Seema—someone who could love Rista like her own child.

Among the unmarried women in our circle, whispers began. Some speculated about Mr. Suren's wealth, some admired his personality, while others considered his social standing.

But Sijal Didi was different. She had an uncanny ability to read people, to see through the masks they wore. Many times, we had witnessed this skill of hers.

Once, in the hostel, someone's money had been stolen. Without hesitation, Sijal Didi had identified the culprit just by reading her face—and sure enough, she recovered the stolen money.

She could always tell who was sincere and who was merely pretending, who wore a smile that didn't reach their eyes.

That's why, in jest, we often called her our very own CBI officer.

Her sharp gaze lingered on me, but she had already sensed my reluctance. So, instead of speaking directly, she chose to hint at things in a roundabout way.

Meanwhile, Bhai's departure abroad had been confirmed, which meant I had to visit Hyderabad to see him before he left.

Seeing Bhai and Gouri Bhauja after so long filled me with happiness. But what made me even happier was meeting their daughter, Mamun. Time had slipped by unnoticed—her babbling, her tiny tottering steps, and the rhythm of her playful conversations with her dolls and toys made me realise just how much had changed.

Time!

How swiftly it moves, how indifferent it is to

everything! It overwhelms all but is never overwhelmed. It makes people laugh and cry while it rushes forward like a river, detached and unconcerned. It bewilders but is never bewildered. It brings misfortune to others but remains unaffected itself.

How selfish time is!

A gentle hand on my head pulled me out of my thoughts.

"Hey, Jhara! Where are you lost?" Akash Bhai's voice rang behind me.

Absentmindedly, I murmured, "Just thinking about time… how it slips away from our hands. Isn't it the greatest deceiver?"

A faint, weary smile flickered on Bhai's face.

Indeed! Time belongs to everyone, yet it belongs to no one. It holds the power to enchant, to captivate, and yet, it cunningly evades our grasp.

Bhai's voice, laced with quiet wisdom, echoed my own unspoken thoughts. He called me *mother*—a term of endearment he often used for me—and his aged appearance gnawed at my heart.

My brother.

A part of my soul. The one I love more than myself. The guiding light of my life from childhood till today. He is the keeper of my memories, and every word he speaks is like the sacred sound of a conch shell.

And yet… how close we are, and how far Apart.

Born of the same blood, raised in the same house, yet now, we have no claim over each other's lives. Even if he wants to, he cannot say *yes* to my *yes*. And despite his *no*, I cannot stay any longer.

What a contrast!

There was a time when his words were law to me—

when his permission and orders shaped my world. I obeyed him without question, without hesitation.

Now, I have travelled all the way from Sikkim just to see this brother of mine.

But we are like two parallel passenger trains, running on our own tracks—close, yet never crossing.

Bhai said, "I knew it, Jhara—you would definitely come before I left India. And if you hadn't, I would have gone to Sikkim to see you."

I sat down, drained. Bhai must have thought I was crying. Perhaps I should have—shedding a few tears might have offered some relief. But my eyes felt like dry riverbeds, parched from witnessing too many storms, too many losses.

Bhai moved closer and gently ran his fingers through my hair. "You know," he said, his voice heavy with resignation, "whether I stay in India or leave, it makes no difference. I have already failed in my role as the eldest son. I couldn't be there for our parents, for our siblings. Your Bhauja has built a wall between us—I on one side, all of you on the other. So tell me, what difference does it make if I go?"

I had already read Bhai's mind—his unspoken grief etched deep within him. Though she had torn our family apart, isolating our parents and grandmother, at least they had been spared from seeing this day. Had they been alive, what unbearable pain would they have endured?

I changed the subject, steering the conversation toward his company, Bhauja's plans, and updates on Biny Apa and Sony Apa.

Yet, even as Bhai spoke, his words barely registered. My mind drifted, caught in the relentless tide of time. How swiftly life had rearranged its scenes—one moment blending into the next, each event, each wound appearing and vanishing like passing shadows in a flickering play.

Perhaps the night had aged beyond its prime. Bhai rose to his feet, stretching slightly. While praising Gouri Bhauja's cooking, he carefully entrusted us—the three sisters—to Vikas Bhai's care. Vikas Bhai nodded in silent acknowledgment, his expression carrying the weight of quiet responsibility.

Bhai turned to me with a wistful smile. "Jhara, I'm so happy to see how much you've steeled yourself over time. My sentimental princess, my little daughter, is no longer the weepy sort—no more July showers! I can't tell you how relieved I am."

His words lingered in my mind. *Tears bring relief, but a sky heavy with unshed rain suffocates with its sultriness. How unbearable!*

As I bid him farewell that day, a stray thought crossed my mind—*Was this the last time I would see Bhai?* Who could say? He left with a heavy heart, burdened by the unfulfilled duty of arranging my marriage. But that sorrow had never been mine to carry. I had never feared a difficult life without marriage.

Instead, I had chosen to live with my own identity, to stand on my own without dependence. I would be fine—wherever life placed me, with or without anyone's support.

And if fate led me to cross paths with Vinit again, what would I say to him?

I still hadn't deleted his number from my phone. Sometimes, I felt the urge to call him, but I never did. I would stare at the digits on the screen, my fingers hovering over them, yet I couldn't bring myself to press 'dial.' Perhaps the number had changed by now.

A wave of shame washed over me. How deeply I had loved someone, as if he had belonged to me—when, in truth, he never did.

I forced my thoughts into submission. The bond of brotherhood in this family had always been fragile; expecting anything more was futile.

Gouri Bhauja urged me to extend my leave, to stay a few more days. "Who knows when we will meet again once we leave this place?" she said.

I looked at her and smiled. "Maybe my father had a premonition when he named me Jharana. Sometimes I wonder—was my name chosen to match my fate, or did fate shape itself around my name?"

Gouri Bhauja fell silent. There was nothing left to say.

The next day, I returned to Sikkim, to my place of work. Lately, the present felt like my truest companion. My workplace had become an extension of me, familiar and comforting. And dearest of all was this Apartment—shared by thirty unmarried women, a space where no one pried into anyone's personal life.

Perhaps we had all reached an age where such questions had lost their relevance. If someone understood, they understood. If not, it hardly mattered.

Sijal Didi, ever perceptive, had built this world with quiet wisdom. She made sure we stayed in good spirits, offering tight hugs to anyone who seemed downhearted. Beyond her warmth, she nurtured resilience in all of us, instilling strength and moral courage—reminders that we belonged to ourselves before anyone else.

13

Once again, Rista was admitted to our hospital. It wasn't serious—just an ordinary fever. But Mr. Suren, panicked as always, insisted on getting her admitted. She stayed for three to four days, and in that time, the hospital became more than just a place of treatment—it became a familiar refuge. Mr. Suren seemed at ease, knowing Rista was safe while he was at work, as if the hospital belonged to him. Rista often joked about it too. She knew that every time she fell ill, she was brought here, no matter how minor the illness. To her, it was as natural as home.

Yet, a peculiar question often lingered in my mind. Rista always said her mother had died, but according to Seema and Sijal Didi, the truth was different. Her mother had left Mr. Suren when Rista was just three months old due to irreconcilable differences, and they had legally separated. Whatever the past held, my heart ached for Rista. *Had her mother been there, would she have been admitted to the hospital over a slight fever?*

She had grown up with Seema's love and care, but things had changed. Rista struggled to bond with her new caretaker, Dona. She missed Seema's warmth, and it showed.

That day, I spent a long time with her. Her sweet, endless chatter filled the air, tugging at my heart. She was upset about being discharged the next day. Pouting, she insisted, "Can't I just go to school from here? Is there any problem if I stay with you?"

Sijal Didi teased, "You can't stay with us. This Apartment is only for unmarried ladies."

With a sharp reply, Rista declared, "Aye! I'm unmarried too, and I promise to remain unmarried forever."

We burst into laughter. Sijal Didi, amused, said, "There's an eligibility age. Once you reach it, you can stay with us."

Rista took her words seriously. With innocent determination, she said, "Alright then, I'll finish my studies, find a job, and stay here with you."

Her words made me drift into thought. *How naive she was! Would she still say this if she understood the winding, unpredictable path of life?*

Sijal Didi consoled her, "Rista, you live so close to us. You can see us from your window. Just call out, and we'll be there whenever you need us."

Like a good girl, Rista nodded silently. She left the next day but not before whispering, "Aunty, to be honest, I love having a fever. Do you know why? Because then, I get to spend time with you and Sijal Didi for a long time."

Everyone called her 'Didi,' but to Rista, I was 'Aunty.' Her words made me smile, yet I could read between them, feel the emptiness she carried in her heart.

I didn't know why, but lately, I had developed a deep affection for her. An attachment beyond reason.

Whenever I had free time, I would visit her. She would sit by my side, doing her homework, playing the Casio, or simply playing with her toys—as if I were her guide, her friend, and her beloved Aunty.

No one can defy God's will. Otherwise, what name

could I give to this inexplicable bond between Rista and me?

Whenever I found some free time, I would frequent to her. Sitting by me, she would do her homework, play the cashio and play with her toys too as if I was her guide, friend and her beloved aunty.

No one can go against God's will. Had it been not so, what name could be given to the relation between Rista and me?

14

My friendship with Mr. Suren existed only because of Rista. He often planned outings on my days off, and the three of us would spend time together. More often than not, he would invite me for lunch or dinner. He was a man of few words—perhaps shaped by the weight of his personal struggles.

At times, I wanted to ask about his life, about Rista's mother, and where she was now. *How could a mother live without her child? Did she never long to see Rista, even once?* Or had Mr. Suren kept her away? But I never dared to ask. His demeanor was always measured, his boundaries carefully drawn. He had extended his hand in friendship solely for Rista's sake, never stepping beyond that line.

There were moments when I felt like opening up to him—sharing my story, my past, my uncertain future. But the impulse vanished the moment our eyes met. I became speechless. *How could I confide in a man who had never once asked where I came from or who was waiting for me back home?* Perhaps, to him, I was nothing more than a source of comfort for his daughter.

Then, one evening, a phone call from Vikas Bhai struck a deep chord in my heart. His voice was weary yet firm.

"Jhara, please agree to this proposal and let us live in peace."

His words felt like a wound cutting through me. How could he even suggest such a thing? *Did he really believe I would accept a man fifteen years older than me—a father of two children—as my husband?*

My mind reeled. I could hear his voice from the other end, steady yet insistent.

"Jhara, you don't understand," he said. "After Bhai left for abroad, your responsibility rests on me. I've already given my word to him—a very wealthy businessman."

A suffocating weight settled over me. *Is this what they thought of my life? A burden to be handed over?*

He continued, "Listen, there's something else you need to know. I'm his business partner—we work together. So please, don't refuse."

His words stung, but I wasn't just angry at Vikas Bhai—I was more frustrated with my fate. *Why does life keep turning against me like this?* I am not a burden on anyone. I have a job, I support myself, and I am saving for my future. *What setbacks do I have? Why do they act as if my life needs to be 'fixed' through marriage?*

That day, I confided in Sijal Didi about the proposal. She gave me a response that resonated deeply:

"People become more restless about an unmarried woman's future than the woman herself. Families treat an unmarried daughter like an unsolved problem, as if she's a burden that must be passed on. But Jhara, you've reached an age where you can decide for yourself."

Her words strengthened my resolve. I refused the proposal.

But they were persistent. Vikas Bhai, unwilling to accept my decision, used Gouri Bhauja as an intermediary. At the time, I failed to see through their plan. Gouri Bhauja tried to convince me, coaxing me into agreement, but I stood my ground.

Then, one day, Vikas Bhai called again. His voice carried an urgency that unsettled me.

"Gouri Bhauja's mother is seriously ill. She wants to see you. Please take leave for two days and come."

I hesitated, suspicion creeping into my mind. *Was this another ploy?* I didn't trust his words. But then, Gouri Bhauja herself called, her voice sincere.

"Jhara, Mother is eager to see you. Please come."

Among all my family members, if there was anyone I still trusted, it was Akash Bhai. And after him, it was Gouri Bhauja.

Her words swayed me. And against my better judgment, I decided to go.

Wasn't this another "Man or elephant—Ashwatthama is slain" kind of deception? I had my doubts. Was Gouri Bhauja covering up for Vikas Bhai's lie?

Still, I decided to go—for two days only. I had deep love and respect for Gouri Bhauja's mother. After my own mother's passing, she had given me the kind of selfless, unconditional affection that was rare in this world. I could never forget her warmth.

That was the only reason I went.

The last time I had visited Hyderabad, I had spent all my time with Akash Bhai, barely managing a few words with Aunty. *This time, I will dedicate all my moments to her*, I thought. Age is fleeting, and who knows how many more chances we will have?

But the moment I saw Aunty, my suspicions hardened into certainty.

She was not sick in the least. In fact, she looked perfectly healthy.

Seeing me, she broke into a delighted smile and embraced me warmly. "I just can't believe you came all the way here upon hearing of my illness! Today, I realise the depth of your love for me."

Her affectionate words stirred something deep inside me—a painful reminder of my mother's love.

I spent most of my time by Aunty's side, but the truth revealed itself soon enough. That day, Vikas Bhai introduced me to a man—the so-called 'suitable match' they had chosen for me.

The moment I saw him, I knew.

He was a bulky man, his presence commanding but unappealing. His expensive attire and the luxury car he arrived in screamed of his wealth. And that was all there was to him—his business, his bank balance, his multiple houses in different cities. That was the entirety of his identity.

Vikas Bhai, mesmerized by the man's status, stood by him in admiration.

Then the man spoke, his voice as direct as it was dismissive.

"I want to marry you because my two sons need the right guidance. Without it, they will go astray."

I didn't need to look at his face to understand his attitude. His words were enough.

He wasn't looking for a wife. He was looking for a governess, a caretaker for his broken family.

Even without stepping into his life, I could see the cracks running deep.

He went on telling his story, indifferent to whether I cared to listen. Vikas Bhai supported him wholeheartedly, nodding along as if the man's words were gospel.

Both Vikas Bhai and Gouri Bhauja took turns trying to convince me. *He is straightforward, wealthy, and caring,* they insisted. They weren't just presenting a proposal—they were attempting to reshape my thoughts, to mould my will according to their design.

Vikas Bhai's enthusiasm was almost feverish. I could see the real reason behind it—his business ambitions. He wasn't offering me a future; he was bargaining with my life for his own gain.

Anger surged within me. Unable to hold back, I blurted out, "Vikas Bhai, how selfish can you be? You're willing to throw me into an abyss just to secure your business interests?"

They both froze, staring at me, momentarily speechless. Then Gouri Bhauja recovered, her voice turning persuasive.

"Jharana, you're misunderstanding us. We only want what's best for you. You're not getting any younger. At this age, it's wiser to compromise than to wait for an ideal match. Besides, Mr. Patnaik is a gentleman—he'll be a caring husband."

I felt like laughing at the irony of her words.

And what exactly is your definition of a caring husband, dear Bhauja?

I wanted to ask her, *Have you ever had a single moment of comfort in your marriage? You've worked tirelessly, taken up jobs here and there, kept this house running—have you ever been truly valued for it? Has Vikas Bhai, with all his whims and irresponsibility, ever rewarded you for your sacrifices?*

You married him after knowing him so well, yet even you couldn't fully understand him. And you expect me to blindly follow your advice?

I swallowed my words. There was no point in saying them. Instead, I simply said, "Give me some time to think it over. I'll let you know once I leave."

Just then, Gouri Bhauja's mother, who had been quietly listening, finally spoke.

"Jhara is not a child. She should not be forced into anything. She's independent, earning her own livelihood. Let her decide for herself. And besides, what's so wrong with remaining unmarried? It's better to stay single than to be deceived."

Her words were like a balm on my wounded soul. For a moment, it felt as though my mother was speaking through her. Overcome with emotion, I embraced her tightly.

Aunty understood me in a way no one else did. My love and respect for her deepened.

But then, Gouri Bhauja finally revealed the crux of the matter.

"Do you know, Jhara? There's a bigger problem. If Vikas Bhai doesn't work with him, things could get complicated. Your brother has borrowed a substantial amount from him." She hesitated, then added softly, "The man is slightly older, yes, but he has a good heart. After all, what does a man's appearance matter? Didn't you see Vinit?"

Her words struck like a dagger. She had unknowingly scratched a wound that had barely begun to heal.

I clenched my fists, forcing down my emotions. I couldn't be angry at her—what choice did she have? She was caught between her husband's desperation and the supposed 'burden' of an unmarried sister-in-law. In her own way, she was trying to navigate both.

Poor woman. She was just another victim of circumstance, just like me.

I remained resolute.

After that, Gouri Bhauja called less often—her

conversations abruptly cut off after a few words. I found myself questioning the very definition of relationship. *Is this truly what connection means?* In her eyes, perhaps, I was misunderstood—a mistake, despite my deep love for her.

These days, Sijal Didi grew especially close to me. Whenever I felt wounded, I would confide in her, and she'd gently console, "This is only temporary. In ten years, you won't face these issues." With a reassuring emphasis, she added, "Jhara, isn't it a hundred times better to marry Mr. Suren than to accept a man with two sons? He's an honest officer—a respected man in this community. And while Rista adores you, I would never rush you into a decision. Study Mr. Suren a little longer, and then do as your heart desires."

I still couldn't understand why I'd come to consider Mr. Suren one of my intimate friends. Could I possibly see him any differently?

"It's all God's desire," I replied, putting an end to the discussion.

Rista, on the other hand, seemed to stake her claim on my heart. Along with my own responsibilities, I found myself compelled to care for her. Every time I encountered something delightful—a girl her age in a pretty dress, a new book, or a toy—I would think of her. I began buying little things, all because my thoughts kept drifting back to Rista.

Sometimes, I wondered who Rista truly was to me. There was no conventional bond between us, yet she represented hope in a loveless world. Her face would light up with unspoken joy whenever she saw me; her smile, radiant. She'd run to me, wrapping herself around me like a tender vine.

Our feelings often spoke without words.

One evening, accepting Rista's invitation, I joined Mr.

Suren and her for dinner at their home. Rista asked, "Why didn't you become a teacher at our school? It would make me so happy."

In a light-hearted tone, I replied, "Then why not arrange a job for me there? I'd gladly leave here." Mr. Suren chuckled and said, "I truly value both fields—education and nursing."

At that moment, the delicate fragrance of fresh tube roses filled the air, and, almost involuntarily, Vinit came to my mind. I recalled the days when his father had been ill, his reluctance to accept a nurse as his daughter-in-law, and the silent support Vinit offered. So many memories rushed in, and I found myself unable to focus on the rest of Mr. Suren's words.

Then Rista grasped my hand and said, "Hello, Aunty! PApa is trying to tell you something." I suddenly felt embarrassed by my absent-mindedness. Mr. Suren had been asking why I worked so far from home. Since he'd never pried into my personal affairs, I had replied openly, "After my parents passed away, there was nothing left that felt like home. All my siblings are lost in their own worlds now. My job—that is where my home is."

My voice was steady, free from agony, but Mr. Suren's expression was a blend of compassion and surprise. Perhaps, for the first time, he truly saw the loneliness that defined my life.

Trying to lighten the mood, he said, "Maybe that explains your deep bond with Rista... It's nothing but God's design."

Rista turned to me, her voice carrying a tinge of maturity beyond her years. "Aunty, wouldn't it be wonderful if we could stay together? Not just for now, but forever."

By then, Mr. Suren had moved to the washbasin.

I recalled Sijal Didi's words from that day after I returned from Mr. Suren's house. "Jharana, if you consider me a well-wisher, then for Rista's sake, I'd say—marry Mr. Suren."

Once again, my mind swarmed with questions, tangled in a web of yeses and nos.

Mr. Suren admired my profession—he had said so once. Rista insisted she couldn't live without me. On the other hand, Vikas Bhai and Gouri Bhauja were rigid in their advocacy for that wealthy businessman. Sijal Didi, however, saw things differently. "Marriage isn't always essential," she had said, "but for you, if a motherless child finds a mother and a lonely man finds joy, isn't that reason enough?"

I gazed into the distance, lost in thought. If marriage were truly so simple, why had so many women sought refuge here? They seemed to be silent witnesses to a harsh truth—that countless women like them had crossed the so-called marriageable age and had been labeled, stamped—UNMARRIED.

Sijal Didi led me near a room. It was Rona Didi's. She was packing her belongings. Today, she would move to the Apartment across from ours.

I was stunned to learn from Sijal Didi that Rona Didi had just had a registered marriage. At fifty!

"With whom?" I blurted out.

Sijal Didi read the questions on my face. "For companionship, Jharana. They will be each other's support. The man has diabetes, thyroid issues—many ailments. And yet, Rona married him, fully aware of everything."

Through a gap in the curtain, I watched Rona Didi, methodically packing her things, preparing for a new beginning.

On the way back, I wanted to ask Sijal Didi—what had compelled her to remain unmarried? But the words stuck in my throat.

Did it even matter? Maybe there was no grand reason. Maybe it was family obligations, personal struggles, divine will—or simply the cruel irony of fate.

Just then, a call from the Labour Room interrupted my thoughts. Duty called, and Sijal Didi left.

I headed to the Surgery Ward, where I was assigned for the night. The patient in Bed 5 was writhing in pain, his moans piercing the air. His wife, a frail woman, pleaded with me in a soft, desperate voice.

"Didi, please... do something to ease his pain."

As I administered the saline and a sedative, I reassured her. Her husband finally slipped into sleep. She sat beside him, watching him intently, as if afraid to blink.

I was about to settle at my desk when Rista's voice reached me.

"Aunty, I can't sleep."

I sighed, already suspecting the reason. "And what were you doing till now?" I asked, a little annoyed.

She hesitated. "Were you watching TV?" I pressed.

"How did you know?" she whispered, surprised.

"I always know."

She giggled softly.

"Go to bed right now," I said, firm but affectionate. "I'm off duty tomorrow, and you have no school. But you must get up early and study for your exams."

"Okay, Aunty," she agreed like a good girl.

"And PApa?" I asked.

After a pause, she said, "PApa has been in bed for a long time. Do know why, Aunty?" "He takes sleeping pills." Then, lowering her voice, she admitted, "One day,

I asked for one too, but he refused. Said they weren't for children."

A shiver ran through me as she continued, her voice eerily calm.

"But I'll take them when I grow up, Aunty. So I can sleep well, too."

"Hey, stop that nonsense, will you? I'll never come to you if you keep talking this way. Now go to bed like a good girl." I said this sulkily, my voice firm yet weary.

"Aunty, good night!" she called softly before retreating to her room.

Her words lingered in the air, leaving an ache in my chest. Poor Mr. Suren—relying on sleeping pills to get through the night. A man surrounded by wealth yet drowning in loneliness.

Perhaps this is the way of the world. Every life carries its own burdens, woven together with fleeting joys. Good days slip away unnoticed, but sorrow—sorrow sits heavy, pressing down like an unshakable weight, crushing the fragile glasshouse of the mind. Under its burden, even the strongest head bows—before society, before fate, before the Almighty.

What does Mr. Suren lack? And yet, he trudges forward, bearing his grief in one hand and the joy of a loving daughter in the other. I finally understood the depth of his unhappiness. He had once confessed—if Rista had been a son, his worries might have been fewer. She was growing up fast, nearing an age when a mother's presence would be irreplaceable. Only a mother could guide her through the confusion of adolescence, teaching her the unspoken rules of the world, helping her discern right from wrong. A mother's wisdom shapes a daughter's understanding of life—teaching her to recognize the difference between a rock and a flower, to navigate the thorns hidden beneath beauty.

A house without a mother is not a home. It is a wilderness.

If Rista's mother had been there, would Mr. Suren have rushed her to the hospital for every minor ailment?

Lost in these thoughts, my mind drifted, and eventually, sleep came to me.

That night, I had a strange dream. I was Rista's mother—caring for her, embracing her playful, exuberant nature, enduring her tantrums with patience. She called me *Mummy*, her voice filled with warmth and trust. My days revolved around her; there was no hospital, no patients, no responsibilities beyond her. Just the two of us, cocooned in our little world.

The dream lingered in my mind throughout the next day, consuming my thoughts. Conflicts and confusions clashed within me, waging a silent war. A chorus of *yeses* and *no's* echoed in my head, making me restless. I felt weak, unable to understand why my thoughts were taking such unexpected turns.

It was as if a voice from deep within me whispered, *"Jhara, whose pain are you measuring while you sit atop your own mountain of suffering? You stretch your small umbrella to shield others, yet you stand exposed—battered by the sun and rain."*

I shuddered. Whose voice was that? No—it was my own. The voice of self. I needed to shake it off.

Just then, Mr. Suren's call interrupted my turmoil.

"I have something to discuss with you. When can you give me some time?" His voice carried an unfamiliar gentleness, a weight of unspoken emotions.

I hesitated briefly before replying, *"I'm free this evening. No duty."*

"Okay. I'll be home, waiting for you."

The line went dead, but I remained still, the phone pressed absently against my ear, as if expecting to hear something more.

I didn't know why, but his words stirred something in me. My mind kept circling back to the dream. Do dreams seen before dawn really come true?

The day slipped through my fingers. I flitted from one thought to another, unfocused, detached from reality. My work suffered, each task a blur of half-hearted effort. My mind was a restless tide—scattered, lost, drowning in something I couldn't quite grasp.

A shiver ran through me, as delicate as the rustling of new leaves in a gentle breeze. What would Mr. Suren say? Would he really ask me to become Rista's mother? And if he did, would I refuse outright, or would I take time to consider?

Whatever my answer—yes or no—I would consult Bhai first. He would likely agree, but Vikas Bhai? He would undoubtedly object. Gouri Bhauja would pull a long face, she would be shocked that I accepted Mr. Suren's rejecting their business partner's proposal.

A storm of uncertainty raged in my mind, accompanied by a drizzle of apprehension. Yet, despite the turbulence, Mr. Suren's words—*'Okay. I'll be home, waiting for you.'*—lingered like a quiet melody, soothing my restless thoughts.

I had visited that house countless times for Rista, but today felt different. For the first time in a long while, I put effort into my appearance. Just then, Sijal Didi appeared.

"Are you going to Rista's?" she asked. "Come back soon—you have Rona's duty." She started to leave but paused, looking at me intently. A slow smile spread across her lips. "Wow! You look stunning."

I stepped closer. "Mr. Suren has called me for an important discussion."

A knowing light flickered in her eyes. "In my opinion, you should say yes," she said, her voice warm with conviction. "I've known Mr. Suren for ten years—he is a rare gentleman. And you… you are the perfect mother for Rista."

I couldn't meet her gaze, though there was no shame in me—only the quiet weight of my own honesty.

She gently caressed my head. "Life is full of twists and tides," she murmured. "If we face them with courage, they become stepping stones. If not, life turns into a barren desert. And remember, everything is predestined. Whether you call Him God, Allah, Jesus, or Narayan, He has already sketched the design of your life before your birth. It is our sacred duty to accept it with humility."

I understood what she meant.

She left without waiting for my response. I stood there, gazing at the sky—it had never looked so beautiful. Two exotic birds soared above, conversing in a language only they understood. A creeper, entwined around a tree I had never noticed before, was bursting into bloom. Strange… I had passed this place so many times, yet I had never seen these blossoms. What were they called? What kind of flower was this?

For the first time, I truly saw them.

I was oblivious to the murmurs of the outside world. Silently, I knelt beside the tree, my fingers tracing the delicate tendrils of a creeper, its tiny, enchanting, rosy blossoms swaying gently. A sudden urge arose—to ask someone its name. But there was no one around.

The verdant evening stretched its arms in quiet embrace. Two birds perched nearby flapped their wings and soared into the sky, vanishing like fleeting thoughts. Before dusk could fully settle, the electric lights flickered on, casting a golden glow over the surroundings.

Mr. Suren sat waiting for me in a garden chair, the artificial fountain before him swaying in rhythm to the soft strains of music. The water, shimmering under the changing hues of light, pirouetted like a dancer lost in a trance. Behind him, an artificial hillock stood beneath drifting clouds, a silent spectator to the orchestrated spectacle.

I couldn't help but admire Mr. Suren's aesthetic sense.

As if reading my thoughts, he asked, "How do you find the hillock and the fountain? Beautiful, aren't they?"

I smiled in quiet appreciation.

A slight smile played on his lips as he mused, "Modern man must lose himself in artificial beauty."

I cast him a questioning glance. He gestured to the orderly. "Tea, coffee, or something cold?"

"Anything will do. I have no preference," I replied.

He burst into laughter. "Do you know, Jhara, people who can manage with anything are often the most unhappy?"

His words caught me off guard. Were my unspoken thoughts so transparent, my emotions laid bare like an open book?

As if to turn an unread page, I quickly said, "No, no! Nothing like that—I just mean I like everything. Tea, coffee, or a cold drink, it doesn't matter."

His gaze lingered, unreadable. Then, with the same air of quiet mystery, he remarked,

"People who claim to love everything often love only themselves. And when love does come to them, it slips away—just as easily as it arrived."

His words made me pause. Did he know about Vinit? Had he heard whispers of my past?

I hadn't even noticed when the orderly had brought the coffee. Mr. Suren handed me a cup and silently sipped from his own.

I broke the silence. "Where is Rista? I don't see her. Isn't she home?"

"She's studying."

I raised an eyebrow. Studying? That didn't sound like Rista. She wasn't the kind of girl to stay buried in her books when she knew I was here.

As if reading my thoughts, Mr. Suren said, "You're surprised she hasn't come out despite knowing you're here, aren't you?"

"Yes, of course! She never sits quietly inside. And since when did she start studying by herself?"

"She's not doing it willingly," he admitted. "I told her to stay inside until I call her. I needed to talk to you first."

Every word of his carried an air of mystery, but I kept my expression neutral.

Then, as if concluding a matter already decided, he said, "You'll leave after dinner tonight."

I objected instinctively, though I wasn't sure why. Something about this conversation unsettled me. He had called me here for something important—yet he hadn't said what it was.

His next question caught me off guard.

"Jhara, have you ever felt the agony of losing something after having it?"

I met his gaze and replied with quiet composure. "Everyone does, sooner or later. Parents, joy, childhood, the love of siblings—everything comes and goes. And yet, we live on. We laugh, make others laugh, and, standing on the past, we look toward the present, letting our gaze stretch toward the horizon of the future. Strange, isn't it? Life's journey ends while we're still busy collecting its mixed experiences."

He leaned forward slightly, his voice measured. "Then, can we not make a decision before life's journey ends?"

I frowned, unsure of his meaning. The question lingered in my mind as he rose and walked inside—perhaps to Rista.

Was this why he had called me here? To discuss a decision? What decision?

Had he carefully placed a marriage proposal before me?

Should I agree to it?

Somewhere along the way, I had become drawn to Mr. Suren. His presence, his quiet strength, his refined sensibilities—they fascinated me. But what I admired most was his unwavering love for Rista. Anyone would acknowledge the depth of his devotion. Raising a three-month-old baby alone was no small feat. Behind everything in Rista's life—her studies, the birthday parties she attended, even the dresses she wore—was Mr. Suren's guiding hand.

I remembered Seema once saying, "No matter how carefully I dress her, her father never rests without adding the finishing touch."

That single detail spoke volumes.

And now, I stood at the crossroads of a decision I wasn't sure I was ready to make.

No matter how busy he was, he never failed to check on Rista over the phone. Truly, a man's face reflects his soul, and his concern for her spoke volumes about his character.

How could Rista's mother leave such an understanding husband?

Seema often said, *"Mr. Suren is like a god."*

A storm of thoughts swirled in my mind. Could I ever give my consent to Mr. Suren without consulting Akash Bhai?

I had visited his house countless times in the past few months, yet he had never hinted at anything. If this was the first time he was opening his heart to me and I refused, it would surely hurt him.

His words echoed in my mind—*"Can we not take a new decision before life's journey ends?"*

The meaning was clear. A shared decision. A new beginning. A family.

Had he given me only the brief moment it took him to return from Rista's room to make up my mind? What else could this be, if not a proposal?

And if he asked me directly, what answer would I give?

I resolved to say, *"I will answer after speaking to my brother."*

Moments later, Mr. Suren returned to the lawn with Rista. Seeing me, she exclaimed, *"Aunty, I knew you were here! But PApa didn't let me come out—he said he had something important to discuss with you."*

I pulled her into a hug. Her small, warm hands clasped mine tightly.

Mr. Suren watched us, then said, *"Jhara, your bond with Rista must be from many lifetimes; otherwise, how could she love you so deeply? Sometimes, I feel she loves you even more than she loves me."*

Rista frowned. Running between us, she wrapped her arms around her father. *"That's not true! I love both of you equally."*

Our eyes met. His gaze held something unspoken—

something raw and full of meaning. I wasn't sure what he saw in my eyes, but I saw his, brimming with emotion.

A sudden shiver ran through me as the cool mist from the artificial fountain touched my skin. It was like the first drop of unexpected rain—a thrill unlike any I had known.

I thought, *If a man could make you feel this way at the slightest touch, wasn't he the right one?*

Rista, holding my hand in one and her father's in the other, tugged us forward. *"Come inside! I have so much homework."*

Slipping his hand free, Mr. Suren gestured toward me. *"You go. Jhara ma'am will help you. I don't understand your lessons; I'd be of no use."*

Rista turned to me, eyes wide with curiosity. *"Really, Aunty? Are you more qualified than PApa?"*

I bit back a smile.

Before I could answer, Mr. Suren chuckled. *"Oh, definitely! Don't you see how easily your Aunty gives injections one after another? And your PApa? He shudders at the mere sight of a needle!"*

We all burst into laughter and walked inside together.

Later, as I sat with Rista at her study table, Mr. Suren disappeared into his room.

That night, as I walked home, I carried more than just my thoughts—I carried his words, each one like a verse of poetry resonating in my heart.

But against my will, another voice crept in.

Vinit had once spoken to me like this too.

His words had once enchanted me just as much.

Then?

Was I about to make the same mistake again? Was I walking into another unknown realm of sorrow?

Once again?

15

My colleagues were gossiping about Rona Didi—some criticizing her, others condemning her husband. Among them, many had already crossed the so-called marriageable age.

But all of them fell silent when Sijal Didi spoke. Her voice, calm yet firm, carried a weight no one could ignore.

"Everyone in this world has their own path to follow. No one can force another to walk alongside them in life's journey. So, no one has the right to judge Rona's personal choices."

I was deeply moved by her words. How measured, how seasoned they were! Sijal Didi always astonished me with her wisdom.

Our hostel housed nearly a hundred unmarried women, 53 of whom had long surpassed the conventional age for marriage. Yet, not one of them lacked beauty. Some still radiated a youthful charm that time had not diminished.

Sijal Didi was one of them. A face as delicate as a betel leaf, an aquiline nose, large expressive blue eyes, and lips that seemed to belong to a masterful painting. But beyond her physical beauty, it was her sincerity, her compassion, and her ceaseless energy that made her extraordinary.

Whenever she walked into a room, she brought with her a flood of warmth and happiness.

That evening, she and I were in the duty room. The hospital was abuzz with urgency—a serious patient, an important man, had been admitted. The pressure was immense, and we had been on our feet all night.

At some point, exhaustion took over, and I dozed off, my head resting on the table.

A soft voice woke me.

"Here, have some coffee."

I opened my eyes to find Sijal Didi standing beside me, two cups in her hands. She smiled, motioning for me to sit up.

As we sipped, she sighed. *"The poor man finally fell asleep after hours of pain."*

I nodded, lost in thought. Suffering—whether physical or emotional—was an inevitable part of life. A circle incomplete without its shadows.

"Do you know, Jhara?" she continued. *"None of his family has come yet. A young man admitted him after finding him in critical condition. He told us that the old man has been a widower for five years. His two sons live abroad."*

I glanced at the beds. I had been comparing two patients all night—bed number six and bed number seven.

One was a renowned public figure, the other an ordinary man.

Crowds swarmed around the VIP patient, whispering in hushed tones, eager for updates.

But the man in bed number seven lay alone, his eyes following the visitors with quiet longing.

Poor fellow. His own blood had abandoned him.

What must he be thinking, watching the endless stream of well-wishers across from him? What pain must he be feeling at the stark contrast?

Sijal Didi sighed. *"What really is the value of human bonds in this world? If even sons can distance themselves from their fathers, whom can we truly call our own?"*

I responded indifferently, *"There are many people in this world who remain unwanted despite having a family."*

Setting her empty cup aside, she looked at me with a thoughtful smile.

"At least we have each other. That, too, is a kind of blessing."

I nodded. It was true.

Placing her hand over mine, she said gently, *"I believe that no matter how far Jhara goes, she will never forget her Sijal Didi."*

There was a quiet confidence blooming in her eyes.

I smiled. *"Why, Didi? Are you planning to send me away?"*

She laughed, *"Not too far. Just across the boundary wall."*

I understood what she meant, but I chose to change the subject. *"Didi, it's time we changed the saline for bed number three. You should rest for a while."*

She sighed but didn't push further.

Then, just as I was leaving, she added softly, *"Jhara, you never take these things seriously. But listen to me—it would be wise if you accepted Mr. Suren's proposal."*

Her words lingered as I walked away, slow steps weighed down by unspoken questions.

Why was she so insistent lately? Had she once ignored such a chance in her own life?

But I couldn't ask her that.

After tending to bed number three, I walked over to bed number seven.

The old man lay still, helpless. The doctors had already said he wouldn't survive. His belly was swollen unnaturally, his limbs puffed, his face a pale mask.

And yet, in his sleep, his expression held a desperate will to live.

His breathing was ragged, but he still pleaded with the doctors, *"Please... save me. I want to live."*

I was startled by his determination.

His neighbouring patient turned to me and whispered, *"Didi, will this old man die in a day or two? I overheard the doctors… Please shift me to another bed. I'm scared."*

I reassured him. *"Don't worry, we are here. You have nothing to fear."*

The old man's forehead was damp with sweat, though the room was cold. His skin had lost all colour.

Would the morning even come for him?

A few minutes later, his face twisted further. His breathing grew uneven—his final struggle.

I called the doctor. But by the time we connected the oxygen, it was too late.

He had breathed his last.

We had the phone number of the young man who had admitted him. I called immediately.

His reply stung.

"I admitted him, that's all. I can't take responsibility for the body. Do whatever you want."

The words cut like ice.

But this was not new.

I had seen it before, over and over again.

The sweepers came. The body was taken away.

And just like that, a life ended—discarded like garbage.

For some, death brings mourning, tears, and remembrance.

For others, there is no one to say goodbye.

16

Rista was unwavering in her demand, and it left me conflicted. She insisted on an outing to North Sikkim, and Mr. Suren, too, urged me to join.

"Jharana, I have something important to tell you," he said.

I couldn't help but smile inwardly. *Important?* He had said the same thing before but never quite revealed what it was.

"Please, go ahead," I encouraged.

He shook his head. "No, not today. I'll tell you during our North Sikkim tour, amidst an enchanting, idyllic setting—when the snow-capped peaks reflect upon the still blue waters of Gurudongmar Lake. Only then will I open my heart to you."

A tremour ran through me, as if my heart had been startled. *That day, too, he had spoken, yet withheld the vital part. He had drawn a boundary—a line separating my past from my future.*

What was it that required such an ethereal setting to be revealed?

Mr. Suren burst into laughter. "Hey, what's wrong? You look pale. Are you scared? Tell me, do you trust me?"

His words unsettled me. I wasn't sure how my face looked, but I hated the idea of him thinking I didn't trust him.

I wanted to say, *No, I don't doubt you. But I am in such a state of confusion that I don't know where to place my next step. I fear that the ground beneath me might give way, swallowing me whole into an abyss.*

But the words never left my lips. I lacked the courage.

There was something elusive about his words, shrouded in a quiet mystery.

"Jharana, you must come for Rista's sake," he continued. "She insists it won't be fun without you. She won't enjoy the beauty of the place unless you're there."

Perhaps I had been too serious. It suddenly felt as if he was using Rista's name to persuade me.

"Sorry, Jhara," he said after a pause. "It seems you don't trust me. Fine then, I'll make arrangements for Rista's trip. Sijal Didi will accompany you both. You three go and enjoy."

Without waiting for my response, he walked away.

A sting of insult rose in me. *Was he testing me? Analyzing me like a psychologist? Had I made a mistake?*

I hadn't intended to offend anyone. *Then why did it feel as if my thoughts were somehow flawed? Had I unknowingly hurt a respectable man like Mr. Suren?*

Back in my room, my mind was tangled in a web of restless thoughts. *Will he not come?*

I stood before the mirror, my thoughts circling him—his words, his unspoken expectations, the weight of something unsaid. Setting all of that aside, I looked at myself.

Was I really this serious? Or did my face betray emotions I hadn't meant to show?

If my expression had carried even a hint of rejection, he must have been hurt.

I stared at my phone screen, surprised to see Mr.

Suren's number flashing. Hesitating for a moment, I picked up the call.

His voice carried a quiet urgency. "Jhara, have I said anything that upset you? If I have, please forgive me."

I remained silent. His concern seemed excessive for such a trivial matter.

"Are you angry with me?" he asked.

"No." My response was brief, almost dismissive.

He sighed. "Listen, Jhara, I never intend to hurt anyone. And I don't expect anything from you. I only ask for a little love—not for myself, but for my daughter. Trust me, I don't know why she loves you so deeply."

There was a heaviness in his tone, a sadness that lingered between his words.

Something in me softened. I couldn't hold back. "Don't take it that way. I never thought of you like that. I'll be happy too if I go with Rista."

"Okay. I'm making the arrangements," he said and disconnected, leaving no room for further conversation.

I stared at the phone, my mind spiralling into confusion. What did Mr. Suren really want? What was he trying to say? Did he expect me to step into the role of Rista's mother? Would I? And even if I did, what would my place be in his life when, as far as I knew, he and Rista's mother were still legally bound?

A wave of uncertainty swept over me. I thought of Biny Apa, Sony Apa, and Akash Bhai. Would they approve? Would they understand the turmoil in my heart?

Lost in my thoughts, I barely noticed Sijal Didi approaching.

"Jhara," she said, "we have leave tomorrow. Mr. Suren has planned a trip to North Sikkim for us. He's not coming. Rista insisted on going, so he's made all the arrangements."

Her words struck me like a sharp jolt. My heart clenched. Had Suren misunderstood me? Had he changed the plan because of what I said?

Sijal Didi continued, unaware of the storm inside me. "Alright, I need to rearrange the duty chart since we'll be back late. Let's start early."

She left, but my thoughts remained tangled.

The agony of losing a dear thing on all of a sudden made me restless.

The idea of going with Suren had left me uneasy, yet the news of his absence now sliced through me like a cold blade. Why did it hurt? Was it disappointment? Longing? Perhaps, in that enchanting realm, I could have found myself in a fleeting, intimate moment—one where his melodies would have woven through the air, filling my heart with a joy I had never known before. And maybe, in return, I would have shared with him the half-forgotten stories buried within me. Maybe, amid the mountains and winding roads, fragments of memories, whispers of unspoken words—woven together with music could have been a new story—one that I had never written before. A new manuscript!

But where did it all lead now? I couldn't deny the restlessness brewing within me—the weakness of my own discontented heart. A part of me wanted to call him, to ask if we could postpone the trip to another day, perhaps next week when I felt more at ease. But then, there was Rista. How could I disappoint her? She must have been brimming with excitement, counting down the hours until tomorrow. This entire plan had been put together just to bring a smile to her face.

And then, just before dawn, everything changed.

Sijal Didi, all set for the trip, suddenly received an

urgent message—she couldn't leave the hospital. The Health Director was arriving, and her presence was mandatory. With no other choice, she informed both me and Mr. Suren.

Despite my deep affection for Sijal Didi, I couldn't suppress the surge of elation at the news of her cancellation. A strange realisation dawned on me—how little we understand ourselves at times. Are we truly so selfish, so adept at disguising our desires behind layers of pretense? Perhaps, at our core, we are always in an unspoken competition, driven by the need to fulfill our own hidden wishes.

Though I was more than ready for the trip, I feigned reluctance in front of Sijal Didi. She insisted, saying Rista would be heartbroken if I didn't go.

Then, right on cue, my phone rang. It was Mr. Suren.

I hurried downstairs, and the moment Rista saw me, her face lit up with uncontainable joy. It was as if she had been waiting for this moment forever.

As I slid into the car, Suren glanced at me and said, "I had no choice but to come. If Sijal Didi had informed me yesterday, I would have cancelled the trip."

Something in his voice lingered—regret, hesitation, or something more? I couldn't quite tell. But I knew one thing for certain—it wasn't the full truth.

For the first time in days, I saw them—the father and daughter—truly happy. There was a lightness in the air between them, something effortless and unguarded. They had never been like this before.

And for the first time since coming to Sikkim, I was outside the hospital, seeing a world I had almost forgotten existed. It was hard to believe that beyond the stark white walls and sterile corridors, there was such untamed beauty.

Above us, the deep blue sky stretched endlessly

over the snow-capped peaks. A glacier cascaded down the mountainside, shimmering like a frozen river, blurring the lines between earth and sky. The crystal-clear waters of Lake Gurudongmar reflected the towering peaks, a mirror to the heavens. The vast, open field surrounding it only added to its otherworldly charm. Was this a glimpse of paradise?

I stood still, lost in the infinite masterpiece of nature—mountain peaks standing like ancient guardians, their snow-covered summits whispering secrets to one another. Their icy breath brushed against my skin, sending shivers through me.

Mr. Suren brought the car to a halt, cutting the engine. We stepped out, standing side by side, gazing at the breathtaking landscape. The sweet murmur of a distant river hummed in the air, a melody that resonated deep within. The dreamlike atmosphere tugged at my emotions, unspoken thoughts swirling within me.

A pair of slobizon birds suddenly took flight, their wings slicing through the crisp mountain air. Rista squealed with joy, running ahead to follow their path, her laughter echoing against the silent peaks.

Turning to Mr. Suren, I murmured, "Thank you. It's only because of you that I got to witness this celestial beauty."

But he shook his head, his gaze following Rista. "No, Jhara," he said softly. "Not because of me. Because of her."

"Indeed! Rista is the bridge that connects our minds," I said with a smile.

"Oh! It's too cold." Rista pulled her shawl tightly around her face, her little nose peeking out. Shivering, she and I hurried back into the car. Mr. Suren followed, starting the engine to warm up the space.

"Hey, Rista," he asked, glancing at her through the rearview mirror. "How do you like the place?"

Rista's eyes sparkled with excitement. "It's unbelievably beautiful! But… is there no school here? Let's build a house! You, I, and Aunty will live here together."

Her innocent words filled the car with warmth. Suren chuckled, shaking his head. "No, no. You and I… Aunty has her hospital. Her patients are waiting for her. Besides, can she stay with us forever?"

Rista pouted. "Why not, Aunty? Why can't you stay with us? Don't you love us?"

Suren, sensing the weight of her question, skillfully changed the subject. He began explaining the science behind glaciers, their formation, and their slow descent over time. As he spoke, I found myself listening intently. For the first time, I was learning things I had never known before.

After some time, we stopped at a roadside restaurant, where the warmth of hot soup melted away the mountain chill.

Rista's eyelids began drooping. "Feeling sleepy?" I asked gently.

She rubbed her tiny fists over her eyes, determined not to admit defeat. "No! I want to take pictures."

I smiled. "Me too. Let's not miss the chance to capture these beautiful moments."

We clicked several photos—scenic landscapes, playful poses, stolen moments of joy. Then, an impromptu game of *Antakshari* began—Rista versus the two of us. Laughter and melodies filled the air, wrapping us in a cocoon of happiness.

But time, like the fleeting sunset, slipped away too soon. It was time to head back.

As we settled into the car, Rista curled up in the back

seat, exhaustion finally claiming her. I moved to the front beside Suren. Within minutes, she was fast asleep, her face peaceful.

The silence between us was comfortable, yet laden with unspoken words.

Suren's voice broke through the quiet. "Jhara, what's your plan?"

I turned to him, startled. "What do you mean?"

He glanced at me briefly before repeating, "Haven't your siblings decided anything about you?"

A sudden heaviness settled in my chest. I remained silent.

"You're working so far from home… Don't your brothers and sisters think about you? Where are they in your life?"

The pages of my past fluttered wildly in my mind. As I tried to gather them, I spoke, my voice softer than I intended. "After my parents passed away, there was no home left—only places I lived in, places that became home for a while. My siblings were caught up in their own lives. The ones who stood by me, who felt like family… they became my own."

Suren sighed. "No matter how easily you say it, Jhara, a person sees their own reflection in life's mirror every day. You can't deny it."

I met his gaze, my voice steady yet distant. "The mirror always tells the truth. But sometimes, dust gathers on it. And if, while wiping that dust, the mirror slips from your hands? What then? It shatters. And the reflection staring back at you is no longer the same—it's fractured, unfamiliar."

A faint smile played on Suren's lips. "They say it's not good to look into a broken mirror."

I pondered over his words. Was he speaking in riddles? Or was he leading up to something deeper?

Then, out of nowhere, he asked, "Jhara, do you know about Rista's mother? You must have heard from Seema… even Sijal Didi knows."

I nodded. "Yes, to some extent."

Suren slowed the car slightly, his hands gripping the wheel as if bracing himself.

"Rista is growing up," he said after a pause. "I'm out of the house most of the day. I don't like leaving her in the care of strangers. You understand how important a mother's presence is for a child her age, don't you?"

I chose my words carefully. "Can't she… be brought back?"

He let out a deep, weary sigh. "Do you think I haven't tried? I did everything I could. I even took Rista to her, hoping she would change her mind. But nothing worked. I lost."

His voice carried the weight of a battle fought too many times, each time ending the same way. The mountains stood tall around us, silent witnesses to a conversation that had only just begun.

I didn't know what to say—my heart was verflowing with sympathy. Ah, poor Suren! Smart and strikingly handsome, a well-respected figure in society, Suren carried himself with an effortless charm. But above all, it was his calm demeanour and quiet strength—his ability to truly understand others—that set him Apart. A man like that… how could anyone walk away from such a husband and ever find peace elsewhere?

Trying to offer him a sliver of hope, I said gently, "Rista was just a little girl back then. Maybe… maybe you could try visiting her again, this time with Rista. Who knows? Perhaps it might soften her heart."

He gave a faint, brittle smile. "She doesn't even answer Rista's calls anymore," he said quietly. "With what hope should I go to her now?"

His words carried the weight of quiet despair. I could sense how helpless he felt—like someone trying to solve an equation that had no solution. What could I possibly say to that? Suggest a second marriage—for Rista's sake? Even the thought felt too crude, too soon.

So I said the only thing I could. "Sometimes, only time can mend what feels broken beyond repair."

Suren looked away, his voice flat and distant. "People cling to time and God, as if they are lifelines. But hope… hope died a long time ago."

His words, soaked in sorrow, made something sink inside me. So many things I wanted to say rushed through my mind, but none of them made it to my lips. I couldn't find the courage. I stayed quiet.

Perhaps my silence pressed too hard on him—because suddenly, he shifted the conversation.

"Doesn't your brother want to come back to India? Or is he planning to settle abroad for good?"

"My brother never really had wishes of his own," I said quietly. "The day he married a woman like my Bhauja, he surrendered all his desires into the flames of the wedding fire. Since then, he's just been… existing. Living like a machine."

Suren's tone grew darker. "Jhara, women like that— they're nothing less than a curse to the people around them. They can't find peace, and they won't let anyone else have it either. My wife is exactly like that. Restless, bitter, always unpredictable. I even consulted a psychiatrist once, but she refused treatment. Instead, she lashed out at me."

Suren's voice carried an unfamiliar vulnerability.

He had opened up to me with raw, quiet intimacy. In my mind, I found myself recalling Seema's words—they matched his. Every word he spoke now was a mirror of what Seema had confided in me earlier. Despite the pain, despite the rejection and humiliation, he still loved his wife more than he loved himself.

I couldn't help but wonder how easily people discard the treasures they already have, blind to their worth. A man like Suren… any woman would be proud to call him her own. And yet, the one who had him could never see his value.

He let out a long, weary sigh. "Let's leave all that. I only worry for Rista now. Nothing else matters."

His words left me distracted, thoughtful. A question lingered at the edge of my lips—*Didn't the wish for a companion? Someone to walk beside him through the rest of life's journey?* But I didn't ask. And maybe I didn't need to.

Suren looked lost, his voice suddenly turning fragile. "Jhara, I need your help… for Rista. Will you help me? I know you won't let me down."

He looked so vulnerable in that moment—his strength drained, his forehead damp with sweat despite the chill in the air. I wanted to say it—wanted to wipe the sweat from his brow and whisper, *Have faith in me. I'll walk with you through every shadow, every sorrow. I'll help you repaint the canvas of your life, brush away the pain and loneliness.*

But I said nothing.

And still, deep down, I believe he understood. Even in my silence, he heard my answer.

That evening, after returning home, I called Akash Bhai to share my new decision. He didn't object—in fact, he encouraged me with a warmth that eased my heart. One by one, I informed Biny Apa, Sony Apa, and Gouri Bhauja. Sijal Didi, hearing the news, was overjoyed.

They were all my well-wishers. With their support, new thoughts began to bloom within me, fragile yet hopeful. A quiet joy seemed to wrap itself around me like morning mist—light, gentle, full of promise.

Without waiting for an invitation, I went to Suren's house. He wasn't home—his orderly told me he'd be late. I was still in the corridor when Rista's sudden voice startled me. "Aunty, do you know? PApa told me I'll always be with you. No one can ever take me away from you."

She looked radiant, her eyes sparkling with a sense of belonging—as if she had discovered a new relationship, something precious. What had Suren said to her, I wondered, that filled her with such confidence? How had he framed it? Even so, I felt a strange hesitation hearing those words from a child's mouth—so tender, yet so heavy with meaning.

Rista tugged my hand, pulling me toward her father's room. Although I had visited their house many times, this was the first time I was stepping into Mr. Suren's bedroom. With the authority of a seasoned homemaker, Rista declared, "Look, Aunty, PApa's room is messier than mine!"

The room wasn't exactly dirty, but it was scattered—books and papers were strewn everywhere, in no particular order. Photographs of the father and daughter were scattered too—one propped on a table, another stuck to the wall, yet another buried under a pile of books. They were placed randomly, from the drawing room to Rista's room.

But there was not a single photograph of Rista's mother.

Why? Had Suren removed them out of bitterness? Or had he hidden them, fearing they might disturb Rista? The question lingered in my mind, unanswered.

Crossing a silent boundary, I began tidying up the

room on my own. I dusted the photographs and arranged them neatly, giving the space a quiet sense of order. I wasn't afraid or hesitant. It felt natural—like I belonged there.

Later, I fed Rista with my own hands and took her to bed. From the cupboard, I pulled out her night suit and handed it to her. After she changed, I gently wiped her feet and applied lotion to them, the way a mother would.

Her new caretaker, Bijal, and Suren's orderly, Rahul, along with a few others, watched me in silence. They didn't say a word, but their eyes said everything. In their gaze, I could sense it—they already saw me as someone taking the lead role in this household.

Suren wasn't home, yet they asked me to stay for dinner. Their requests were kind, genuine. But I quietly declined, and left.

17

Several days passed. Rista would come to me, and I to her. That was the rhythm of our days. It wasn't that Suren and I didn't see each other—we did. He never said much, but often mentioned that he felt assured about Rista, knowing I was around.

The domestic staff—Rahul, Bijal—had begun looking at our connection with new eyes, as though something unspoken was quietly taking form between us.

Then one day, quite suddenly, Rista said, "Aunty, do you know what they were saying? That you'll stay here with me, become my mummy, and go to the hospital for duty from here!"

Her words caught me off guard. A strange chill passed through me, though I masked it with a smile. I tried to change the topic, hoping she'd forget. But Rista was not one to be easily swayed. She tugged at my sleeve insistently, her voice full of childlike urgency.

"Tell me, Aunty! Say yes—please, say yes!"

I smiled faintly and said, "Maybe you were my daughter in a previous life."

Resting her little face on my lap, she replied softly, "In this life too, I am your daughter."

Her innocent persistence, her questions—*Why won't you stay? Why can't you be my mummy? Why shouldn't we live here together?*—discomposed me. Still, I tried to reason with her.

"See, Rista, I have a job. I can't do everything while working full-time at the hospital."

But she countered with childlike logic. "Rahul Bhaiya is here. Bijal Didi is here. You just be with me. I'll have lunch with you after school. I'll sleep, play, and study with you."

It wasn't her words but the trust, the confidence, the sense of belonging in her eyes that overwhelmed me. It was deeper than anything she could articulate. And that very day, something unusual happened.

Mr. Suren asked to meet me privately—not at his house, but at a distant CCD. The invitation unsettled me slightly, but I couldn't bring myself to refuse.

We met at the appointed time. The cafe was quiet, unfamiliar. No known faces around. He showed me an envelope. His face was pale, his voice low. "Richa has sent the divorce papers. On her own."

There was a fragile sorrow in his tone, and his eyes were filled with a kind of silent despair. For the first time, I sensed how deeply he had loved Rista's mother.

"I made one last attempt," he continued, "just like you advised. But I failed. Everything I did—every plea, every gesture—was in vain. She's lost in her father's business world now. There's no room for me in her life. She's happy without me, Jhara. Very happy. And I… tell me, am I so unwanted a man that she can't even bear to see me?"

His voice trembled as he poured out his heart, his pain raw and unfiltered. I handed him his coffee and tried to calm him.

"But why, Suren? Why is she misunderstanding you like this?"

He gave a bitter smile. "Some questions, Jhara, have no answers. From the start, she wanted me to be part of her father's business empire. That goes against my principles… and frankly, not everyone is cut out for it. I'm content with my job, my reputation, my simple life. But it wasn't enough for her. She wanted someone who could run beside her father's ambitions. And I—I just couldn't do it. Is that such an unforgivable mistake?"

His words struck deep. I felt the weight of it all—the exhaustion, the futility. Some problems truly had no solution.

He looked away, his voice softer now. "Still, I held on to the hope that maybe—just maybe—she'd return someday. That we'd rebuild our world for Rista. You know, Jhara, I've never thought of any other woman, never even dreamed of one. Only Richa. And yet… she uses my love against me. It's the weapon she knows will hurt most."

His eyes welled up with tears.

I wanted to comfort him, to tell him something that would ease his ache. But I couldn't find the words.

"I respect her, still," he said quietly. "Because she's Rista's mother. And I wonder—if I start a new life with someone else, would Rista forgive me when she grows up? That's why I never considered separation, not seriously. But she… she never hesitated."

His face, streaked with tears, bore the helplessness of a child who couldn't understand why he was left behind.

We had nearly finished our coffee. He rose, and so did I. His car was parked nearby, but instead of walking toward it, he kept going. I called out and reminded him.

He simply gestured toward a nearby Buddhist temple.

We walked to it together and sat in a quiet corner on the temple steps, beneath the soft silence of evening.

Suren remained silent. A strange unrest stirred within me. Why did such things always happen to me? What role was I meant to play in all this? Could I ever truly be an honest life partner to a man burdened with such sorrow?

And beyond all that—Suren loved his wife more than life itself. That much was unmistakably clear from the way he spoke of her. No one could take her place. Not even me.

The place was dimly lit, but I felt no fear with Suren. In the few months I had known him, I had come to trust him deeply—unshakably. Even so, I asked gently, "Should we go now?"

"Do you have any duty tonight?" he asked.

"No," I replied. "No duty tonight."

"Then… can't you stay a little longer?" he said softly.

I don't know what magic his words held, but something in them pulled me closer—an unspoken yearning that echoed my own.

Still, I hesitated. "Rista will be waiting for me. Lately, she relies on me a lot."

"And I rely on you—for Rista," he said with a long sigh. "I know I can go anywhere in the world, with full confidence, because I know she's safe with you."

His words caught me off guard. *Go anywhere?* Was he planning to leave? Was frustration pushing him to abandon everything?

Alarmed, I asked, "Where will you go?"

A faint, hollow smile flickered across his weary face.

"Did you think I'd become a hermit and renounce the world?" he said. "No. You know me better than that. I've always said—everything else can wait, but not my profession. I've been selected for a project in Germany. Three months."

Then he paused, searching my eyes. "If you don't

mind, could you stay with Rista during that time? There won't be any issue. If my mother were still alive, I wouldn't have asked. But ever since she passed, I've felt a kind of loneliness I can't put into words. My father stays with my elder brother now. He'll come and be around, but he's old and... honestly, he depends on others himself. He can't look after Rista. And she—she isn't at ease with anyone the way she is with you."

I nodded slowly. "Don't worry, Suren. Rista is my responsibility. Go with a free mind. It's just three months—it will pass quickly."

A light returned to his face. "Really, Jhara, I'm indebted to you. No one else would do this for my daughter."

He stood up. We walked toward the parking lot. All along the way, Suren spoke—of his marriage to Richa, her coldness, his father's indifference, and the dreams he harboured for Rista.

But beneath all his words, woven through every memory and regret, was an unmistakable thread—his undying love for Richa.

And in the shadow of that love... a quiet seed of jealousy began to take root in my heart.

18

I don't know why sleep eluded me, no matter how hard I tried. Suren's pale face, his hollow eyes, and that heavy, exhausted voice kept flashing before me. There was something about him—a strange, unnamed pull. And yet, I had long accepted that there was no empty corner in his heart where I could seek shelter.

Then why was I thinking about him so much?

Whatever existed between us was only for Rista's sake. When Seema was around, Suren had no reason to worry. But now, with her gone, he wanted Rista to be happy—with me. That was all. Nothing more. So why was I caught in this restless spiral of thoughts?

He never hinted at a new beginning, never offered anything beyond the shared concern for his daughter. I had spent countless quiet moments beside him, and maybe it's natural—for a man so broken—to seek solace in a woman's presence. But even in those moments that bordered on closeness, he spoke only of Richa 's coldness. He let his grief flow into me, filling me with a strange, bitter jealousy toward a woman who had already abandoned him.

My thoughts felt jumbled, irrational. I was angry with my own frail mind. What was Suren thinking? Should I have said something—something real? Should I have taken his hand and told him, *"Don't worry. You're not alone. I'm here for you. Let's walk into a new world together…"*

But even if such words rose within me, something deep and feminine held me back. If he, as a man, couldn't bring himself to say it, how could I?

Still, how could he ask me to take full responsibility for his daughter for three whole months, staying in his house round the clock? Wasn't there a difference between caring for Rista through occasional visits and moving into his home, day in and day out? What did this nameless relationship mean?

A wave of shame washed over me. Why hadn't I asked him—asked clearly—in what capacity he leaned so heavily on me? *If I mean so much to you, then why is there no name, no bond, no commitment?* Or am I just another Seema to him—just more dependable this time?

Dawn crept in through the window. I dressed for my ward duty, forcing my mind to shift gears. I buried myself in my work.

But that day, I couldn't hide from Sijal Didi's eyes.

"You look pale, Jhara," she said softly, her gaze full of concern. "There's a shadow under your eyes. Didn't you sleep well?"

I felt like someone caught in the act of a silent crime. My heart shrank. She reached out gently, stroking my head like an elder sister, and said, "When sorrow is shared, it hurts a little less. Don't bottle it all up. Tell me what's troubling you."

I was flipping through patient records, pretending to focus. But my mind was adrift. *How could I tell her? Should I say, "I think I love Mr. Suren—but he sees me only as his daughter's caretaker"? What do I even say... That I want to ease his pain, bring back the smile he lost long ago, while he remains lost in thoughts of a cruel, indifferent wife?*

And the bitter truth? The man, for whom I kept awake

over, the one who haunted my sleepless night—who will have sound asleep in Germany, having entrusted me with his daughter's life without a second thought.

Sijal Didi eventually walked away. I don't know what she made of my silence. But her quiet departure wounded me more than words ever could. Still, what could I do? A woman caught between love and dignity is always helpless. And I—I was no exception.

Evening. My phone rang—it was Suren. He told me he had spoken to Sijal Didi.

I froze.

"What did she say? I haven't told her anything," I said, feeling a quiet flush of embarrassment rising within me. Suren hesitated, then said, "If you don't mind... we might have to take a different decision once I return." His voice faltered. There was something evasive in his tone, something that hinted at a decision already made but not yet spoken aloud. It unsettled me. Just the other day, he had taken me to North Sikkim—an outing, he'd said—to talk about this new decision. And now? Now, he wanted three more months before he could speak of this "different" path. Why couldn't he just say it? Why did it feel like he was caught in something unspoken, as if life itself had pressed his voice into silence? Why was it so hard for him to admit that he was changing course?

Sijal Didi looked radiant that day, as if a heavy burden had finally lifted from her shoulders. Her eyes sparkled with the quiet joy of someone delivering long-awaited good news. She said, her voice gentle and wise, *"Even a creeper, denied the support of a tree, can still bear flowers and fruit while crawling on the ground. The tree should never underestimate the creeper—it can still protect its own identity."*

Then she added with warmth, *"Mr. Suren holds deep*

love and respect for you. He wants your companionship. He's only asking for three months. Once he returns from Germany…"

She had touched me that day not with words alone, but with a tender layer of affection that seemed to settle on my very skin. I was overwhelmed with gratitude—for her love, her sensitivity, her quiet strength.

How deeply she cared for me, though we shared no blood. In many ways, she felt closer than a sister. She could read my turmoil just by looking at my face. She saw the ache in my eyes, the silent grief of what I'd lost. And yet, she never spoke of her own pain.

She gave of herself equally to everyone in the ward, not just to me. But perhaps that's why she felt compelled to make a strong choice on my behalf—to be a voice of care, when mine was lost in uncertainty.

I hadn't seen or spoken to Suren in the last two or three days. Later, Sijal Didi told me that he was feeling shy after confiding in her. I, too, was burdened by a strange awkwardness. Even though Rista had begged me to come over, I couldn't bring myself to visit his house. My steps faltered, as though I'd committed some great mistake.

Sometimes, I felt I had crossed the age for marriage, and that it was somehow shameful to marry now. The thought gnawed at me.

Then Rista came, persistent as ever, her questions piling on my heart. "Why didn't you come to see me?" she asked again and again. And then, with a child's fearless sincerity, she looked into my eyes and said, "You'll live with me forever as my Mummy, won't you?"

Her words struck me like a tremour. My body trembled, like the rustling of a tender leaf in the wind. What was I supposed to say to her? How could I answer something so pure and unguarded?

Holding my face in her tiny hands, she asked again, more firmly this time, "Is it true? Tell me. Are you going to stay with me forever? After PApa comes back...?"

To dodge the question, I said lightly, "What if I bring a good Mummy for you?"

She instantly stamped her little feet, furious. "No, no, no! Never! No one can be like you. I want *you*—only *you!*"

She sat beside me, her voice soft but full of certainty. "You know, PApa asked me for permission. I was so happy! Look here—you must not say no."

Her eyes sparkled with hope and excitement, and I was swept into a quiet storm of memories and questions. I found myself combing through my past, tracing the strange path that had brought me here. Had I ever imagined something like this? Maybe fate's most meaningful gifts are the ones we never plan.

Rista's return stirred something deep in me. The conviction that Mr. Suren was different from others took root quietly but firmly. Her unwavering faith in me, set against his hesitant heart, left me torn. And somewhere deep inside, a voice was whispering, *"Your true purpose is to bring joy to these two. Maybe now is the time to embrace it."*

Suren was preparing to leave, and yet he hadn't called or sent word—not even once. Only Rista had told me, "PApa is leaving this evening."

Just then, Sijal Didi appeared, as if by intuition. "Let's go meet Mr. Suren. He's leaving for three months," she said.

I wanted to, but my lips formed excuses. She insisted. And finally, I went with her.

When we arrived, Suren was already ready to leave.

In the meantime, he had arranged for his father to stay and look after Rista.

Turning to Sijal Didi, he said, "I'm leaving Rista and my father in your care."

His voice was steady, but his eyes betrayed him. He avoided looking at me, and something about that moment felt strange—heavy with unspoken words. A strange apprehension took hold of me, as if we were on the verge of a mistake we'd come to accept too easily.

He called Rista close and whispered something into her ear. Then, hugging her tightly, he stepped into the car.

I stood there, silent, like stone. Rista's eyes brimmed with tears. I lifted her into my arms and waved at Suren. .

But that day—yes, that day for the first time—I saw something in his eyes. A shower of unspoken affection. What lips fail to say, eyes convey effortlessly. The silent voice of the heart speaks loudest through a glance.

While I stood there, lost in the depth of that moment, I watched him vanish down the road.

Sijal Didi, too, had read him well. We spent a little time speaking with his father, while Rista chattered on, singing our praises before her grandfather.

Just as we were about to leave, Rista ran inside and returned with a small packet in her hands. "PApa said you should open this on the coming Sunday," she said, placing it in mine.

I looked at her, puzzled, then around, unsure how to respond. I left with Sijal Didi, never even managing to thank her properly.

On the way, Sijal Didi kept praising Suren, gently nudging my thoughts toward him. But one thing kept playing in my mind—*Why had he asked me to open the packet on the coming Sunday?*

I had half a mind to hide it away in the cupboard and forget it altogether.

But then Sijal Didi laughed and said, "Hey, Jhara! Have you forgotten? This Sunday is your birthday!"

19

Indeed!

Rista had asked about my birthday a few days earlier, but I never imagined that she and her father were quietly planning such a sweet surprise.

Sijal Didi, glowing with admiration for Suren, said warmly, "Just look at him, Jhara—how thoughtfully he's planned this. He left a gift for you a whole week in advance. Really, you have to give him credit..."

Trying to hide the flutter of emotions stirring inside me, I responded with mock annoyance, "What was the need for all that? I don't care much for such formalities."

But truthfully, that day, I missed Suren more than I could admit. The thought of three months without him felt like an eternity stretched across my heart. Even the city looked distant, stripped of its usual charm.

My thoughts wandered, comparing him to Vinit. With Vinit, love had always felt like performance—a carefully recited "I love you" that echoed with selfishness.

Love, I realised, is not a formula to be solved like a difficult math problem. It doesn't need grand declarations. It moves quietly, like an unheard symphony that seeps into the soul.

Mr. Suren never tried to impress me with sweet words. He never sought stolen glances or lonely moments to his advantage.

And yet, in his silence, in the space between our conversations, I had found something real—something deeper than spoken love.

This time, I shared my decision with all my siblings—without hesitation, without fear. No one showered me with blessings or enthusiasm, but neither did anyone raise objections. Only Akash Bhai wrote back, his words heavy with sorrow. He lamented that he might not be able to witness the beginnings of my new family anytime soon. Yet, he promised that if he ever returned to India, his first visit would be to see the home I'd built with love.

Still, his words echoed within me long after. I yearned for Akash Bhai to perform the *samarpan* ritual—to place my hand into Suren's and bless us with flower petals and kind wishes. How deeply I wished to step into Suren's home under the protective grace of his blessings. But fate has always played its own game with me—an irony I've grown used to.

Sony Apa, in her usual teasing tone, said, "Oh, how convenient for you! No need to learn how to build a family—it's already built. You've even become a mother, without going through labour. Truly, how fortunate!"

Biny Apa was more cautious. She asked if I had looked into Suren's past carefully, fearing that I might be walking into something deceitful. "Be careful, Jhara," she warned.

Gouri Bhauja said gently, "You've grown wise enough to know right from wrong. Whatever you choose will be the right path." But Vikas Bhai's words carried a sting. "You couldn't understand Vinit in two years, but now you think you know a divorcee in a few months? It's your choice…"

Their words swirled together, forming a strange harmony of doubt, sarcasm, and concern. They were my own, my family—and yet, they felt so distant, their warmth held at arm's length. Strangely, those who were not tied to me by blood—Sijal Didi, Rista, and even Suren—felt closer, as if some unseen thread had bound our souls across lifetimes.

In Suren's absence, Rista leaned on me for even the smallest of needs. The domestic staff looked to me for guidance, treating me as if I were already the head of the household. Suren's father, too, grew fond of me quickly. In just a few days, he began to share his thoughts with an ease that touched me.

One afternoon, he spoke of Rista's mother. I sensed pain in his voice, deep and old. According to him, Suren had endured much because of her. Yet even after Richa's cruelty, he hadn't let go of the hope that she might change. Holding my hand gently between his palms, he said with quiet desperation, "Mamma, only you can heal this family. I worry so much for my poor boy. He's been through hell since marrying Richa. Her coldness, her whims—they've broken him. One who couldn't love her own child, how could she love anyone else?"

I had no words for him, only silent listening. In truth, could I shoulder the weight of this broken family? Could I ever fulfill their hopes, mend their pain?

Then Suren called. He asked about Rista, about his father's health, about the house—his tone carried a trust so complete, as though he had left his world in my care. After I updated him, he asked softly, "Jhara, have I burdened you?"

That single question carried the weight of tender humility. His voice felt so near, so dear—I almost replied, *It's your absence that burdens me.* But shame held back the words.

He paused, then continued, "You know, Jhara, ever since I confided in Sijal Didi, it feels as if you've become the closest person in my life. I've suffered a lot—it must have been His will. But now, He's given me the greatest gift: you. With you, I want to begin again. A new life. A new world."

Sleep crept gently over me that night, like a lullaby woven with dreams. A new world, a new family—I was already wrapping myself in this budding bond with my heart and soul.

That day, after returning from Suren's home, I found myself unusually absent-minded. My heart was restless, counting down the days with a quiet, eager impatience—waiting for Suren's return.

20

That day, after receiving my salary, I went to a mall. I wasn't drawn to ornaments or glittering displays; those things never held much appeal for me. I bought a few beautiful sarees—simple yet elegant.

Back home, I stood in front of the mirror, draping each one over my shoulders, one after another. I was taken aback. *So glamorous?* I blinked at my own reflection, almost not recognising the woman staring back. *How could this be me?*

Among my small purchases was a suit piece I had picked up for Suren. I had no idea whether he would like it, but while selecting it, it had felt as if he were right beside me—smiling, nodding in approval. That quiet thought warmed me.

Sijal Didi was even more delighted than I was, bustling around like a proud guardian. Her joy was radiant—as though this was her celebration too. Suddenly, she opened a small box and held out a gold jewelry set. Her eyes twinkled as she said, "How do you like it, Jhara? It's for you."

I stared at her, stunned. "What is this, Didi? For *me*? No, no… I don't want it. Your blessing is enough. That's my real ornament. Please keep this with you."

Her smile faded, the brightness of her face dimmed in an instant. In a low, almost hurt voice, she said, "I know…

I'm no one to you. But if Biny Apa or Sony Apa or even Gouri Bhauja had given it to you, would you have refused? I'm not your family, after all."

She turned to leave, her disappointment hanging heavy in the air. My eyes brimmed with tears. Rushing forward, I wrapped my arms around her tightly. "No, Didi, don't say that. You're *closer* to me than they are… but this set, it's so expensive…"

She cupped my face gently, her palms warm and soft, and wiped away my tears. "Oh, silly girl," she murmured. "It never came to any use for me. My mother had it made, just for me. But look at me—those days are long past. I've crossed that age. You are my all now. If you wear it, my mother's soul will rest in peace."

I stood there, motionless, overwhelmed. Her words touched something deep within me. I felt humbled and blessed, yet a strange heaviness settled in my chest.

She took my hand and pulled me toward her room. Opening a carefully wrapped box, she revealed a rich red silk saree, its threads shimmering with warmth. There were other sarees too—each lovingly preserved, meant for a bride. She showed them to me one by one, her face glowing with joy.

But I couldn't take my eyes off her. I gazed at her, unblinking, as if seeing someone else entirely.

In that moment, Sijal Didi wasn't just my guardian. She was my mother. My long-lost Ma had returned in her— her care, her pride, her unspoken love. The ache of years welled up inside me.

I wanted to cry out, to call her *Ma* with all the longing stored inside me. But the words stuck in my throat.

Tears spilled freely down my cheeks, and I was drenched within.

I opened Suren's gift on my birthday. Inside was a beautiful photograph of Rista and me—captured in a moment so tender, it felt like time had paused. Suren appeared in a few of the pictures too, his presence quiet but significant. There was also a saree, folded with care, and a silver vermilion case tucked beside it. The case gleamed softly, already filled with vermilion. A strange warmth coursed through me, almost like a shiver—startling in its intimacy.

Then I found the birthday card. Just a few lines, hurriedly scribbled in his handwriting. But they undid me.

"I feel I've crossed many milestones in life. Today, I stand before one I never thought of reaching. And here—my body, mind, and entire being—refuse to move forward."

I went to Suren's house carrying a box of sweets and chocolates. I bowed before his father and touched his feet. With a warm smile, he placed his hand gently on my head and blessed me. Rista's joy knew no bounds. There was a quiet excitement in the air—an arrangement was underway at their house, just for me.

The dining hall was decked with balloons, all at Rista's insistence and under her grandfather's supervision. A cake sat beautifully on the decorated table. It was the first time in my life that someone had celebrated my birthday like this.

Born into a low- middle-class family, I had never experienced the luxury of such celebrations. On my birthdays, my mother would offer a homemade cake and kheer to God. My grandmother, with her betel-stained smile, would press a crumpled ten or twenty rupee note into my hand and say, "Take this, my dear, buy some sweets for yourself."

I would tease her, laughing, "How many sweets can

this buy? Once I eat them, there'll be nothing left for you all!"

She would chuckle and reply, "Alright then, wait until next year. I'll save more and you can buy yourself a new frock."

But her promise always remained just that—a promise. Our family was constantly juggling a deficit budget. Akash Bhai used to say, "Wait until I get a job—I'll give you everything you ask for."

Ah, my Akash Bhai… my poor, loving brother. I wondered if anyone even remembered my birthday today. Just as the thought crossed my mind, Suren called and greeted me with a cheerful, "Happy Birthday."

I had drifted somewhere far away in my thoughts when Rista tugged at me gently and said, "Hey, Aunty, where are you? Cut the cake, please!"

With a smile on my lips and tears brimming in my heart, I celebrated my birthday—for Rista's happiness. After the cake cutting, I took her out for a little outing. All through the day, my mind wandered back—back to my childhood full of small joys and unspoken sacrifices, to bonds that time had faded, and to the silence that now stretched between siblings who once shared everything.

21

How swiftly the three months were passing! A strange blend of anticipation and emotion stirred within me. A new chapter of life was about to begin. Even Suren's father shared in the excitement—but none more than Rista, who was overjoyed.

The house kept changing, little by little, following Suren's directions from afar. Though physically absent, his presence seemed to shape every corner. His ideas found colour and form here, as if he were already home.

And then, he came back. The house came alive with even more decorations, buzzing with warmth and activity. But this time, I don't know why, I felt shy around him. I couldn't bring myself to meet him after his return. Rista kept calling me, but Suren gently stopped her from insisting—and that quiet restraint, that thoughtful care, drew me even more toward him.

His composed demeanour, his disciplined masculinity, and his measured joy transported me into a world I had never known.

One day, Rista chirped, "Do you know, Aunty? PApa brought so many pretty dresses for me, and a walkie-talkie too! And… he brought lots of gifts for you as well! But he won't show them to me—he said they're in your new cupboard!"

Hearing her, my heart fluttered—not for the gifts, but

for the tenderness behind them. That thoughtfulness, that love… it sent a thrill through me. I had never dared expect so much from life.

Suren fixed the day for our meeting. I would go to his house only then. In the presence of an advocate, we would sign the papers, with Sijal Didi and a few close well-wishers standing witness. By then, all formalities regarding his divorce from Richa had been completed.

My mind was at peace, free from doubts. The speed with which everything had settled amazed me. But I took it all as a blessing from God—and I was grateful.

As part of my duty, I informed Akash Bhai, Vikas Bhai, Biny Apa, and Sony Apa. Everyone except Akash Bhai promised to be there on that special day. Their assurance made me deeply happy. Their presence would be my pride. I had already arranged for their stay.

Every night has a morning—and with it, a new beginning. Days pass. And how dreamlike the joyful moments are! How effortlessly they blur the sorrowful tales of yesterday, as if washing away all despair.

Sometimes, I felt like telling Vinit about my new beginning. But it seemed meaningless. He was like a torn letter—there was no use trying to piece it together and read it again.

I welcomed every decision of Suren with full-hearted respect. Nothing felt forced. His choices felt like my own—natural, warm, and right.

There was a wild eagerness in me to see him. But he had said, firmly yet tenderly, that we wouldn't meet until the day he had chosen. That day would mark the beginning of our shared destiny.

We were both waiting—for that one blessed moment. The dawn of a new life was just within reach.

22

Building sandcastles on the beach is easy—but even easier is watching them vanish under the crashing tides. Everything disappears in the blink of an eye.

Who could have imagined that Suren would meet with an accident?

It felt as if the sky and the earth collapsed into one, drowning me in a sudden deluge. A voice inside me cried out, *"Will I ever reach that new world I had been yearning for? Or has it sunk in this flood of sorrow?"*

He had suffered a serious head injury and slipped into unconsciousness.

The news spread like wildfire through every corridor of our hospital. Immediate arrangements were made for his treatment. Everyone sprang into action. Amid the darkness, faint flickers of hope still glimmered—lightning behind storm clouds. I waited for the sky to clear, for the storm to pass. In my mind's eye, I still saw the beautiful home we had imagined together. But now I wondered—had I been dreaming of walls built not from brick and mortar, but from fragile clouds of fog?

The most heartbreaking part was—there was no road accident, no reckless moment. He had simply slipped while trying to hang a beautiful painting on the wall of what was to be *our* room. He fell and struck his head. He was brought into our hospital unconscious.

I found myself blaming fate.

I cared for him with every ounce of strength I had. There was no weariness in me—only a quiet contentment that I could do something for him. Yet everything around me felt hollow, unreal, like a dream slipping through my fingers. At home, his aging father and little Rista looked like frozen statues, lost in silent grief. They had fallen into a stunned silence. How could I console them?

Rista would cry softly one moment and then suddenly break into shrill screams the next. Her sorrow tore through the air. Suren's father, too, was searching for someone to lean on, someone to absorb his pain. He clung to me as though he had waited for me to arrive, believing that I alone could offer him some measure of comfort.

My sense of responsibility deepened. I buried my own pain and gave all my time to Suren, to Rista, and to his father.

I lost all sense of days and nights.

Rista couldn't sleep without me, so I stayed beside her every night. I had to feed Suren's father myself—he wouldn't listen to anyone else, wouldn't take a bite unless I coaxed him. One evening, Rista pulled me into what was to be our new bedroom. Everything there was fresh and untouched—the bed, the dressing table, the carpet. On a small shelf, a framed photograph of Rista and me sat together, glowing with warmth and innocence.

We were so close to a beginning.

But maybe God had not kept such happiness in reserve for me.

My colleagues and Sijal Didi tried to console me, saying, "Don't lose hope. Everything will be fine. Suren will recover. Even if it takes time, your marriage will happen."

I had never seen Suren this closely, not even after

all those shared moments—at his house, in coffee shops, during our trip to North Sikkim, or while sharing meals in hotel rooms with Rista between us. I could never meet his eyes for long; if they caught mine by chance, I'd turn away, flustered.

But now, he lay before me, silent and still—and I couldn't look away.

Now, for the first time, I was seeing him this closely.

I sat beside him after administering the saline. He lay there with his eyes closed, sleeping peacefully. Not a trace of pain touched his calm face—it was as if he had surrendered himself to a deep, undisturbed slumber. After a while, he would stir and open his eyes, only to recoil slightly at finding me so close. I had observed his behaviour for days—so composed, so unlike others. Truly, a man of restraint.

I gently wiped the beads of sweat from his forehead. Fear gripped me. Nightmares hovered before my open eyes. What if something happened to Suren? His father would be devastated. Rista would be lost. And I...?

Suren is the best man—no, the last man—in my life. I cannot imagine another. There could never be anyone else.

Unknowingly, my fingers caressed his face. Tears welled up and rolled down without restraint. I kept blaming fate, over and over again, unable to hold back the grief swelling within me.

Then, suddenly, a hand touched my head. I startled and looked up.

It was Dr. Ayush.

I had never expected to see him—not like this, not now. To be honest, I hadn't even thought of him these past few months.

"You're surprised to see me, aren't you?" he said

softly. "Don't you remember? I once told you—whenever you needed me, I'd be there. You didn't call me this time, but I came anyway."

The way he said you—it was affectionate, familiar, intimate. Yet I couldn't help but wonder: how did he know I was here? How did he find me?

"You didn't inform me," he said, as if reading my thoughts. "But I know everything about you. I heard from some doctor friends here—about Suren, about you."

I had no words. My tears fell silently, splashing on my feet—unruly, uncontrolled, as if seeking comfort, forgetting time, place, or propriety.

"There's nothing to fear," he said gently. "Dr. Matthews—the best neurosurgeon—and I are handling the case. You're lucky, Jhara. Your brother is with you."

In that moment, it felt as if Akash Bhai himself had come to me through Dr. Ayush's voice.

As we stepped outside, I understood—Akash Bhai had told him everything. About me. About Suren. Even about our marriage.

I shrank a little in front of Ayush, embarrassed. Yet I felt a strange happiness stir within me. There was something in knowing that someone had spoken for me, that someone had offered me social legitimacy.

Ayush's quiet strength calmed me. His words planted a small, stubborn hope inside me—Suren would recover.

Still, I couldn't sleep that night. I stayed awake, whispering fervent prayers into the dark, clinging to that one line Ayush had spoken:

"Suren will be alright."

That morning arrived with a different hue, a kind of stillness and tension I had never known before. It didn't feel like an ordinary morning—it felt like it had a face, a presence, watching me quietly. Suren was scheduled for surgery in just a few hours.

Ayush had reassured me the previous night: *It's a small clot—simple procedure. Nothing to worry about. The chances of success are nearly a hundred percent.* But logic and reassurance don't always hold up against fear.

Sijal Didi had stayed close, never leaving my side. Rista, too, was unusually stubborn that morning, refusing to go to school. After much coaxing, she finally agreed, but I couldn't bring myself to go on duty. I was trembling, not from fatigue, but from sheer nervousness. It was as if I had shed my professional skin—I wasn't a nurse that day. I wasn't the calm, composed person people saw in the ward or the operating theatre.

Instead, I sat there like a worried family member, shaken by every passing second. Outwardly, I tried to appear composed, but inside, I quivered like a new leaf in a mild breeze.

The bond that had quietly blossomed between us— between me and Suren—was no longer a secret. Everyone in the hospital had sensed it. One by one, my colleagues dropped by to comfort me, to offer their strength and a few quiet words of hope.

When Suren was finally wheeled into the operation theatre, I returned to my room and sat in silence, hands clasped, whispering frantic prayers.

A while later, Ayush came out of the OT with a soft smile. "It's done. Everything went well. Nothing to worry," he said.

His words, simple and steady, were enough to ground me. Slowly, I began to feel myself again.

It was one of Ayush's best qualities—his deep discomfort with sadness. He couldn't bear to see someone upset and always tried to lift the heaviness in the air with his warmth.

He still kept in touch with Akash Bhai, Vikas Bhai, and Gouri Bhauja. I, however, remained the exception, a fact I often pointed out with mock irritation.

Later that day, we went together to Suren's house. I introduced Ayush to Suren's father, and he seemed genuinely pleased. He spent some time with Rista, and I could see how deeply he noticed the little gaps—the spaces where I had quietly filled in, in their home.

"I'll tell my wife everything about her," Ayush said softly, as we watched Rista play. "They'll be happy knowing how well she's doing."

He promised to stay in Sikkim until Suren recovered. His friend—another doctor—would be back in two days. I felt nothing but gratitude for him.

When we returned to the hospital, a man and woman were seated in the waiting hall outside the ICU. They looked tense and tired. I might not have noticed them had one of my colleagues not quietly pointed them out.

"They're Suren's father-in-law and wife," she whispered.

A strange uneasiness swept over me. I don't know why, but I felt suddenly cold, like something was about to change. I walked straight to my room while Ayush went inside the ICU. Thankfully, my colleague had been discreet; Ayush hadn't heard her mention them.

Later, Sijal Didi came and gently explained what was happening.

Suren's father-in-law wanted to shift him to another hospital. He was adamant—his son-in-law's recovery mattered more than anything, even though the surgery had been successful. Despite Ayush's clear declaration that

Suren was out of danger, his wife and her father insisted on moving him.

Their distrust felt like a quiet slap. The room suddenly felt heavier.

I had heard everything, yet I couldn't bring myself to look at Sijal Didi's face—as though I had committed some grave mistake.

Sijal Didi said quietly, "Do you know, Jhara? That woman is strange… She has no sense of decorum. She's been shouting at the doctors and nurses for no reason. I think she's mentally disturbed… Maybe they're legally separated?"

I remained silent, pretending I didn't know. I didn't have the strength to process what was unfolding, let alone what I should do next. I felt disoriented, lost—like a bird with aching wings, fluttering in a sky without direction. Only my thoughts soared, grazing the distant horizon.

And then, the next morning, Rista said, "Grandfather and Mummy have come," she said over the phone, her voice trembling with urgency. "They're insisting on taking PApa away. Aunty, please… please say no."

Her words barely faded when Suren's father took the phone from her. His voice, too, was unsteady. He repeated the same request.

Even though I was buried beneath silent grief, I somehow managed to speak with a calm voice. "No. His condition is stable. The doctors still want to observe him before discharging."

In a softer tone, I asked, "Are they at home?"

"No," Rista replied. "They're saying all this over the phone."

I was stunned. Is this what human bonds have come to? Suren's house is just across the road from the hospital—

it's visible from the balcony. And yet, his mother doesn't want to even see her daughter? Or Suren's aging father?

My mind was a battlefield of conflicts. Suren had said the divorce papers were already signed a few days ago. If that's true, then what is the purpose of this performance? Why now? What do they really want?

Still, I knew my own footing was unsteady. I doubted every decision, every thought, as if each one could crumble at the slightest touch.

Sijal Didi, with her calm assurance, urged me to be patient.

Dr. Ayush added, "As he was regaining consciousness, he kept asking for Rista."

Not for me. Only Rista.

So… has he forgotten me?

Dr. Ayush must have sensed the shift in me. He placed a hand on my shoulder and said gently, "He's recovering, Jhara. Give him time. Slowly, he'll remember."

But then another question rose, unspoken yet heavy: how did they know about Suren's condition in such detail? And why were they so insistent on bringing him back, even after the divorce?

Despite everything, I couldn't bring myself to meet Suren—not even as his nurse. It felt like I had become an unwanted presence. As if an invisible river now flowed between my yesterday and today. I stood on this shore, watching the world I once dreamt of on the other.

Even Dr. Ayush, with all his warmth and concern, couldn't reach the sealed chambers of my heart. I respected him deeply, yet in my mind, he always took the place of Akash Bhai. And I could never let anyone else sit in Akash Bhai's place.

Maybe this bond—this closeness—is like a gentle

drizzle falling on parched land. It seems to wet the surface, but beneath it all, the earth remains dry and cracked.

So, then… who truly belongs to whom?

Whose shoulder can I lean on?

Where do I pour the monsoon of tears I've been carrying?

I took the photograph of my parents out of the cupboard—a faded picture, yet still alive with their warmth. Pressing it to my face, I didn't just cry—I accused. I held them responsible, whispering through trembling lips, *Would it have been so wrong not to bring such an unlucky girl into this world?*

I didn't notice Sijal Didi until her hand gently touched my shoulder. That single touch brought me back to myself. My tears seemed to seep into hers. I crumbled, weeping like an endless July rain, my head buried in her lap. She sat silently, unable to find words. Sometimes, life presents us with such moments—where no one can fix anything, only sit beside us in shared helplessness.

Eventually, I wiped my tears and sat up. "Didi, could you assign me to the orphanage duties for a week? I need to be away from here."

She understood without questioning. She too felt it would be unfair—for me to linger here without truly being present in my role. So, she made the necessary arrangements.

The orphanage wasn't far, but it felt worlds away from the ward, the ICU, and my room—each of which now carried too much weight. I didn't even want to step into my room again.

I had been posted at the orphanage before, but this time, everything felt different—sharper, more intimate. I found myself watching the children with a new depth, with a quiet attentiveness. Sometimes, a person drifts through life unknown, yet with a strange and sacred passion. In those quiet moments, I began to reflect on my own place in the world—in what way have I been fortunate being given a name, and being born into a known bloodline?

During this time, Rista called me often. But I couldn't bring myself to meet her. I was adrift, sailing a boat too unsteady to carry anyone else. How could I let her board this wreck with me?

Yet, even in my distance, I was restless for her— aching inside. She was part of me, no matter how much I tried to let go.

So I threw myself into work, clinging to routine like a raft. I left the rest to Time, to Fate, and to God.

My week at the orphanage had come to an end. Sijal Didi reassigned me to the ward for the physically handicapped. It was a bit removed from the main building, but we still met regularly—she made sure of it. Every evening, she came to sit with me, and we had dinner together in quiet companionship.

Before his departure, Dr. Ayush came to see me. His face was unusually somber, his silence heavy with things left unsaid. Maybe he already knew everything. Maybe he just didn't have the courage to speak about it. I could sense the weight he was carrying. Suren's wife, it seemed, was still determined to reclaim her husband.

A question burned in me—*Had Suren asked for me? Had he searched for me, even once?* But I couldn't bring myself to ask. I lacked the strength to either hear or answer.

Still, Ayush spoke, as if reading the silence between us. "I've seen it in his eyes, Jhara," he said gently. "He's searching for you. There's a look in him… like unspoken words that rise and fall at the edge of his lips, never quite crossing over."

I didn't let him say anything more. Emotions stirred within me, but I had learned the art of suppression. I wore my practiced mask—a dry smile, empty and polite.

Time had trained me well. I knew how to shift a conversation, how to lighten a heavy moment, how to make everything appear normal. My circumstances had seasoned me in this strange performance. I had mastered the technique of hiding my wounds behind measured words and an even tone.

Dr. Ayush took his leave quietly. On any other day, in any other state of mind, his sad eyes might have pierced my heart. Maybe his unspoken disappointments had found a place inside me, transforming into the tears. I no longer cried.

But something was different now. I didn't feel the pain of his absence. I couldn't even ask when he'd come again.

My mind felt frozen, yet a part of me still longed to see Suren and Rista—just once. Could I, somehow, find out about Rista's mother through someone discreet? Did Suren know she would return before their legal separation was finalised? Was that why he had asked me for time?

Whatever the reason, I couldn't bring myself to distrust Suren—not even a little. There was something in him, something sincere, that set him apart. That was why I had come to both love and respect him.

The sky outside had turned somber. I had never seen such a heavy, sorrowful sky since arriving here.

Someone was calling me. I snapped out of my thoughts. After freshening up a bit, I stepped out of my room.

Though she was a stranger, any woman in my place would have instinctively known—this was Rista's mother, Richa.

We entered the room together. I gestured for her to sit, but she refused. She stood stiffly, her face hard, her expression filled with annoyance—perhaps even disdain.

Then, without warning, she broke the silence.

"Aren't you going to ask who I am? Or why I'm here?"

Her sudden voice startled me. My throat went dry, and a wave of heat washed over me—I was sweating, dizzy. Was I about to faint?

Perhaps she sensed it. Her voice softened slightly as she continued,

"There's no need to be afraid. Do you think I've come to punish you? I know everything. Just a while ago, my husband was looking for you. Aren't you going to see him?"

I wasn't prepared for this—for her words, her presence, or the questions they raised. So I stayed silent. I had no answer, no strength to meet her gaze. My head dropped, heavy with the weight of unspoken thoughts.

She looked at me squarely and said, "You must already know—there's been no divorce between us. Yes, I wanted it a few months ago, but it was never finalised. And now, I've changed my mind. I no longer want to leave my husband. That's why I'm here—to make things clear.

Don't try to enter our lives under any guise. If, in a moment of emotion, you've started dreaming of something, erase it. Take it as nothing more than a nightmare."

She kept speaking, her words sharp and cold. I sat there, unable to respond, unsure of what to say.

I felt as if I had been branded with the shame of the vilest criminal in the world. To her, I was probably just a desperate woman—someone who, enchanted by Suren's looks, his money, and his social standing, had tried to steal what wasn't hers.

My silence only seemed to infuriate her more. Her voice rose in anger.

"What is it that you want? Money? A house? Someone to lean on?"

No matter how hard I tried to compose myself, the tears defied me and streamed down my cheeks.

She sneered, her voice laced with contempt. "What's your education? What do you know about legal rights, about marriage? It's not that easy to take someone else's husband and build a life. Keep that in mind.

My husband. My daughter. They are mine—*only* mine. Stay away from them. Make sure not even your shadow touches their lives."

And with that, she stormed out, like a whirlwind leaving destruction in its wake.

I collapsed onto the bed, sobbing uncontrollably. A storm of emotions surged within me, stealing my breath. For a moment, I wished I could tear myself apart—anything to numb the humiliation, to silence the ache clawing at my chest. But I couldn't. I just lay there, broken, drowning in a pain that had no name.

Sijal Didi came. I had endured just enough to face her tender presence, to accept her soothing touch without flinching. The sky outside had quieted after a furious downpour. In much the same way, I had calmed myself—if only on the surface.

I said to her, "Once I had to leave Hyderabad for Vinit. Do I now have to leave Sikkim, my place of work?"

"Leaving a place for someone never solves anything," she replied gently, stroking my hair. "You have to stay and struggle through the pain. One day, Jhara, you'll see—you've won."

Perhaps I was losing the equation between losing and winning, tangled as I was in my sighs. I had never competed to win—neither in school, nor at work, nor along the winding road of my life. And I had never proposed a marriage to Suren. He was the one who had wanted me—wanted me to be his partner, to care for Rista, to bring order to his disordered world. And me? I was only ever the one to bear the blame, the humiliation. Richa had flung her words at me like stones, sharp and wild. I took them all, silently—without a word, without complaint.

Two days later, a friend told me that their belongings were packed and ready to be shifted from Mr. Suren's house. "Perhaps they're leaving," she said. "It's his own house, not government quarters. I wonder why they're vacating. Maybe they're taking Rista and Suren's father too."

I listened passively, as if none of it concerned me anymore—as if my identity with that family had vanished. And yet, some quiet corner of my mind and my eyes kept searching—for one. Maybe I'd never meet Rista again in this life. Maybe she, too, had looked for me. Maybe she hadn't been given the chance to say goodbye.

But I was building strength again, little by little. Each day I met a brave new world through the bright, curious eyes of children. My mornings, though shadowed with sorrow, were never lifeless. There was always movement, always the hum of something beginning again.

My siblings had come to know what happened. They directed their dry sympathy toward me and their harsh judgment toward Suren. Their sympathy meant little to me, but their blame—unfair and unknowing—hurt deeply. How could I explain to them? They believed Suren had made hisdecisiononlyforRista'ssake,tokeepherclose,tocareforher. But no matter what anyone said, I couldn't hold anything against him. Yes, Rista was the bridge between us, but Suren had never used her to manipulate me. I still held the same respect for him—and I always would.

Some days later, I returned to my old Apartment. From the balcony, I could see Suren's house and the garden. One quiet afternoon, I stood there, gazing at it. The old security guard paced near the gate. The flowers bloomed in their usual colours, but to my eyes, they looked faded.I found myself searching for the little butterfly that used to flit around the gate— The one who would call me, whispering over the phone from behind the rose bushes, "Tell me, Aunty, from where do I see you?"

From the balcony, I used to search for her. She would dart playfully from behind one tree to another, teasing me with her little game of hide and seek. Sometimes behind the creepers, sometimes peeking from behind a trunk—my Rista, my dearest.

Today, I walked up to the gate, lost in thought. The security guard looked surprised.

"No one's home," he said, puzzled. "Didn't you know? They came, and everyone left with them."

As I opened my mouth to ask who *they* were, he seemed to guess.

"Would you like to walk around the garden, Ma'am?" he asked politely.

He had seen me there many times before. Without hesitation, I smiled faintly. "No... I was just wondering if the seedling I planted had grown any new leaves."

A gentle lie. Spoken softly. And with that, I stepped inside.

The house, now abandoned, sighed in silence with

the garden. I wandered through the overgrown paths, searching for the seedling—but it was gone. Not even a trace remained.

How could it have survived? A seedling needs the right soil, the right warmth. I had planted it in the wrong climate, under a sky that did not welcome it. My hope had withered long before it had the chance to bloom.

I paused, gazing up at the closed window—the one that was supposed to be mine. I was sure he had decorated it, just as he had begun weaving dreams that mirrored my own.

Of course, Suren loved his wife. But she had hurt him—again and again—pushing him away, breaking his trust. And yet, perhaps she repented. Why else would she return to take him back?

I stepped out through the gate. The guard said nothing. Perhaps he read the silence in my eyes.

I turned once to glance back at the campus. Rista's laughter lingered in the air, her voice echoing—sometimes clear, sometimes faint. I knew they were illusions.

Let her be happy with her parents. Let their broken home rebuild its strength.

There were no tears in my eyes. No grief in my heart. No bitterness in my soul.

No hesitation. No regrets.

With quiet strength and steady steps, I moved forward—without looking back.

Sijal Didi was waiting for me, as if she had known. She seemed concerned, anticipating that I would have broken down upon seeing Suren's deserted house.

I smiled at her, though it felt unfamiliar. She looked startled.

"There's nothing to worry about, Didi. I'm alright,"

I said. "If one chooses to leave the straight road for an untrodden path, one must be ready for thorns. I've returned from that path. Now the road ahead is straight and clear—there's nothing to fear, no chance of stumbling."

Feigning not to have heard me, she said, "Our new hostel is being inaugurated today."

"Yes, Didi, I know. We should get ready soon."

"Are you aware of the new rules?"

"Yes, I am. Some modifications, I believe. It's good—will help avoid misunderstandings among the residents."

We had reached my room by then. The new rules were about the allocation of rooms—decided by lottery, ensuring fairness between married, unmarried, aged, and middle-aged residents. A step toward equality, without room for complaint or resentment.

Dr. Ayush was present for the inauguration. After the ceremony, he came to meet me. I noticed the faded sympathy in his eyes, and the uncertain rhythm in his voice as he tried to comfort me.

"Please don't take me as an outsider," he said. "I'll always be there for you. Don't hesitate to reach out if you face any difficulty."

His words drifted past me like a gentle breeze. I replied calmly, "There's no need. I am no longer a creeper looking for support. I've already grown strong."

Surprised, he gazed at me. Then, with a softness in his voice, he added, "Jhara, we'll never leave you alone. We'll find someone truly right for you. Our happiness lies in seeing you happy."

There was sincerity in his tone—no pretension, no selfishness. He spoke with the care of an elder brother.

I couldn't help myself—I burst out laughing. When it faded, I said, "Do you really think a woman must marry to live with dignity? The number of unmarried women in this hostel surpasses that of the married ones. And there are married women too, who are forced to live as if they were alone. So what does marriage guarantee?"

"To me, marriage is like a glass house—fragile, beautiful, but prone to shatter with the slightest touch. And sometimes, one must continue living inside, wounded and bleeding."

Dr. Ayush interjected before I could finish, "Not always. Look at us—my wife and I. We don't tread carefully around each other. We live with mutual love, with respect, and our bond only deepens. Marriage isn't just for this life, it's for many. Don't waste your life mourning Suren's love."

I remained silent. Arguments serve little purpose—they only breed tension.

Besides, I couldn't bear anyone criticizing Suren. I had seen the human in him. Whatever happened, I never blamed him. Only fate.

It wasn't just Dr. Ayush. My siblings, my brothers-in-law—they all seemed to think that life wouldn't be complete unless I married. Their well-meaning worries echoed around me like thunder from a cloudless sky.

But my heart no longer wept. Once the mind turns to stone, no rain can soak it. The rock simply lets the rain pass.

I had grown to love solitude. Sympathy from others felt more like an intrusion than comfort. It irked me, especially when anyone mentioned Suren. But one presence kept surfacing in my mind, gently yet persistently—Rista. She danced along the edges of my thoughts, laughing, making me laugh, speaking in soft tones, listening intently. The touch of her small hands on my head felt like a breeze from spring—sweet, soothing, and full of life.

The world, I had come to realise, was a shifting blend

of light and shadow—a mix of good and bad, where people crossed paths in various roles, like a never-ending game of hide and seek.

Under the new hostel regulations, Barsha became my roommate. She was a woman of few words—a quiet presence. She didn't interfere or intrude, didn't indulge in idle gossip. I silently thanked God for sending me a companion who understood the unspoken boundaries.

Barsha was new here, and nobody knew much about her. She followed a simple rhythm: go to duty, return, make her bed, eat, and then lose herself in a book until sleep arrived. Among her possessions, books outnumbered everything else. She was a true bibliophile.

There's a certain charm in hearing something from someone who rarely speaks. That's what happened with Barsha. I often felt like talking to her, asking her things, but her silence held me back.

Curiosity stirred among our colleagues. Whispers floated through the corridors—some said she was married, others insisted she wasn't. They turned to me for answers, accusing me of hiding something. But how could I reveal what I didn't know?

Eventually, it came out—Barsha was from a Hindu family and had presumably crossed the conventional age for marriage. I began to see reflections of myself in her. There could be countless reasons for not marrying—neglect from family, heartbreak, disinterest in worldly ties, fate. In my case, it was neglect.

After our parents passed, no one remained who truly belonged to me. My siblings were absorbed in their own worlds. What followed can't be pinned entirely on anyone. Life unfolded in a series of vague, untraceable causes.

Vinit drifted away, looking down on my profession.

Some invisible force snapped the fragile thread that could have tied me to Suren. Relationships—siblings, relatives—became like driftwood floating on a flood-swollen river. That river swept everyone to separate shores, while I remained adrift.

It's not that I was never offered a shore. I was. But every time I reached for one, another current pulled me back into the depths. Now, in these endless waters, I've stopped hoping to touch the ground.

One quiet evening, Sijal Didi said to me, "Do you know, Jhara? Barsha has been full of praise for you. She's happy she got a roommate like you."

I was surprised—and elated. Admiration, especially from someone like Barsha, felt like a balm. Everyone craves appreciation. Criticism, no matter how truthful, often weighs heavily.

But what touched me most was that she didn't say it to my face. That, to me, made it genuine. Too often, people praise you in person only to turn around and twist your story behind your back. They take liberties with your life, interpreting your choices in ways that serve their gossip. But Barsha didn't. And maybe that's why her silence spoke louder than any words ever could.

That small gesture of appreciation had quietly planted a seed of affection in me. Sometimes, I found myself watching her with quiet curiosity, a fondness I couldn't name out loud. I borrowed good storybooks from her collection and devoured them one by one. She never minded.

There was something in her composed lifestyle, in her quiet dignity, that made me hesitant to reveal even the slightest hint of my growing attachment. So, despite sharing the same room, a subtle distance lingered between us—like a curtain neither of us dared to pull aside.

One night, I awoke abruptly. Her bed was empty. Puzzled and slightly concerned, I tiptoed to the balcony. There she was—Barsha—standing still, gazing at the desolate road beyond the railing. Her figure was motionless, but her laboured breathing betrayed the tears falling in silence. She was crying.

A part of me longed to approach her, to stand beside her in that stillness and offer something—anything. But I couldn't. I turned back and slipped into bed as quietly as I had come. Sleep evaded me. For the first time, I truly understood that beneath someone who seems as unyielding as stone, there can flow a hidden spring of sorrow—soft, secret, and persistent.

She returned a while later, sat against the corner wall, her body folded inward like someone cradling an unseen wound. I watched silently, her anguish pulsing in the air between us. Was her fate as ironic as mine? Had she too been betrayed by love, by life? There's a peculiar strength that comes from seeing your own pain reflected in another—it soothes, it reassures. For a moment, I wanted to rise and ask her, to console her, to open that closed door between us. But her guarded expression returned to my mind, and I hesitated. Perhaps, like me, she was simply trying to find rest. I don't know who fell asleep first.

The next morning, she was preparing for duty with her usual composure. Yet something lingered on her face—a trace of the night's tears, the puffiness around her eyes.

Unable to hold back, I finally asked, "Barsha, are you feeling okay? Your face… it looks a little swollen."

She looked at me calmly, and with a soft voice said, "No, nothing of the sort. I'm quite fine." Then she slipped on her apron and left.

I sat there, thinking—how thick and impenetrable

the darkness is behind people's composed masks. What storms lie behind their silences? What tangled sighs, what unspoken griefs?

But morning had arrived, and the brightness of the day began washing away the heavy thoughts of night. I lost myself again in the usual rhythm of hospital life—reading patient charts, administering injections, adjusting oxygen masks.

Yet even then, when sleep broke by chance in the middle of the night, I'd glance at her bed. I could see, in the faint light, a face marked with tears. Again and again. It became clear—there were chapters within her she had chosen to keep sealed.

Six months passed.

New flowers had bloomed in Suren's garden, tended now by a new gardener. His world had filled with laughter, the stirrings of a new family. Meanwhile, a thin layer of dust had begun to settle on my memories of him.

Time, for me, felt as though it had paused—its hands fixed on a single moment. Same work. Same walls. Same days and nights. A perfect circle of repetition. Nothing had changed—not in my appearance, not in my job. Only one thing had shifted—I had grown a little more inward. A little more mature.

Lately, I found it difficult to connect deeply with anyone. Everything around me felt artificial—conversations seemed rehearsed, smiles too well-curated. It felt as though everyone wore a mask, playing roles in a grand theatre of pretense. The gap between appearance and reality grew more visible to me with each passing day.

Perhaps this shift in me had not gone unnoticed, because I sensed my realisations echoed in Sijal Didi's concern. She tried her best to cheer me up, to bring back the version of me that smiled more often. If there was anyone in this world who felt truly mine, it was Sijal Didi. Her care was steady, without conditions, like a soft shawl laid across tired shoulders.

One day, she came to me unexpectedly, a note of urgency in her voice. "Do you know, Jhara? Barsha is not unmarried—she's married," she said.

I stared at her, stunned. "But... she doesn't wear bangles or the vermilion. I thought she was Hindu."

"I've only heard this much," she replied. "Nothing more. But the source is reliable—it can't be false."

My curiosity grew restless. If she truly was married, why had she never once mentioned her husband or family in these six long months?

I began watching her more intently, drawn to her silence as though it were a riddle waiting to be solved. I laughed quietly at myself—was I becoming like a diligent student, desperate to unlock some secret knowledge?

Then, unexpectedly, the chance arrived. Barsha fell ill—typhoid. Her fever ran high, and at times, she would slip into delirium. It was during one of those feverish nights, as I sat beside her coaxing her to sip fruit juice and gently administering medicine, that she murmured a name—Chandan.

It felt like a key, suddenly dropped at my feet.

Chandan. The name echoed in my mind long after she had drifted back into fevered sleep. Who was he? A husband? A lover? Someone from her past she had buried deep?

Something had cracked open that night—not just in her mystery, but in the wall between us.

"Who is Chandan you keep calling for?" I asked softly.

"My son... my three-year-old son," she replied—perhaps consciously, or perhaps lost in the haze of fever.

I was stunned. Barsha—so quiet, so self-contained, someone who seemed untouched by any worldly attachment—had a son? She had always appeared as an unmarried woman, and yet...

"Is he... with your husband?" I ventured, my voice hesitant.

She turned her face to the wall, gave no reply, and soon drifted into a restless sleep.

Her fever had spiked again. Sijal Didi came and sat beside her, gently stroking her forehead with cool hands. We stayed by her side through the night, guarding her sleep like sentinels of silence.

Though we now knew she had a son, there had never been any signs of a married Hindu woman—no bangles, no sindoor. We quietly assumed her husband was no longer alive.

At dawn, when her fever had somewhat subsided, Sijal Didi gently asked, "Barsha, with whom have you left your son?"

"In the orphanage," she murmured, her eyes glistening with tears.

Sijal Didi's voice grew tender, yet firm. "Why, Barsha? Why did you hide this from us for so long? And more than that—you know our orphanage here is a good one. You could have kept him close. You could see him every day."

Barsha gave a small nod. Her silence, at last, was a soft agreement.

Though the fever had broken, she looked utterly exhausted. She refused food, her energy drained. I coaxed her into eating two slices of bread and sipping warm soup with her medicine. After that, she slept soundly through the day.

By evening, Barsha had woken up, still pale but more at ease. Sijal Didi returned, bringing a bowl of pudding she had prepared herself. She sat close, offering it with quiet affection.

Barsha reached out, took her hand, and said with genuine warmth, "You and Jhara have done so much for me... I've troubled you both."

Sijal Didi feigned a scolding tone, though her eyes were soft. "What do you want then? That we lie still and don't trouble you when *we* fall sick?" Then, more gently, she continued, "We live away from our families now—this is our family. We must learn to share each other's joys and sorrows. Sorrow shared is sorrow halved. Joy... joy rarely gets doubled. Too often, envy shadows it. But sorrow— sorrow can be soothed when someone simply listens."

She touched Barsha's shoulder.

"Talk to us, Barsha. Let us help. Bring your son here, to our orphanage. You'll feel lighter. You'll feel peace."

"Yes," she replied, her consent wrapped in that single, quiet word.

Barsha was fast asleep. I sat there, lost in thought, wondering how God burdens each soul with their own share of sorrow. Ah, poor Barsha... Her husband must be gone from this world. What other reason could there be for her child to grow up in an orphanage?

Suddenly, my own suffering felt smaller in comparison. Maybe it was a blessing that I never married— who knows what grief might have awaited me?

Chandan, Barsha's son, came to mind. The poor child had never known a father's love. And though his mother lived, he was still far from her. I couldn't help but think of Barsha's constant worry about his future. How would she manage to guide him through this harsh, unforgiving world? Perhaps that's why she had folded into herself—turning silent, like a stream that flows without a sound.

Sijal Didi joined me and began recounting stories of many girls—some quietly inspiring, others unbearably tragic. Woven between them were faint, unspoken threads of her own.

Her father had once financed the education of a poor man's son, even sending him abroad for higher studies—under a mutual understanding that, upon his return, he would marry Sijal. But when the young man earned his degree, he chose another path. He fell in love with someone overseas, married her, and settled there—leaving behind the promises made, the trust given, and the girl who waited.

For seven long years, Sijal Didi waited—hoping, believing. When hope finally withered, something in her shifted. The pain crystallized into resolve. To her, the entire fraternity of men began to seem like a brotherhood of betrayers. From that day forward, she vowed never to marry, channeling her strength into work, silence, and self-reliance.

"But, Didi," I asked, "how could you then want me to marry Mr. Suren? On what basis?"

Returning to the present, she replied softly, "Oh no—Mr. Suren is not that kind of man. His wife has made his life unbearably bitter. I believe he's not at peace. He's a good man, truly."

Her words left me adrift in thought. In such ironies of fate, who can be blamed—the man or the woman? The happiness of conjugal life is a kind of lottery. If fortune favours you, joy is yours; if not, you live in quiet deprivation. Some spend their lives in compromise.

Lately, I had grown accustomed to letting go. I began to see Suren as a fleeting dream—a figment from my subconscious. That dream, like all dreams, had broken as morning broke, and I returned to the numbing rhythm of hospital duties. I was not alone; many girls like me dream, but not all dreams come true.

Surely Barsha must have dreamed of a home, a husband, and children. And Sijal Didi too—she must have imagined the return of the man her father had trusted, dreamt of a life with him as her partner. But dreams are fragile, and human wishes, more often than not, go unanswered.

Barsha's story was unlike any other—and we might never have known the truth, had her husband not shown up at the hospital. Rumours had circulated for months: some claimed he was dead. Even Barsha, once, had quietly confirmed it. So, when we saw a man asking for her outside the duty room, searching with anxious eyes, we were stunned.

But Barsha refused to meet him. She sent word that she wasn't on duty.

When I came into the duty room, I couldn't hold back. My voice carried a trace of irritation as I asked her directly, "Barsha, how can you call him dead when he stands very much alive? For a Hindu woman, a husband is everything—her bangles and vermilion mark are sacred symbols of that bond. Is it right to erase him so easily?"

Barsha didn't flinch. Her voice was steady, her eyes sharp. "Maybe he's alive for the world," she said coldly, "but he's dead to me. He died the night he refused to accept our child—his own flesh and blood—and abandoned the newborn at an orphanage. And when I protested, he threw me out of the house, kicking and beating me like an animal."

Her eyes blazed with fury and contempt. Her whole body shook with a storm I hadn't expected.

I had never seen her like this before. For a moment, I was frozen—too shaken to know how to calm her. Still, I made her sit down and gently offered her a glass of water, my hands trembling. I hadn't been prepared for such an eruption—for the raw, unhealed wound behind her silence.

After calming down a little, Barsha said, "You did the right thing by not getting married. Tell me—how many women are truly happy in this male-dominated society of ours?"

I couldn't accept her words so easily. Her remark unsettled me. Instantly, several examples flashed through my mind—my two elder sisters, Dr. Ayush's wife, and a colleague who married late in life. They all seemed content in their marriages.

But then again, is there truly a formula for a happy conjugal life? Perhaps not. Perhaps it's something a woman must learn as she steps into it. Fortune is fickle, beyond the reach of logic or control. It is God who holds the equations of joy and sorrow, and we must live what is written for us.

Viewed from a distance, happiness often seems like a beautiful mountain—serene, inviting. We believe others are living better, more fulfilled lives. But who can ever tell when the landscape will shift, when the next storm might come?

That day, as I tried to console Barsha, I couldn't help but feel a quiet sense of gratitude. I had been spared that kind of torment. Before ever knowing the pain of captivity, I had the chance to fly—untamed, beneath the open sky. A bird learns to live with the ache in its wings, but the true anguish of a cage is not the stillness—it's watching other birds soar freely while you remain grounded.

Barsha had fallen asleep crying a lot. Sleep, while settling in my eyes, dodged away by and by. Barsha's face was as clear as a rain washed sky.

Many days slipped by in silence. None of us brought up Barsha's husband—neither did we ask, nor did she ever speak of him. Barsha seemed like a still, rippleless pond. But there was a world of difference between the calm surface and the murky depths below—like the deceptive clarity of water hiding the heaviness of silt at the bottom.

Barsha's son came to our orphanage at Sijal Didi's request. The moment we saw him, we were surprised by how instinctively drawn we felt to the boy. He had his father's nose and eyes, but his mother's soft complexion. Looking at him, Sijal Didi murmured a quiet wish, *"May he never inherit his father's nature."*

Time was shifting, slowly changing its tune. My past felt dry and faded, like an old photograph losing colour. At work, I blended in with my colleagues, finding a strange comfort in staying busy. But in quiet, solitary hours, the past would catch me off guard. Whenever it did, I'd carefully distract myself—because I believed that lingering at a stumbling block would never help me reach the end of the road. The path ahead was long, and no one else could walk it for me. I had to move forward—for myself, and only for myself.

Sometimes, we spoke about our work, and each time, I felt a quiet pride in my profession. I considered myself truly fortunate. I held deep respect for the turn my life had taken. Everything—from tending to patients and adapting to the rhythms of hospital life, to my unwavering sense of duty—mattered deeply to me.

Here, among tears and smiles, the quiet drama of life unfolds—birth and death playing out side by side, with sweets shared in joy and shoulders offered in sorrow. Even when I'm not personally connected to the departed, a strange heaviness lingers in my heart for a while, despite all the self-consolations I try. Perhaps it's because, in this place, everything feels like a part of me.

For that, countless sleepless nights and early mornings pass without hesitation. Time slips away—no one knows where it begins or where it ends. Unlike us, it never tires.

Sometimes I feel as though time has no heart. Everyone longs for it, but it longs for no one. We try to grasp it, but it rushes past like the wind, deceiving us all. As if by nature, it resists being tied to anyone.

It makes us laugh, makes us weep—and then drifts away with a cold, indifferent glance.

If only we could borrow even a fraction of time's detachment, perhaps not even the shadow of sorrow could touch us.

23

I saw a girl around Rista's age today. She reminded me of her so vividly that it tugged at something deep within me. My bond with Rista may have lasted only a few months, but it rooted itself firmly in my heart. Even now, I can't forget her.

Whenever I catch sight of someone who resembles her, I can't help but stare, as though time might fold back upon itself and return her to me. An ache rises—this restless urge to say just a word or two. And when I do speak to someone like her, my eyes brim with tears. I remind myself again and again that she no longer belongs to me, that our paths have diverged. I try to be strong.

At times, I even feel hurt—strangely sulky. When she was here, just a few meters away, she would call me often. But now, though she's far away, she doesn't call even once. I don't have her number, but she remembers mine. I've kept it unchanged—like I've kept myself—waiting, hoping. Doesn't she understand that?

Eventually, I settle my thoughts. Perhaps it's not her choice. Maybe her mother has placed restrictions on her. Maybe she's no longer free to make even a simple phone call.

While thinking of Rista, I'm suddenly reminded of my nephews and nieces. I long to rush to them, to wrap them in my arms and hold them close. But their parents never think to call me. Not even once. It feels like I've been erased from their lives. Perhaps they no longer want me. I yearn to hear them call me *Mousie* or *Piusie* again, to hear their voices... but that too remains a quiet ache. The bond of kinship seems to be fraying.

Barsha had just returned after visiting her son. She looked drained, her eyes clouded with unspoken sorrow. As she lay on the bed, she muttered, "It's good I brought him here. Otherwise, travelling that far just to see him would've been so difficult."

One day, catching her in a slightly lighter mood, I gently asked, "Do you ever think of going back to your husband?"

She sat up, leaned against the wall, and replied with quiet conviction, "No. Never. He's dead to me. The torture he put me through still smoulders under my skin, like a wound that refuses to close. Do you want to see, Didi?"

Before I could answer, she pulled back her clothing and uncovered her back. I gasped. My God—deep branding scars. The skin had wrinkled and puckered, yet the pain they held felt raw and recent.

"Man or monster?" I whispered in disbelief.

"A *monster*, Didi. A monster," she repeated, her voice hollow. Then she showed me her knees and thighs—though the wounds had healed, the cut marks remained, stark and unforgotten.

I trembled. My eyes welled up. "Barsha... how did you bear all this without a word?"

"There was no escape," she said, her voice a low murmur. "But the moment I found one, I took it. I left with my son. I wiped the vermillion from my forehead and shattered the bangles with my own hands. I will never return to him. Never. He doesn't come for me—not even to see his own child. He only comes for the salary I earn. That's all I am to him now. And that's why I've severed every tie. I won't go back. Not now, not ever."

She said all this in a single breath, then turned away and wrapped herself in a sheet, curling into silence. The agony-filled pages of her life's novel seemed to flutter open before me. Though some lines blurred through the mist of my tears, their meaning was heartrendingly clear.

Days rolled on.

Barsha was no longer the quiet shadow she once was. She had begun to speak more—sometimes too much, as if releasing a lifetime of silence. Amid her words, she once said, "Joys, when shared, often spark envy. But sorrows, when shared, lose some of their weight."

Experience, I realised, shows us the way—sometimes as steady as a lamp, other times as sudden as lightning. And with each of our own scars and stories, we kept moving forward. The sharp sting of old grief began to dull as we passed each milestone.

But some marks—etched deep—refused to fade. They returned with memories, like shadows cast by the past, uninvited but unforgettable.

24

Years passed by in such quiet, unhurried manner. New faces arrived, grew familiar, and eventually faded into the background. Some bonds were formed, others quietly dissolved. I no longer cared to keep track of them.

Sometimes, when I reflect on how far I've come—from the innocence of a tender heart to the resilience of a mature mind—I can't help but laugh. The journey between the two is vast, and only now am I beginning to truly feel its weight.

Dr. Ayush still visited from time to time. These days, his words carried no trace of sympathy—and I didn't seek it either. I had grown past the need to share my sorrows in mournful tones, not just with him, but with my siblings as well. I told them all the same thing: I'm doing well.

I am the empress of my own little empire. I don't wish to live under anyone's shadow.

But if there's one person who helped me find this strength, it's Sijal Didi. She has been more than a guide—she is my lighthouse, steady and unwavering, guiding my fragile ship through the vast, unpredictable sea of life.

She is my inspiration. She is my strength.

Some days, we would sit together during those quiet, desolate hours, sharing light conversations. She always encouraged me to stay strong and let go of the past. With her comforting words, she gently wiped away the bitterness I held toward my siblings.

To her, no one is truly ours or not ours in God's creation. Even a motherless orphan, she would say, finds care and grows with the love of strangers. Through others, he comes to understand the true meaning of human compassion.

And truly, her words began to soothe my wounds. The love, care, and wise counsel I never received from my own sisters, I found in Sijal Didi.

My sisters were quick to pass judgment, branding Suren a betrayer without trying to understand the full story. But they didn't spend even a day with me to help rebuild the shattered pieces of my heart.

I alone know how I survived those turbulent days and nights. Only Sijal Didi stayed by my side, comforting me, never once blaming Suren. She understood his helplessness—how he had been cornered by circumstances.

Not once did she speak ill of him. Instead, she reminded me to keep moving forward, to continue doing my 'karma' with faith and resilience.

The sudden phone call from Dr. Ayush unsettled me. Though the news of his arrival was welcome, the reason behind it took me by surprise. This time, he wasn't coming alone—he was bringing his brother, and the purpose was to offer me a marriage proposal on his behalf.

At that moment, I felt as though I had outgrown such propositions. I tried to express this to him, but he wouldn't listen. His quiet insistence left me feeling cornered.

I couldn't help but wonder—why was Dr. Ayush offering me this 'gift' of marriage? Did he see me as someone so pitiful, so broken, that I needed to be rescued? Was I truly that helpless in his eyes? After all, I had a job that kept me grounded, a roof over my head, a steady salary to sustain myself, responsibilities that gave me purpose, and colleagues who filled the silence with warmth. What more was I supposed to need?

Perhaps he saw things differently. He had confided in Sijal Didi about his intentions. Her response was calm and firm: "The wounds from her recent heartbreaks haven't healed yet. I don't think she's ready to consider another proposal. It's better to let her be—for now."

But her words didn't deter him. Ignoring her advice, he arrived, his so-called brother by his side.

Frankly, I was disheartened. For the first time, I asked myself: does losing one's parents turn you into an object of pity? Was that how others now saw me—someone to be 'fixed' or handed over, out of sympathy?

Dr. Ayush, knowing my family history all too well, perhaps couldn't help but feel this way. But I wasn't ready to accept a marriage meant to patch over my brokenness. Not when I was still gathering the pieces myself.

A tea party had been arranged at a particular venue. Dr. Ayush had suggested that both Sijal Didi and I attend. True to her word, Sijal Didi arrived on time, ready and waiting for me.

Seeing me somewhat subdued, she asked gently, "Aren't you ready yet?"

I replied with a quiet "Yes," which made her pause and look at me more closely, surprised.

Taking in my minimal makeup and plain appearance, she murmured with a hint of disbelief, "What is this…?" Wonder flickered in her eyes.

I simply nodded while locking up the room, and she didn't press the matter. We left in silence. From my demeanour alone, Sijal Didi could sense my disinterest. She knew I was going only to honour Dr. Ayush's request—not out of any personal enthusiasm.

My thoughts about marriage had grown cloudy, weighed down by doubt. I was merely managing the situation, not stepping into it with hope.

At the venue, Dr. Ayush introduced his brother to me.

The gentleman looked sharp and well-composed. I could tell Dr. Ayush had spoken highly of me. The man said, "Indeed! This profession is built on sincerity and duty. Without devotion, it loses its soul—and society pays the price. Truly, I admire those who honour it."

His words rang clearly, but something about his voice and appearance tugged at my memory, like an echo from the past. It created a strange illusion—an uncanny familiarity I couldn't place.

He asked me a few polite questions. I responded calmly, without keeping track of his reactions or wondering whether he was pleased with my answers.

Sensing my unease, Sijal Didi excused herself on the pretext of some work. I glanced at Dr. Ayush, silently requesting to leave as well.

But the gentleman stopped me. "Won't you ask me anything?"

Dr. Ayush chimed in with a smile, "It's better if you both talk privately," and stepped away.

We were left alone.

He began, "I'm Sourav. Do you know, Jhara, Ayush Bhai has spoken so much about you. Ever since I heard about you, I've been hoping to meet you. Honestly, I want someone like you as my life partner—if you agree, that is."

His words sounded rehearsed, like lines from a play. I couldn't help but feel detached. Without letting his enthusiasm sway me, I replied calmly, "Marriage isn't something decided by a simple yes or no. It's something divine—something beyond our will. It rests entirely in God's hands."

"Exactly," he nodded quickly. "I'm not saying we'll have that divine connection instantly. But we can begin by knowing each other—understanding each other. And if it feels right, then maybe we can think about marriage."

I couldn't bring myself to respond. The disinterest stirring inside me was on the verge of surfacing, but I stayed quiet, not wanting to offend Dr. Ayush.

Just then, he returned, as if prepared to say something important.

"Don't be in a rush, Sourav," he said warmly. "You'll be staying here for a few months. It'll give both of you time to know each other better. I truly believe you're a perfect match. But in the end, your happiness is what matters most to us."

I listened to them silently, but deep within, I knew—no flower would ever bloom in the desert of my mind.

That day, after they left, I went on duty as usual. Patient number 17 was writhing in pain. His wife sat beside him, gently caressing his arms and legs, her eyes filled with desperation. There was a quiet, haunting helplessness about her.

The moment she saw Dr. Nirmal, her hope seemed to flicker back to life. Her tearful eyes followed him, her voice trembling with urgency as she asked question after question. "Please, doctor… tell me the truth. Will my husband recover?"

How could I offer her a lie dressed as hope? I had overheard the doctors—he wasn't going to make it. He was at the final stage, far beyond the reach of painkillers or interventions.

Still, I sat beside her, trying to offer what little comfort I could. But she didn't seem to hear me. Her grief had tuned out the world.

Clutching my hand, she began to speak, her words pouring out like a long-held storm. She and her husband had no one else. They had grown up together in an orphanage, built a life from nothing. Their home, their bond—it was all they had. And now, she was watching her world slip away.

Her face was pale with sorrow, her voice barely above a whisper. It was the kind of scene we witness far too often here. Tragedies that carve into our hearts—and then, somehow, we move on, as if forgetting is a part of surviving.

In moments like these, amid such raw helplessness, I often wonder: is life anything more than an illusion we try to believe in?

Here in this hospital, the illusion wears thin. The sorrow is real, and the distance between life and death—so terribly short. We don't need to be told the meaning of pain. We see it. We breathe it. And we carry it quietly, every day.

A little while later, the patient closed his eyes. His young wife, barely nineteen, rested her head on his feet, staring at him with innocent, speechless eyes. She didn't blink. Hunger, thirst, sleep—everything had abandoned her, as if she were no longer part of the living world.

From the records, I knew she was only nineteen. Her husband, twenty-four. How could a girl that young—who should still be waking slowly in the soft comfort of morning beds—bear such a brutal shock?

After returning from the ward, I shared her story with Sijal Didi. My voice trembled with emotion as I said, "How will that girl live alone if anything happens to her?"

With a dry, knowing smile, Sijal Didi replied,

"Everyone is alone in this world. For some, loneliness shows. For others, it stays hidden. But in truth, we're all alone."

That day, I was on duty at the orphanage from morning till evening, so I didn't return to the ward. In the evening, I heard the news: the patient in bed number 17 had passed away.

I couldn't recall his face clearly, but her eyes—those innocent, pleading eyes—flashed before me again and again. Her fragile voice haunted me: *"Will my husband recover?"*

I couldn't eat that night. I felt deeply unsettled. *Poor girl,* I kept thinking. *Where did she go? What happened to her? What will she do now?*

A colleague, sensing my unease, said, "She will be working here at the hospital. Though no one has officially asked for her consent yet."

The next day, I learned she was indeed still in the hospital. With the help of a few people, the cremation had been carried out. Even after death, a man needs the help of others. And somehow, help always arrives. God makes arrangements through the hands of strangers—why else would the young man have come here at all?

She sat in silence, unmoving, like a statue. No tears in her eyes. No words on her lips. But her stillness shouted grief. Everyone around her was filled with quiet sympathy. I too was breaking down inside.

Perhaps sorrow was written too deep into her fate. Deprived of parental love, denied the bond of siblings, and now, the one person she clung to—her husband—was gone too.

I was filled with resentment—towards life, towards fate, towards God.

Did He do the right thing by taking away a young man like him, and not those whose bodies are twisted in endless pain, who pray each day for release?

I was furious with her unknown parents—who had abandoned her in an orphanage, yet must still be alive somewhere in this vast world. *Fie upon their hearts,* I thought. *Fie on the name of such parenthood.*

God never spares anyone when it comes to sorrow. He distributes grief according to what He believes each person can endure. But such things instill a quiet dread—a fear of what married life might bring.

25

I couldn't stand Sourav's presence—it felt jarring, almost repulsive, especially when my mind was still clouded with grief. He had invited me to join him for dinner, but I declined. Still, he wouldn't take no for an answer. There was a kind of sulky persuasion in the way he insisted, as if my refusal only spurred him further.

Though known to be a competent doctor, Sourav spoke far too much, with the persistent chatter of a boy. He was headstrong, unrelenting. It was Dr. Ayush who had recommended him for the job here. In truth, Dr. Ayush wanted me to accept him—not just professionally, but as a life partner. I resented that kind of guardianship, especially in matters of marriage.

One day, out of sheer frustration, I confided in Sijal Didi. I even said something unkind about Dr. Ayush—words born out of irritation. Sijal Didi, with her calm wisdom, tried to make me see reason. She reminded me that Dr. Ayush was, at heart, a good man.

But I couldn't shake off the feeling that he was thinking too much, too often, about me—when I had reached a point where even the word *marriage* felt jarring, like an off-key note in a quiet room. No wonder I bristled every time I saw Sourav.

That day, Dr. Ayush kept calling me—again and again. He was full of praise for Sourav, brimming with new hopes about *us*. Eventually, worn down by his persistence, I agreed to have dinner with Sourav.

During dinner, Sourav bombarded me with all sorts of questions. He was eager to know why I wasn't interested in marriage. To my own surprise, I spoke openly—unfolding the pages of my past without hesitation. He listened.

When I spoke of Suren, his face clouded with sadness. His empathy for Suren's helplessness was genuine, and his curiosity about Rista was almost childlike. As I spoke her name, my eyes filled with tears. It was as though her name was embedded in every sigh of mine. Blood ties aren't always what form bonds—some relationships take root in pain, in care, and in memory. And they endure.

Hope is a fragile thing. When someone shows a little understanding, a glimmer of shared emotion, you start building castles in the sand. That night, Sourav's sympathy for Suren and Rista planted quiet hopes within me. I began to believe—perhaps he might help me find Suren's address. Maybe he would even bring Rista to me.

The dam of long-buried grief had cracked open. I kept talking, one story after another tumbling out. I even showed him a photo of Suren and Rista, and described Suren's house in detail.

In that moment, something shifted. Sourav became a friend. A real one.

After that evening, he never brought up the marriage proposal again.

But our friendship didn't go unnoticed. Dr. Ayush grew suspicious. He began questioning me—relentlessly. He had once been so hopeful, and now he had turned somber, his thoughts weighed down by my uncertain future. Eventually, he promised to stop interfering. And for a while, things were quiet.

But life doesn't wait for us to be ready. It doesn't wait for full moons or new moons to change tides. Things happen—swiftly, without warning—and in an instant, everything shifts. Dreams, plans, and possibilities burst like bubbles. Something unforeseen strikes, and you are left stunned—nothing more than a puppet in its grip. It happened like that.

Sijal Didi's sudden illness sent a wave of concern through us all. A woman so full of life, always on her feet, suddenly rendered still—it was jarring. It shook me to the core. The news of her heart attack struck the hospital like lightning—sharp, unexpected, and devastating.

How could it happen to her? She who lived by the rules of wellness—disciplined meals, daily yoga and pranayam, never missing a routine check-up. She was the embodiment of health, a guiding light for us all. And yet, even she wasn't spared.

In just a day and a night, her vibrant presence faded into silence. And then, she was gone.

For me, it was as though the universe itself had stalled. The sky disappeared. The ground slipped away. I had faced loss before—my parents, others dear to me—but nothing compared to this. No grief had ever hit with such brutal finality. Losing Sijal Didi felt like losing a piece of my soul.

The entire hospital stood frozen in time. The usual bustle—the echo of footsteps, the murmur of patients, the steady rhythm of care—all went mute. Even the wind seemed to pause, as if holding its breath. From the orphanage came the muffled sound of crying—raw, broken, and unbearably real. It was as if the very air had thickened with sorrow.

Aside from one distant nephew, no one from her family came. The cremation was carried out by the hospital staff—those who had become her true family in the absence of blood ties. With hands trembling and eyes full of tears, we bid her a final farewell.

She left this world wrapped not in rituals, but in love—quiet, unspoken, and deeply felt.

Sijal Didi's nephew came to collect her belongings after all the final rites were completed. But something left everyone in quiet astonishment—a single sheet of paper tucked inside her passbook. On it, she had scribbled two sentences, dated long ago: "All my belongings, including my clothes, should be donated to an Old Age Home. My entire savings go to the orphanage. No one has any claim over them."

In the cupboard, I found a neatly wrapped packet. Inside it lay a Benarasi silk saree—carefully folded, lovingly preserved. My name was written on the wrapper in Sijal Didi's familiar handwriting. I had already picked it up before anyone could hand it to me. Pressing it to my chest, I broke down. It felt as though the very soul of Sijal Didi was nestled within those folds.

I had once returned that saree to her—after everything fell Apart between Suren and me. That day, it was Didi who broke down. She had always appeared strong in front of me, shielding her pain, but I later came to know how much she had wept—hiding away, unable to face me without her eyes trembling. She was my pillar through every storm, but inside, she was crumbling. I hadn't noticed then how deeply my sorrow had become hers.

Now, I found myself aching for her constantly. The hospital, the orphanage—they still stood where they always had, but everything felt hollow. Lifeless. Like a cremation ground after the mourners had left.

For days, I couldn't focus on anything. Her voice

echoed in my mind—her consolations, her scoldings, her unwavering affection. Even her silences haunted me.

She used to say, *"No matter how far you fly, you can't escape life's storms. Difficulties will always be your companions. But if you choose, you can face and resolve them right here."*

And once, with a smile in her eyes, she added, *"If you step into the sea, you must expect the tides. How can you enjoy the sea bath if you're afraid of the waves? Life, too, is a dance between light and shade—a never-ending game of hide and seek. Joy and sorrow come hand in hand. Bow slightly, let the storm pass, and then rise. With patience and courage, the world is yours."*

Each word she spoke carried the weight of lived wisdom.

I had visited the old age home and the orphanage. The place was wrapped in a grief I could no longer bear. In every corner, in every face, I could feel her presence—quiet, warm, and constant. It was her true home. These people were her family, though she had never built one through marriage.

I remembered her once saying, *"Relationships don't grow just under roofs and within four walls. They need wide skies to breathe. The ground beneath our feet is heaven enough if our hearts are open. That is where we become truly related."* And she lived that truth. Every hospital staff member, every child, every abandoned soul—she had woven them into her own chosen family.

That night, I locked myself away in my room, distancing myself from the others. I stared out through the window. The moon hung incomplete in the sky, as if waiting to become whole. I had turned off my phone—there were no duties calling me. Only thoughts, swirling restlessly.

A knock at the door broke through the stillness. I opened it. Shobha, my colleague, stood there.

"Dr. Sourav is calling you," she said. "He's in the duty room."

I sighed inwardly, reluctant, but followed her anyway.

Dr. Sourav was alone when I arrived. I stood quietly. He looked at me, as though he could read the turmoil I was carrying. Softly, he said, *"This is the way of the world, Jhara. No one has power over Death. You, of all people, know this— you've worked in a hospital long enough. I know Sijal Didi's passing has left us all shaken."*

Tears slipped down without warning.

In that moment, I felt a truth rise within me. *I am not like everyone else. I'm just a fragile creeper, and she was the tree I clung to. Without her, I don't know how to stay upright.*

And even though I didn't want to say it aloud, the words of the last sentence fell out on their own.

"You're right," Sourav said gently, "but even after the tree falls, the soil remains. Can't a creeper still take root in that soil? Your duty—and the world around you—can be your support now. You have responsibilities. How will things carry on if you collapse like this?"

His words brought a flood of tears to my eyes.

Without saying much more, he stood up and softly wiped my tears with his handkerchief. Then, in a low, reassuring voice, he added, "If you truly loved and respected Sijal Didi, then have patience. Focus on your work. You know as well as I do—her soul will never find peace if she sees you in this condition."

I understood every word he said. But I was not myself anymore. Despite my best efforts, I couldn't stop the wave of grief rising within me. I carried her presence like a second skin—everywhere I turned, I saw her face, heard her voice.

Sourav gently caressed my head. His touch brought me back to myself, slowly. I stepped back, trying to regain composure.

"I didn't even want to take the night duty," he said with a faint smile. "But I had to cover for Dr. Prasant. You know me—I never object, it goes against my principles."

"I'll take over then," I said quietly, readying myself to leave.

"Take care," he murmured, and walked toward the ward.

Later, back in my room, I couldn't sleep no matter how hard I tried. After tossing and turning for a while, I got up, switched on the light, and began tidying the cupboard. But even that brought no relief. I pulled a book from the shelf and turned its pages. Reading calmed me slightly. Then I stepped out to the balcony.

The night had laid its dark veil over the silent mountains, yet their silhouettes stood steady against the sky. A few birds on the pine branches murmured in their secret tongue. *If only I had wings,* I thought, *I would have flown to them.*

Once, standing right here, Sijal Didi had said, *"Do you know, Jhara? I don't know why, but I love the mountains and the pine trees. They are as much mine as this hospital and the orphanage."*

A cold breeze passed, brushing my face with its icy fingers. I remembered reading somewhere that a soul lingers in the places and things it once loved. *Then perhaps… she is still here.*

And if she were really here, would she have allowed me to stand out like this at night? No, she would have scolded me gently, made me return inside.

I turned to go. Just then, a colleague approached from

the Duty Room. She saw me and smiled teasingly. "Waiting for someone?"

I didn't appreciate the joke, but I replied calmly, "Sleep wouldn't come."

Perhaps sensing something in my tone, she softened. Taking my hand, she said, "I know you're grieving for Sijal Didi. But what can you do? Life has to go on. Why don't you take a few days off and go home? A change of place might help."

I just nodded, saying nothing. She didn't really know me. If she had, she wouldn't have said that.

That word—home—kept echoing inside me, throbbing like a wound.

And my mind wandered, all the way back... fifteen years ago.

To a time when *home* meant a courtyard lit with morning smiles. When Ma, Bapa, Grandma, and all of us siblings filled the house with laughter. When joy was as common as the sun rising. Our noons were filled with laughter and games, and our evenings echoed with the chorus of our prayers. After that, we would gather around to study together, as the night slowly tiptoed in, drowsy and gentle. Oh, time... Oh, life...

Back then, there was everything—home, happiness, and the warmth of sibling bonds.

And today? There is no home. No happiness. No trace of that once unshakable bond of love among us. Time's storm has shattered that nest. The little birds have flown, scattered to different skies. And how could they return, having lost their direction? Even if fate made them cross paths again, could there ever be the tenderness of those dear old days?

I dragged my unwilling feet back into the room.

Barsha was fast asleep. Under the soft glow of the night lamp, I stared at her peaceful face. So much sorrow lay folded behind her closed eyelids, and still, she slept deeply. Why couldn't I?

I lay down, pulling the sheet over myself. Everything was still—except for the ticking of the wall clock. It seemed to whisper to me in the hush of the night: *"Stay a while. Don't sleep just yet. Let's talk. Let's share what's buried deep inside."*

In the rush of daytime, we never notice the clock. But in these quiet, solitary moments, its ticking feels like a heartbeat—echoing mine.

I don't remember when sleep finally came.

Morning arrived with Barsha's soft call. I had to be at the orphanage.

I got ready in a hurry. Barsha handed me a glass of milk. I took it silently, knowing I had no choice but to drink it.

On the way to the orphanage, my thoughts lingered on Barsha.

Truly, what a remarkable girl. At first, I hadn't thought highly of her. My impression was vague, tinged with doubt. But once I came to understand the emotional turmoil she had endured—and the heavy silence of her circumstances—my heart softened. A deep affection grew within me.

Sometimes, we fail to see people for who they truly are. And in that blindness, we often misjudge, get hurt, or hurt others. That's what happened in my case. Not just me—others had judged her too. But despite everything, it was her quiet tenderness that drew me in. In the absence of Sijal Didi, she had been especially caring toward me.

Her respect for Didi was profound. It was out of

that reverence that she brought her own son to stay at the orphanage.

As I entered the orphanage gates, Sijal Didi's memory clung to every corner like mist.

How devoted she had been—how lovingly she'd built this place from scratch, nurturing it with dreams and untiring passion. Her one goal had been clear: to raise these children into kind, capable human beings.

Now, in her absence, everything felt hollow—even the hospital, once alive with her presence.

It was strange, but I felt as though I saw her in the eyes of the children. Their laughter, their touch—it was like being touched by her all over again.

Still, I could not settle the storm within. Yes, the earth drinks in rainwater patiently. But even it has a limit. And when that's crossed, the excess flows away in restless streams—gliding, spilling, flooding.

That was me. This body and this mind had taken in so much sorrow, so much grief, that I could no longer name it. It had all blurred into a shapeless ache. I was restless, as if I had nowhere to stand. And yet, duty remains. Like the Earth, carrying the weight of countless burdens, yet never ceasing to spin. Perhaps it is from her that humans have learned endurance.

So I moved through the day mechanically, performing tasks with a hollow diligence.

When I returned to the hostel, I saw Sourav waiting for me at the Reception.

"Would you mind stepping out for some snacks?" he asked gently.

I shook my head, meaning no. I really didn't feel up to it.

He added, "I haven't eaten since morning. Come—at least for me?"

Eating had slipped my mind completely. Everything had, for days now. Still, absentmindedly, I agreed. Perhaps I said yes just because he asked.

We walked to a quiet restaurant nearby. Sourav looked at the menu and asked me what I'd like.

"Your choice is mine," I said softly.

We started talking about the orphanage. But the very things I was trying to forget kept resurfacing. I couldn't help it—Sijal Didi's name came up. Sourav noticed the shift in my tone, and with a careful tact, he gently steered the conversation elsewhere.

He was observant. He could tell when I was fully present—like when I spoke passionately about the strengths and shortcomings of our hospital—and when I was completely lost within myself.

The evening passed that way, in gentle fragments.

And when we returned, something in me had shifted.

My feelings toward Sourav had changed—just a little. To be honest, I had begun to see him… as a good friend.

26

Some relationships follow their own rhythm—the plus-minus principle. In such bonds, the question of willingness or unwillingness doesn't matter. They simply exist, shifting between gain and loss, closeness and distance.

After a long time, Vikas Bhai and Gouri Bhauja had planned a family get-together. Biny Apa and Sony Apa were coming too. I also decided to take a few days' leave and join them. When my colleagues heard about it, they were genuinely happy for me. Everyone wanted me to take a break—believing it might offer some peace to my unsettled heart.

Barsha helped me with everything. She booked my tickets online and was unusually attentive to every detail. Her care felt deeper than before—almost protective.

But that very tenderness stirred a strange unease within me. Too much attachment had always frightened me. I felt as though I was preparing to lose something precious... again. The thought angered me. I scolded myself for being so fatalistic—so weak. Was I cursed by the stars under which I was born? What strange constellations governed my life, that every person I held close seemed to vanish midway?

Why did those who came into my life... never stay?

In response to Barsha's growing concern, I withdrew into indifference. But she didn't let it bother her. She came to see me off at the station, though I carried only a small bag. She insisted on holding it herself and handed me some food packets before leaving quietly.

As the train pulled out and her face blurred into the distance, my eyes brimmed with tears.

Why was she drawing me so close? Who was I to her, really?

We may walk together for a while, but eventually, life leads us in different directions. That's how it goes—the cruel, unbending logic of fate.

I reached Hyderabad on time. Everything looked unfamiliar, as though I had forgotten the city's geography. Time had redrawn the map in my mind.

Vikas Bhai picked me up from the station in a car. On the way, he chuckled and said, "You look like someone visiting Hyderabad for the first time. What's with that dazed look?"

I gave a dry smile. "No, no. Everything looks just as it did. It's only the pages of time that have turned."

He laughed, a sound that didn't really belong to the moment.

By the time we reached home, the gathering was already in full swing—Biny Apa, Sony Apa, both brothers-in-law, Biny Apa's son, and Gouri Bhauj's daughter. The children were running around, giggling. The house felt full, alive.

For a moment, I felt a strange thrill—an ache wrapped in warmth.

As I hugged the children tightly, I whispered, "It's you two who brought me here. Otherwise, I wouldn't have come." They wriggled, trying to escape my grip. I had unknowingly smeared years of buried emotions on their soft cheeks.

Biny Apa teased, "Will you just keep hugging the

kids or spare a glance for us too? What diet are you on, Jhara? Or is it rigorous yoga?"

The elder brother-in-law added, "The Sikkim climate has turned her into a model!"

Gouri Bhauj nodded, "Truly! Her complexion is glowing."

"She's maintained herself well," said Sony Apa.

To that, Biny Apa laughed, "Why wouldn't she? She only has her job. The rest of us are drowning in family chaos."

I smiled through their banter, holding back the tide inside me. Not one word about what I had endured. Not a single gesture of empathy.

They saw my face, not the pain behind it.

At one point, I brought up Sijal Didi. As I spoke about her with quiet reverence, Sony Apa cut in with a laugh that didn't belong.

"Oh Jhara, the childishness in you still lingers. You say she had no one in the world—fine. But who would've taken care of her in old age? It's good she passed peacefully. There's no need to mourn her."

Her words pierced me. Was she mocking my grief? Or warning me not to expect anything from them?

Is that what they all think—that I am a burden waiting to descend on their lives?

Do they already see me… as too much?

The topic branched out like a giant tree- sprawling, messy, with too many leaves. Biny Apa said, "Really, Jhara, if you keep waiting and choosing like this, time will slip through your fingers. You'll end up a spinster. Listen to me—agree to marry now." Picking up the cue, Gouri Bhauja added, "I had brought a perfectly good proposal. But Jhara didn't accept it."

Suddenly, Biny Apa's eyes lit up, like she was about to hear the unfinished twist of a suspenseful film. "Oh yes—what about Suren? Is he living happily with his wife now?"

Before she could finish, Sony Apa interrupted, "Hey, Jhara, you're such a fool. How could you even think of marrying someone who already had a daughter?"

Gouri Bhauja, not wanting to be left out, steered the conversation in another direction. "As far as I know, Suren is a good man. But forget it—let the chapter close. Whatever happens is God's will."

I just sat there, barely listening to their opinions, letting their words skim over the surface of my thoughts. I had nothing to say. I didn't know what effect my silence had on them—if any.

Trying to lighten the mood, Vikas Bhai joked, "Let bygones be bygones. Now that we're all gathered, we should find a match for Jhara!"

I chuckled. "Oh, Vikas Bhai, do matches fly around like butterflies for you all to catch?"

At that, both my brothers-in-law burst into laughter. The atmosphere, which was turning serious, suddenly became light again.

Later, everyone made plans for an outing. I chose not to go. I stayed back. What a relief! I sighed, grateful for a moment of quiet. I felt like I belonged to a different world—one untouched by this noise, these constant opinions.

They left in a hurry, the house falling into disarray in their absence. I began tidying up. As my hands moved, my mind wandered to the past—Hyderabad. That city still held fragments of my memories, dreams that had withered before they could bloom.

Yet, Hyderabad taught me much. I encountered many

kinds of people—both within my family and outside it. My once-fragile mind had grown stronger, even if it remained enclosed in the shell of its past.

The man I had come there for, who once dreamed of making me a doctor, was now far away. I couldn't become what he wanted, but his dream still lingers in the corners of my memory.

Akash Bhai's face flashed before me. Despite his tiredness, he always supported my studies. He loved us—but also kept us in check. I owe him everything.

Even now, when he calls, it's the same: "Jhara, take care, be strong, be happy." That's all. As if he has no other words left for me. What more could he say?

I remember his face—drawn and quiet. He used to send photos by mail. In each of them, Bhauj's smile gleamed with self-satisfaction, while Akash Bhai's expression seemed faded, like that of a man reduced to a money-making machine. I often wondered: what worth did he have in her eyes, beyond his salary? The day he could no longer provide, she would sever even that bond. Poor fellow!

Ah, Akash Bhai…

My hands kept moving. I cooked dinner and had everything ready when they returned. They were happy to find the house clean and food warm.

Gouri Bhauja laid out the saree she'd bought for me and said, "It looks good on you." Biny Apa and Sony Apa handed me little gifts—as if fulfilling some quiet obligation.

On one side, there was the stench of pride and the undercurrent of broken ties. On the other, a drifting mist of affection and the faint glow of my growing understanding.

I smiled, but it didn't reach my eyes. I didn't really want the gifts, except out of politeness.

"You didn't like them, did you?" Gouri Bhauja asked, noticing my lack of enthusiasm.

The next two days felt dry and colourless. I felt distanced from all of them—like I no longer belonged here. A quiet gap had grown between us.

My return ticket to Sikkim was already booked. I was yearning to go back. To my hospital, my ward, the orphanage—my world. I imagined them waiting for me, welcoming me back with open arms. And I, ready to melt into that world again.

And so I returned.

As I left, I felt no one held any true feelings for me. And I had no longing left for any of them either.

I accepted that I would not live my life pining for people who never truly saw me.

27

I cherished my duty hours the most. Amidst the patients, I could hear the silent voice of life and see the quiet yearning for it in every pair of eyes. Of course, there were moments when the fragile sandcastle of hope crumbled. Life is an endless battle—sometimes we win, sometimes we lose. Yet, one must carry on, regardless of the outcome. From morning till evening, time would slip past unnoticed, as though carried away on invisible wings. Sometimes I wonder—how would people even pass their days if they didn't keep themselves occupied?

Truly, how mysterious is God's creation! Every living being is engaged in some form of work—even the tiniest ant is no exception. If it weren't for Akash Bhai's constant encouragement, where would I be today? Most likely, a burden on my siblings.

I found myself longing for Akash Bhai—he was like God to me. The apple of my parents' eyes. Poor soul! What did he receive in life except the bitterness of sacrifice, like Neelakantha, swallowing poison for the sake of others?

Sourav's voice snapped me out of my thoughts. "It's been two days since you returned, and only now do I see you," he said, pulling up a chair. "Had a good time catching up with your siblings?"

"Those days are gone," I replied quietly. "Now,

everything feels like a matter of formality—measured, polite, distant."

He blinked, clearly surprised by my tone. Trying to soften it, I added with a faint smile, "Lately, I've felt like an outsider among them. My presence doesn't seem to matter much anymore."

Sourav burst into laughter. Once it died down, he said, "That's the thing with unmarried girls—they get too sentimental without reason. They begin to feel like the family has stopped loving them. But trust me, it's just a phase. A psychological illusion. Get married, Jhara. Start your own family. You'll find new meaning in life, and all this gloom will vanish."

I didn't like what he said. His words sat heavily on my chest. To steer the conversation elsewhere, I asked about the new Superintendent.

"He seems like a man of integrity," Sourav replied. "It was much needed. If someone disorganised had taken over after Sijal Didi's passing, things would've fallen apart. But I hear he's methodical, focused—just the kind of leadership we need now."

"It's alright. Everything will be fine if we just do our duty sincerely." Sourav got up and left. I sat there for a while, thinking of him. Had I really been unfair in my anger toward my brothers and sisters?

Sourav hadn't faced such complexities in life—how could he possibly understand mine?

Barsha came to me with a glass of milk and gently urged, "Please drink this, Didi." Her face looked pale, drained. Something about her expression unsettled me. Was she unwell?

"I'm fine, Didi," she said, her eyes brimming with tears. "But he… he's very sick."

Could a heart once filled with resentment soften like this?

Trying to make light of the moment, I teased. "Why are you worried about him? He severed ties with you long ago."

Barsha suddenly burst into tears. "Didi," she sobbed, "some bonds go beyond rules and grievances. You can't just set them aside, no matter how much you try."

I had never heard her speak this way before.

"Are you crying for the man who never showed compassion to his wife?" I asked, almost harshly.

Two days later, we received news of her husband's death. Barsha collapsed. She stayed on leave for a while. Though we all tried to comfort her, it took her a long time to return to herself. Our sympathy for her son deepened, and so did our understanding of her grief.

Grief brings people closer in ways that joy rarely does. After Sijal Didi, it was Barsha who cared for me the most. She slowly won me over with her quiet strength. I came to love her, not as a colleague, but as my own younger sister.

Time moved on, carrying both sweetness and sorrow in its fold. During this time, Sourav and I grew closer. We would occasionally spend time outside together. I often brought little things for Barsha and her son—clothes, books, toys. Our bond, the three of us, became quietly strong.

It was strange, though, to see Barsha mourn so deeply for a man she once seemed to despise.

One day, Sourav said to her bluntly, "What did he ever give you besides a child? He didn't love you—not even a little."

I had said similar things myself. But Barsha's quiet reply silenced us both.

"Look at me, Didi," she said softly. "Look at my empty hands. My bare forehead. The way I walk now."

She didn't need to say more. I gently changed the subject, but her words stayed with me, echoing long after.

The next day, Sourav surprised me with a question I hadn't expected.

"What if I married Barsha?"

I was stunned. Was he serious? Would his family ever accept this? I turned to look at him, searching his face. But there was no hesitation, no doubt—only a calm, unwavering resolve. His eyes carried a quiet light I hadn't seen before.

For a moment, I felt small before his conviction. The task of speaking to Barsha, of helping her understand, now rested on me.

I could sense the conflict weighing on Barsha's mind. So much sympathy, so much sacrifice—for a man who had given her nothing but pain. I had no personal experience with the intricacies of a husband-wife relationship, so I chose not to dwell too deeply on their past. I decided to leave it to time. And with time, Sourav and Barsha grew closer. He seemed to think of her constantly—his concern for her never wavered.

One day, Barsha confided in me, her voice heavy with emotion. "Didi, I understand everything… but what about my son? What answer will I give him when he grows up? Will he ever respect me?"

Her worries were real, valid. And yet, I couldn't dismiss Sourav's perspective either. He would often say, "There's a long road ahead for Barsha and her son. They deserve a future. What did they ever receive from that man? Did he even know what being a father meant—what fatherly love looked like?"

His words stayed with me. His reasoning was sharp,

but it was his sincerity that moved me most. There was something magnetic in his spirit—something that could easily draw in any beautiful woman. But here he was, devoted to a woman with a child, a woman still carrying the weight of her past. His love, his unwavering commitment, stirred something deep inside me. Were there still men like him in today's world?

The mind is a strange thing—untamed and unpredictable. It always reaches out for what feels just beyond its grasp. I remembered the day Dr. Ayush had casually proposed my marriage to Sourav. Sourav had been open to it. But I had declined. And yet now... why was I feeling this weakness, this vulnerability? Shame on me. What would Barsha and Sourav think if they could see through me? Would Barsha still hold me in regard?

Over time, Sourav's care for Barsha and her son only deepened. Some praised his compassion. Others whispered and judged. But a new life was opening up for Barsha—a life she had never known. She had never tasted the sweetness of a husband's love. Slowly, Sourav's presence began to soothe her long-held wounds. The scars would remain, yes—but the pain was softening.

Still, one shadow lingered in her heart: the fear of what people would say, and the unknown thoughts of her growing son.

That day, we lay quietly on the bed, watching clouds drift lazily over the mountain peaks. A gentle breeze swept through the open window, caressing our faces like a tender memory.

Barsha suddenly sighed, her voice soft and full of wonder. "Didi… how beautiful nature is."

I smiled. "It is," I said. "Because it's God's creation."

Pausing for a moment, she said thoughtfully, "Yes,

indeed. But it is man who has created society and its traditions. Man has built the very social norms and rules that now bind him. Escaping this web is no easy task."

I understood exactly what she meant. Like someone drenched in the rain offering his umbrella to shield another, I said gently, "You shouldn't sacrifice your promising future out of fear of society. Your son won't remain in the orphanage forever. He'll grow up, he'll study, and one day he'll become a man—a man for whom you must live and strive. Have you ever thought of that?"

Something in those words seemed to reach her. Her face lit up with a quiet happiness. Wanting to bolster her courage, I added, "There are many girls for Dr. Sourav, but he chose you. And I think you know why. A man with his mindset is rare. He made this decision with your son's future in his heart."

Sometimes, a wild river changes its course without warning. So too had Barsha's path. She and Sourav were married in a temple, the deity bearing silent witness. All of us, her colleagues, gifted her our warmest blessings. But Sourav's family disapproved of the marriage—though he paid their disapproval no heed.

The carefree blossoms of a new life swayed in a gentle breeze, full of promise. I watched little boats drifting toward the shore. But the ship of my own life? I laughed quietly to myself. My boat, without a boatman, was still afloat— tossing, tumbling, yet somehow moving forward, leaping over waves. Every time it neared the shore, the current pulled it away again.

Then, quite unexpectedly, I received a call letter from a nursing home in Odisha—a place I had applied to two years ago. I had long given up hope of hearing from them. After all, I had rarely received the things I truly wished for.

Whatever I held dear was like a dream—beautiful, fleeting. And like a dream at dawn, it vanished.

The world had turned its face from me. Whatever I was in the past, I remained still: a creeper slithering along the ground, unseen.

The appointment letter startled everyone—Barsha, Sourav, and even myself. Each had their own opinion. But the decision was mine alone.

I returned to Odisha. The familiar embrace of Odia language and life brought me a deep sense of relief.

Sikkim faded into the distance like a few turned pages of a cherished book—its characters once so close to my heart. But even the flames of time could not burn away what remained within me. Sijal Didi's inspiration stood behind me, like an invisible hand on my shoulder, even though she was gone. Her love and blessings followed me like a shadow.

She was my guiding light. Perhaps that's why I didn't let myself grow too emotional when leaving Sikkim. I only felt a quiet ache when I looked for the last time at the house where Suren and Rista once were. My heart was heavy, but my eyes did not tear up.

Life, in its own way, had taught me how to harden a soft heart.

28

I joined a nursing home in Bhubaneswar. Lodging and boarding were available on campus, so I didn't have to stay elsewhere. Though the nursing home was old, it had been recently renovated and looked welcoming. It wasn't very expensive either. Among all the options I had explored, this one appealed to me the most. Something about it felt comforting, as if I had returned home after a long, uncertain journey.

Since the day I left for Hyderabad, I hadn't stepped foot back in Odisha. But being here now, I felt a renewed sense of purpose, an enthusiasm for my work that had been lying dormant. Although none of my family was around, I found myself searching for traces of them—in faces, in voices, in passing conversations. Somewhere deep down, I hoped that one day, by chance, I might run into one of my maternal or paternal relatives, though none were in contact anymore.

The sudden upheavals in our family had severed those ties. The loss of our parents and the abrupt shift in our lives left little room for staying connected. My siblings, unlike me, chose to detach completely. They didn't feel the need to hold on to the past.

Sometimes, I have a wild urge to visit my maternal uncle's village, just to appear unannounced and see the surprise on everyone's faces. I'm sure no one would even recognise me now. I often think of the village pond, more than half covered in red and white lilies, and the towering blackberry tree standing a short distance away. Farther still, the mango grove lay waiting—silent, lush, and guarded in turns by the villagers during summer.

Grandmother, (Aai) would take us there during the summer holidays, carrying along a Ludo board. While she sat watching us play, we'd also keep an eye on the grove. Guarding the mangoes and playing Ludo became a ritual. The first storm of the season was always a delight—it meant a rush to gather fallen mangoes, laughter trailing behind us as we ran barefoot over the damp earth.

Those vacations were magical. The villagers held deep respect for my grandfather's family and greeted us with warm smiles and homegrown vegetables offered out of affection. Their love was genuine, so pure and expectation-free that I'm left in awe even today.

And when I think of them, I think of Shari—Madan uncle's daughter. Though not related by blood, I spent most of my time in their house. Shari and I were inseparable. With her, I learned to swim in the pond, to relish raw green gram legumes, to wander aimlessly and taste wild thorn berries and sweet cane fruits.

During Raja festival, we swung on makeshift swings hung from tree branches, played puchi and bahuchori—"stealing the bridegroom"—with the other girls. Laughter echoed in every corner of that village. When the holidays ended, our hearts grew heavy as we packed to leave. We'd start counting days until the next summer.

Even now, a quiet sadness lingers in me, a sense of loss I can't quite name. Ah, those dear, distant days. I wonder where Shari is now—perhaps married, with children of her own, weaving her own stories of joy and struggle.

Strangely, though, the people I see around me here sometimes feel familiar. Their eyes, their gestures—they remind me of someone I once knew. Amid the rush of work and the unceasing march of time, I still hope—hope to catch a glimpse of a known face in the crowd.

Here, life doesn't pause. Nor does time stumble. It simply flows—quietly, relentlessly.

One day, I was assigned to the Paediatrics Ward. As I moved from bed to bed, I couldn't help but notice the small children—frail bodies, innocent faces, eyes too tired for their age. Their suffering cast a long shadow on their parents' faces. It was as if these children were not just flesh and blood, but their very breath, their souls.

I saw fathers, desperate and worn, trying to save their children by selling off whatever little land they owned. Mothers sat by the bedsides, shedding silent tears, whispering prayers through trembling lips, their hands resting on their children's fevered foreheads. And then there were those who could barely afford a prescription— running tirelessly from one counter to another in search of medicines, holding hope in one hand and a piece of paper in the other.

Scenes like these weren't new to me. I had witnessed them over and over again. Still, each time unsettled me. It pierced through something soft within, and yet I was powerless. All I could offer was my care, my time, and my sincerity. I didn't have the means to support them financially, and besides, such stories unfolded before me almost every day—they had become a painful part of my routine.

What disturbed me more was the indifference of some of the professionals around me. I had seen doctors—stoic, even callous—who showed no compassion for the poor, yet would bend over backward for influential patients. It wasn't just the doctors. From the bearers to some nurses, many shared that same attitude. They acted like bullies in uniforms—pouncing on the helpless like a one-eyed cat tormenting a tiny cockroach—rude, impatient, and dismissive.

They didn't listen to those who couldn't tip them. Their loyalty lay with privilege, not with pain.

The boy in bed number 17 had been admitted fifteen days ago, but despite repeated blood tests, his illness remained undiagnosed. He was nothing more than skin and bones—his tiny frame a mere shadow of what a child's should be. Since the day of his admission, he had kept his eyes shut, unmoving. His mother sat silently beside him, gently stroking his head, her lips murmuring prayers no one else could hear.

His father had approached the doctor with a question, but the doctor, irritated, walked away, muttering something harsh under his breath. Even the sweeper, while cleaning the veranda, threw an unkind remark in their direction, unsolicited and cruel. The indifference, the rudeness—all in the face of such helplessness—shook me deeply.

I went over to the boy's bed and spoke with his parents. It was as though two people adrift in a flood had suddenly found a piece of floating wood. They held onto my words like a lifeline. The father showed me the pile of prescriptions and test reports, his hands trembling. I felt a tightness in my chest.

Within my limited means, I did what I could. I arranged blood for the child and managed to collect some medicines from doctors I knew. Slowly, the boy began to show signs of recovery. Watching him improve brought a quiet joy to my heart.

When the day came for them to leave—though the boy had not yet fully recovered—the mother embraced me, tears of gratitude spilling onto my shoulder. Her husband, head bowed, folded his hands and said, "God must have sent you to us… Otherwise, we would have lost our son."

But I felt it was their unwavering faith and quiet endurance that had brought their son back from the brink. I had done so little.

Before leaving, they gave me their address. Their home, they said, was just seven kilometers from my uncle's village. It was as if someone had lit a lamp in the dark, shut room of my heart. On a sudden impulse, I decided to take a short leave and visit my uncle for two days. The couple was overjoyed when I told them. The woman gently took my hand and said, "If you would bless our poor home with your presence, it would make us very happy."

They left. I stood watching them until they disappeared at the end of the corridor.

A month passed. I had begun making preparations to visit Madinapur on my own, not expecting anything. But to my surprise, the couple showed up, just as they had promised, to take me with them.

Their sincerity moved me. In a world where promises are so easily broken, these two kept theirs—with quiet dignity and simple hearts.

I couldn't turn them away—their warmth, their sincerity, their joy at having me. I stayed at their house for a short while, touched by the simplicity of their affection and the quiet dignity with which they hosted me. After some time, we began our journey to my uncle's village.

No one had expected me to arrive like that, unannounced. Their astonishment was genuine. It felt as though I had struck a forgotten chord in their memory—

like the tune of a song once loved and now suddenly remembered. The old house stood there, just as I had left it, with its familiar courtyard. But inside, three separate ovens burned in three separate kitchens. My grandmother was no more. The children of my uncles were either away studying or working in distant cities. The house, once brimming with voices, now wore a desolate silence.

Only the youngest daughter of my younger uncle was at home, still studying at the local school. My arrival brought sudden excitement. My uncles, seeing me after so long, were deeply moved. "You remind us of your mother," they said, eyes damp with memory. They began recalling stories of my childhood, and I too slipped into the quiet lanes of the past.

I asked about my childhood friends. Some of them came the next day. I hadn't thought much about growing older, but seeing them—with their babies in their laps—I felt as if time had leapt forward in a single breath. Many of them had already returned from their in-laws' homes after their first childbirth. I was still standing at the threshold of my own life's chapters, yet watching them, I felt I had already crossed a few unseen steps.

One of the visitors was Tulasi. I learned that she had returned to her parents' home just a few months after her marriage due to dowry issues. She had come with her brother as soon as they heard I was in the village. In Tulasi's eyes, I saw a reflection of all that we had left behind. Her family had always lived modestly, yet their warmth had never faltered. I still remembered the *Raja podapitha* her mother used to make—no taste since has matched it. And the *Raja paan*, specially rolled for the festival—how could I ever forget that?

Tulasi's father had passed away before her marriage.

At that time, her elder brother Chinmay was still in college, too young to grasp the deceit behind the marriage proposal. Tulasi had been married off to a greedy man, and soon the facade had crumbled. But Chinmay had grown into a responsible man. He now supported the family with his job in a spice manufacturing company. Tulasi's younger sister, thankfully, was doing well after marriage.

Tulasi told me everything in a single breath, the way only an old friend can. She said, "Mother will come in the evening to meet you." I didn't want her to take the trouble at her age. Instead, I insisted on going with them. There were other houses I wished to visit too.

And then, Tulasi shared the news that shook me to the core—Shari was no more.

I was stunned. Shari—the spirited, fearless girl who once swam across the lily-laden pond, who laughed like a murmuring brook, who was everyone's favourite—had taken her own life.

Tulasi explained, her voice trembling, "She had no way out. Amarendra Rout's son promised to marry her, then abandoned her. How long could she carry the burden of that shame alone? At last, she drowned herself in Kain Pokhari."

"Ah, Shari…" I sighed, the name echoing inside me like a haunting refrain.

Back then, I didn't know how to swim, but bathing in that pond was an unforgettable experience. Part of it was covered in lilies—red, white, blue, violet—spreading like garlands across the water. There were three bathing ghats: one for men, one for women, and one for washing clothes. From the washing ghat, the lilies seemed to stretch out in colourful lines, as if someone had arranged them there by hand. It was a deep pond, so long that you couldn't see who was at the other end.

Shari could swim across it with ease. Every day, she would pluck lilies for me. She was bold and generous, ever ready to help anyone in need, regardless of who they were. From fasts to festivals, her presence was indispensable.

I remembered her last words to me: "Jhara, I know you won't marry anytime soon—you're still studying. But my marriage is in February. Who knows if we'll meet again?"

That girl, who once dreamed of building her own world, had left this world too soon. Tulasi and I sat in silence for a while, each lost in grief.

As we walked, Tulasi continued updating me about the village. It wasn't just information—it was like receiving a stack of newspapers filled with stories sweet and bitter, though the bitterness seemed to outweigh the sweetness now. The village had changed. It was divided, full of politics, jealousy, and mistrust. The peace we once knew had vanished. Selfishness had gnawed into the heart of the community. Any friendliness left was only surface-deep—a show, a performance.

At last, we reached her house. Aunty came out and embraced me tightly. If Tulasi hadn't told her I was coming, she wouldn't have recognised me. As I sat beside her, I felt a wave of longing. I looked for my mother in her—her touch, her affection—and found it. Though not related by blood, she felt like my own. I didn't want to part from her.

In that small house, I was wrapped in the love of Tulasi, Aunty, and Chinmay Bhai. And in their affection, I found something I hadn't felt in a long time—home.

I returned from there carrying a mixed load of love, grief, and aching nostalgia. During my two-day stay at Uncle's house, I found myself yearning deeply for my grandmother. Her absence hung heavy in the air. The dishes lacked her familiar warmth; the taste of her ghee-fried *mug dal* lingered on my tongue like a haunting memory. I mentioned her whenever the conversation allowed. But no matter where our talk began, it always circled back to one subject—my marriage.

The uncles and aunts, as if driven by a sudden urgency, kept bringing it up. I felt like I had already crossed the so-called "right age" for marriage. But neither was I interested in it, nor willing to bend under pressure. Life had taught me enough—enough to understand the nature of men, enough to protect myself from illusions. That knowledge had matured within me like slow fire.

It seemed the long-neglected sense of duty toward me had suddenly gripped everyone's minds. They were determined to get me married. The eldest uncle had even taken concrete steps toward it. And then there was Tulasi and her mother, seeing me after years, nurturing new hopes. That spark of a dream had already travelled, like whispered wind, to my uncle and aunt.

I smiled inwardly. How long would these proposals come, one after another?

The next day, Tulasi took me aside, to a quiet, secluded spot, and spoke with an openness that softened me.

"Jhara dear," she said, her voice trembling, "after so long, it felt like a fragrant, cool breeze had entered our home, stirring something forgotten. We were swept into a sudden joy. I saw a flicker of light in my brother's eyes."

I understood. I had already sensed it—in the way Aunty's eyes lingered on me, and how Chinmay Bhai avoided my gaze, as though wrestling with a feeling he couldn't name. His voice, too, had changed. There was a new softness in it, a quiet grace that hadn't been there before.

And then, like a gentle tide washing over a forgotten shore, my memories returned.

In childhood, he would always hand me the juiciest mangoes from the grove, the ones he saved just for me. During games of Bahuchori, he'd help me win, and in Ludo, he was always on my side. I remember the day he tied a swing to the old tamarind tree—simply because I had said I liked it.

As the vacation days dwindled, his presence around me grew more constant, as if he wanted to make the most of every moment before I left. Tulasi and Aunty loved me dearly too. Even now, I cannot forget their warmth. They would walk all the way to the ferry ghat to see me off. Chinmay Bhai would stand silently at the riverbank, watching our boat until it disappeared across the water, as if already counting the days to the next holiday.

"Hey, Jhara, where are you lost, with your face hanging like that?" Tulasi nudged me out of my thoughts.

"I was just remembering," I said softly, "how happy you all were when I came to your village as a child."

Before I could finish, Tulasi interrupted, her voice low and sincere, "We missed you for a long time after you left. Bhai would untie the swing right after you were gone. For days, he'd barely speak. Trust me, Jhara, even though he was young, he loved you very much."

All of a sudden, our visits to Uncle's village came to an end. We left for Hyderabad, and Grandma's stories were left far behind, like echoes swallowed by time. What a beautiful time it was—how warm those friendships, how vivid those days. But time, with its quiet cunning, scatters people like seeds—sending them drifting from one land to another.

Tulasi said hesitantly, "If you had no objection—I

mean, if you agreed—our house would be all aglow, Jhara dear." Her face held the innocence of a child. But I was no longer that naive Jhara. The journey from Hyderabad to Sikkim had hardened me, like stone shaped by storm.

As a child, I would come back from my uncle's village with a restlessness in my heart, a longing to return. But now, I don't feel that tug anymore. No tears well up when I say goodbye—not even to those I once held close. How could I explain that to Tulasi? I have moved beyond their reach.

The years spent in big cities, among people with wide eyes and narrow hearts, have changed me. I was only a kite in Chinmay Bhai's hands once—he held the spool of human connection. But I've flown so far, so long, that the thread feels like it might snap. And when it does, I'll fall—somewhere out of reach, like a story abandoned midway.

Everything felt different now. In the old days, I'd cross the river by boat to reach Uncle's house. But now, there's a bridge. The bus stopped right at Tinikonia square, just a short walk away. Everyone had come to see me off. Even Chinmay Bhai.

He stood beside me, maybe wanting to speak—about the village, its changing face, the challenges, his job at the spice factory. He mentioned a big hospital that had recently come up across the river—suggested I could even work there if I wished. "There are auto-rickshaws," he said, smiling, "you can reach in fifteen, twenty minutes." I laughed and teased, "Do you really think, Bhai, that Jhara would work here?"

We all burst into laughter. Just like that, his quiet proposal dissolved into the air.

Ah, poor Chinmay Bhai! How could he ever understand what was going on inside me?

I had already returned to my real world. Uncle's village no longer cast its old spell over me. The only memory that clung to me now was of someone no longer there—Grandma. Without her, the village felt hollow. Uncle and Aunty's words seemed like a cracked wall patched too many times—nothing could hold anymore. Their talk didn't linger in my heart. It was like a smile from a wall where the colour had long faded—their affection, a performance rehearsed too often.

And Tulasi? I held a bundle of sympathy for her—a silent weight in my heart. Her mother's love, Tulasi's hopeful eyes, the fragile dream she carried of building a world with me—they stood before me like a bare tree stripped of all leaves, shivering in its agony. But I'm at a distance now, unreachable.

And Chinmay Bhai? He is like a boat tied to the other bank—still, resigned—sighing at the new concrete bridge that rendered it obsolete. Did I underestimate him? Did I value him less than Dr. Ayush, or Vinit, or Mr. Suren, or Sourav?

Sometimes I wonder if I'm the one lacking. Perhaps I am a pitcher full of cracks porous, unable to hold anyone's love. I cannot offer even a handful of warmth to another. The whips of time have drained me of sweetness. And now, I live with this faded heart, carrying only the hollowness of a broken vessel.

Still, one has to carry on. I tried to immerse myself in work, hoping it would shake off the cloud of confused thoughts. Barsha would occasionally call me. Her voice brimmed with warmth and gratitude when she spoke of Sourav. She said he had played the role of a true hero—

restoring her pride, giving her a life of dignity, and offering a father's love to her son, who had never known what a father meant. Such a turn in her life felt nothing short of remarkable. The news lifted my spirits. My respect for Sourav deepened. God, in His wisdom, has made man a mix of light and shadow. Society is filled with the selfish, the crude, and the cruel—but thankfully, there are good people too. Otherwise, life would be unbearable. Returning to work in my hometown brought me a deep sense of joy.

29

I returned to my native Odisha in search of *the love of my people*, yearning for a sense of belonging I had missed while living away. Every patient who came to the hospital felt like my own—each face held a story that touched me deeply.

But within a few days, harsh realities began to wound me. The presence of brokers in the hospital system was overwhelming. They were indifferent to the suffering around them. For them, this was a profession—a way to fatten their pockets without a trace of empathy. And then there were doctors who had long forgotten that medicine is a service to humanity. They treated their profession as a business, exploiting patients without a second thought. How heartless they were! People look up to doctors as second only to God—and yet, some played with that sacred trust.

One incident shattered whatever hope I had clung to. A patient arrived at the hospital after selling his last piece of land. He believed that once he was cured, he could reclaim what he had lost—for himself, and for his son. But fate had other plans. He neither survived nor left behind anything for his child. The helplessness of that moment seared through me.

Everywhere I looked, there was exploitation, corruption, deception. It broke my spirit. Why does man turn into a beast? Everyone knew what was happening, yet most chose silence—turning their heads, pretending not to see.

Then came a personal blow. One day, I saw Dr. Biswambar humiliate a poor patient, his behaviour laced with greed. For months, he had been exploiting the man, exaggerating a simple condition as something fatal. He kept prescribing unnecessary tests and repeated X-rays. In the end, the patient and his wife left the hospital disappointed and broken. I couldn't bear it. I consulted with other doctors, and within days, the patient fully recovered. But my intervention came at a price.

Dr. Biswambar turned against me. He poisoned the Superintendent's mind with baseless accusations—claiming I had administered improper treatment and was responsible for unrest in the hospital. The situation spiralled. I was punished for doing what was right.

One colleague warned me quietly, "If you point out others' faults, you'll suffer for it. Everyone knows what's going on—but no one dares speak."

Those words churned within me. So, is that it? Will the voices of truth always be silenced, while the corrupt grow stronger? Will we all remain mute witnesses, watching the decay of what should have been sacred?

Over time, the corruption and exploitation around me became impossible to ignore. One day, a tragedy struck that shook me to my core—a 17-year-old boy lost his life due to gross medical negligence. The responsibility lay squarely with Dr. Biswambar and another doctor. But they suppressed the incident with cold efficiency. Many of the staff knew. No one spoke. It was as if protest itself had been outlawed.

That day left me shattered. The anguished faces of the boy's parents haunted me—their cries echoed in my ears long after they had left the hospital. I couldn't sleep. Grief, rage, and helplessness twisted inside me like a storm.

The next morning, fate struck cruelly. I was the one suspended—accused of administering the wrong treatment, of giving the wrong injections. I had sinned against no one. But I was being treated as the sinner.

I was devastated. I couldn't bear to remain in that place a moment longer. And yet—where could I go? I had come to Odisha with hopes in my heart, full of purpose. But now, everything seemed to fall apart.

Whispers spread behind my back. Some pitied me, some advised me to apologize. "Better to bear the burden than lose the job," one said. "You have to stay silent if you want to survive in this system," said another.

Their words only poured salt into the wound. While packing my things, I muttered, "Apologise? To *them*? To such sinners?" A colleague quietly gestured for me to stay quiet, to not say more.

But I had already made up my mind. I walked out, carrying my bag and shattered dignity. They say there is no smoke without fire. But I had learned a bitter truth: in today's world, smoke can rise without a spark—fabricated, manipulated, weaponisoiuyed.

That thought suffocated me.

By the time I reached the bus stand, I still had no plan. With nowhere else to go, I boarded a bus to my uncle's village. I would stay there until I found another job—until life offered me one more chance to begin again.

I couldn't forget the doctors—their exploitation, their corruption, their cruel, dismissive behaviour. And I resented the hospital staff who bent for money, who called injustice by another name and walked hand in hand with the corrupt.

A month passed at my uncle's house. I hadn't received an offer from any of the places I'd applied to. Wherever I went, nothing seemed to hold. I couldn't stay.

Then, quite unexpectedly, Tulasi came one day with a strange request—almost like a whim, but one that carried weight. She said Chinmay Bhai wanted to marry me. He dreamed of building a life with me, if only I agreed.

That month, I had received nothing but warmth from Tulasi, her mother, and Chinmay Bhai. They treated me like family—as if I had always belonged among them. Chinmay Bhai had always been gentle and quiet, never revealing what lay in his heart. He had never hinted at any affection toward me, not once.

Tulasi's eyes brimmed with tears. She clutched my hands tightly, her voice trembling. "Our home will glow if you say yes, Jhara. We want you. All three of us. Chinmay Bhai cannot be happy with anyone else."

I tried to explain that marriage isn't something to be rushed into like a child's game. It calls for conviction, clarity, and commitment. I had never looked at Chinmay Bhai that way. But what stunned me was hearing that he had nurtured this desire for years—quietly, patiently.

Soon, the village was abuzz. Word spread like wildfire. Aunts, uncles, relatives—everyone weighed in, eager to decide for me. But I stood firm, even though I couldn't clearly explain the reason behind my refusal. Something inside me simply could not accept the proposal.

Everything fell into chaos. Arguments, gossip, whispered judgments followed like a shadow. They called me arrogant. They said I had become too proud, too stubborn—no longer the kind of girl they understood. Some whispered, *She's not like our daughters anymore. She's moved around too much, grown too independent, too bold.*

How can she ever be happy with someone as calm and rooted as Chinmay?

Even Chinmay Bhai misunderstood me. He told me I was no longer the simple girl I used to be. Tulasi and her mother, once so affectionate, now looked at me with cold disappointment. The tide had pulled away, leaving their fragile sandcastle in ruins.

I never imagined our bond would break so completely over one unfulfilled proposal. But Tulasi stopped coming to see me. Chinmay Bhai never asked if I was okay. To my uncles and aunts, I had become nothing more than a defiant, difficult girl.

And so, once again, I slipped into that familiar state of isolation—unseen, disconnected, misunderstood.

As the days rolled on, I encountered more and more of the same kind of people: selfish, small-hearted, transactional. There was no escape from the churn of my unsettled thoughts.

For a few months, I stayed in a village across the river, working at Dr. Nita's nursing home. My uncles and aunts raised no objection. Perhaps they simply didn't want me around anymore.

It pained me—how easily people could twist someone's truth. They saw in me what I was not, and I had neither the power nor the opportunity to change their minds.

After that, no one brought up my marriage again.

No one asked.

Not Tulasi.

Not aunty.

Not even Chinmay Bhai.

Some months later, I heard about Chinmay Bhai's marriage. I couldn't help sulking at Tulasi. She hadn't even sent me a card. Was that too much to expect? It wouldn't have been out of place. Then why? Did they truly despise me now? Did they carry some deep, unquestioned doubt about my character? How quickly Tulasi had undone the bond she once so lovingly built! My eyes filled with tears. A quiet humiliation crept into my chest—but still, I wished them well.

Time turns its face without care for anyone's heart. People move along with it, adjusting their pace, forgetting who once mattered. What once felt familiar suddenly becomes distant. Those who once called you their own look away when their needs no longer align with yours. I often questioned my fate—battered by so many highs and lows. My ties of love with many had frayed beyond repair. People I thought were mine had drifted into cold indifference. As these thoughts gnawed at me, I felt a simmering anger—at fate, at God, at the silence of it all.

My uncles and aunts, once warm and welcoming, now barely tolerated my presence. So I stopped visiting them. All I had left was my job at the nursing home. Even that, I feared, could slip away. Nita Madam—stern, sharp-eyed— kept me on edge. What if one day, she misunderstood me? Misfortune rarely comes alone. If I lost this job, where would I go? There was no home waiting, no shelter left for me. I felt like a ghost in the world—unseen, unclaimed.

For days, I drifted through life, absent-minded and numb. Then, out of the blue, Barsha called.

"Come back, Didi," she said gently. "Join us again."

Her voice stirred something deep within me. I remembered the orphanage—the warmth, the noise, the odd comfort of that place. A part of me longed for it again.

But I was in a fix. I didn't know what to do, where to go. Would I go on living with this tangle of wild, confusing thoughts haunting me every day? I finally opened up to Nita Madam, pouring out my doubts and fears.

She listened patiently, then said with quiet encouragement, "You'll have a better future there than here. It's time you moved forward. The past is waiting for you to make peace with it. You know this nursing home is small—I'm running it with the modest goal of serving the people of this underdeveloped area. But your experience, your skills, they deserve a wider canvas. You should join them again, keeping your future in sight."

I was humbled by her words. I felt small before her vastness. How lofty her ideals were, how kind and selfless! There wasn't a trace of narrowness in her heart.

Then she asked, almost suddenly, "Have you thought about your worldly life? You're growing older, dear. How long will you live like this—alone?"

Her words startled me. Had someone said something to her? Many villagers visited the nursing home. Had they whispered about me, repeating the same old gossip?

Perhaps reading my silence, my downcast eyes, she gently placed her hand on my head. "May God bless you with all happiness," she said. "I've seen few nurses as sincere as you. You're meant for something greater—I'm sure of it."

A few days later, I returned to Sikkim.

It felt as if the place had been waiting for me. The same mountains wrapped in mist, the familiar winding roads, the orphanage, the hospital, and the little Apartment where I had spent so many days and nights.

And then, a quiet question rose in my heart—what truly defines "our own" and "the other"?

How fragile, how misleading, that sense of belonging can be. I had such deep affection for Odisha. But what did

I find in return? The place I called home, the people I held dear—especially my uncles—had all turned their backs. All I carried back was a bitter bundle of experience.

Except for Nita Madam—only she had shown me the face of true humanity.

Sikkim!

It was mine—not just in this life, but in many before it.

Everything embraced me—the mountains, the wind, the familiar smells, and the people. Barsha threw her arms around me, weeping unruly tears of joy. Sourav's face lit up with unbound happiness as he watched our reunion. Yes, the touchstone of separation had proven the strength of our bond.

Before returning, my mind had been a storm of questions. *What would the people of Sikkim think of me now? Would they see me as fickle, as someone who abandoned her place and came back as if nothing had happened?*

But none of those fears came true. On the contrary, their warmth overwhelmed me—as though they had been waiting all along for my return.

Barsha now lived with her husband and son in a new house, while I moved back into my old Apartment. People joked, "See? Even the room waited for you—no one else claimed it."

And it was true. Two years had passed, yet the room had remained untouched. I was surprised—but also quietly moved.

Everything seemed just as it was. Yet, in the midst of it all, I longed for one presence.

Sijal Didi.

She wasn't there—but her memory lived on, glowing within me like an ever burning lamp.

I was first assigned duty at the orphanage. Stepping into it felt like entering a garden in full bloom. The children were like blossoms swaying in cradles of laughter and light. I held them in my arms and felt a joy so divine, so complete, that I didn't wish for anything more.

My energy doubled. My desire to work surged. Work, after all, thrives only in spaces where there is no suspicion, no malice, no inner conflict. When the heart is free, the body never tires.

It didn't feel like a job. The hospital, the orphanage—they felt like creations of my own hands. The patients were mine. The walls, the halls, the gentle voices—everything called me home.

Though the language was unfamiliar, the warmth of the staff and the affection of the children had wrapped me in an unspoken bond. I lacked for nothing. We followed a rotation schedule for duty, and the days passed peacefully.

Then, one day, Rista's call startled me. The number was unknown, but the voice—it was hers.

She was returning, she said. With her father.

Suren was unwell—seriously so.

A chill slithered down my spine. I didn't know what to do. I told everything to Barsha and Sourav, who quickly stepped in to arrange for Suren's treatment.

Just two days later, Rista arrived.

She had changed. Life had drawn harsh lines across her young face. She looked older than her age—not just in appearance, but in the gravity of her gaze, in the restraint of her words.

The chatterbox I had once known was gone. In her place stood a girl who had seen too much too soon.

From her cautious conversation, I pieced together a life carved by hardship.

Her grandfather had died—not because of fate, but because of sheer neglect. Though Suren had recovered physically, his peace was shattered by his wife's persistent cruelty.

The home Rista returned to after Sikkim had become a battlefield.

Her mother had brought in a relative—a man who soon took over the household. Rista described him in quiet, clipped tones. He was dangerous. Manipulative. He exploited their vulnerability.

If she protested, she was beaten and silenced.

Suren, broken and jobless, could do nothing. A helpless figure in his own home.

I was heartbroken after hearing how they had spent the last two years. But gathering my strength, I consoled Rista. Suren's treatment resumed, and we were determined to see him recover.

In a quiet moment, I questioned whether I could shoulder such a responsibility. Rista's education, her future, and Suren's fragile life—locked in a battle with illness— were daunting challenges.

At times, I imagined meeting Rista's mother and asking her why she had taken Suren away from the hospital. But in what capacity could I ask such a question? What right did I have? Rista already knew the truth. She knew how that so-called relative—her own mother—had orchestrated everything to her advantage.

Whatever the past, Suren was improving now, thanks to the doctors here. Their dedication made all the difference. Dr. Ayush had also come, having heard about Suren from Sourav. Their unflinching support helped save him.

Rista had informed her mother of Suren's recovery. But there was no response—not even a word of relief.

Perhaps she already knew the truth: after the stroke, Suren would never be the same again. And that's exactly what happened.

I brought Suren to my room. He was little more than a lifeless form—almost a vegetable. Now and then, he would open his eyes. But it seemed that all faces, all relationships, blended into one indistinct blur for him.

One evening, Rista clutched my hands, tears streaming down her cheeks. "Aunty, never leave us alone," she whispered.

I wrapped her in a tight hug.

"Never," I promised. "I never will."

Sometimes, people make life-altering decisions in a single moment, without knowing what the consequences might be. That's what happened with me.

Barsha and Sourav, both dear well-wishers, discussed it with me. "I've heard from a reliable source," Sourav said, "that all of Suren's property is under his wife's control. She didn't leave him with anything. Only the house near the hospital—that he had registered in Rista's name long ago— is truly his."

Then he asked, "Jhara, can you spend your whole life with Rista?"

"Yes," I answered without hesitation. There was no pretense in my voice. For me, it would be a blessing—a gift— to share my life with her. Nothing could make me happier.

"But what about Mr. Suren?" Barsha asked gently. "Will he never get better?"

Sourav replied, "If he had stayed here and continued treatment, by now he might have regained his speech. His current condition is entirely his wife's doing. Taking him away was a terrible decision. Honestly, it's a miracle he survived the last two years."

It all felt like a movie—the kind where the plot twists to leave you stunned. Barsha, Sourav, and I sat silently, listening as Rista narrated everything with a maturity beyond her years.

Could a woman really be that heartless? The truth was undeniable—Richa Madam's relationship with her business partner, the control he exerted over her, and their inhumane treatment of Suren all came to light.

Our hearts were with Suren.

30

The house registered in Rista's name was being cleaned and set up. I arranged the drawing room, two bedrooms, and the kitchen to my liking. This place—I had accepted it as the final refuge of my life. I was resolved to raise Rista with all the care and love I had within me. And I would serve Suren with the same devotion.

Sourav's words echoed constantly in my mind: *"Jhara, only your care will keep him alive."*

But his words had left behind a shadow of fear. He hadn't said Suren would be cured. He hadn't promised that I would one day live happily with him.

So, then… was Suren just an uncertain future for me?

I had informed my siblings and brothers-in-law of my decision. "Suren and Rista are my family now," I had said. "They are my future."

Though they were clearly displeased, their disapproval did not shake me. I had made up my mind.

I arranged for a neurosurgeon and a physiotherapist for Suren. He lay in his bed with a distant, unfocused gaze, unable to recognize even Rista or me. A strange mind in a familiar body.

But still—it was a new life. Once more.

Barsha and Sourav stood beside me like walls of strength.

Then one day, a sudden phone call from Akash Bhai

caught me by surprise. "Jhara dear," he said, "I have good news for you."

How fleeting the mind is—faster than wind. The joy in his voice took me to places I hadn't dared to dream of in a long time. Was he about to become a father?

But no. "We're coming back to India," he said. "Your Bhauja has changed. She feels lost here, like a fish out of water. She doesn't have the courage to face you yet."

His tone made me smile. I invited him to visit me. Though he didn't object to my choices, I could sense some unspoken worry in his silence—concerns he hadn't voiced.

Life moved on. I balanced my duty with caring for Rista and Suren.

Rista wasn't a child anymore. She had a wisdom beyond her years. She helped in every way she could, always checking if I had eaten, always watching over me. I would hold her tight and whisper, *"Ah, my little mother…"*

A deep river of love flowed quietly inside me. I no longer indulged in regrets or restless thoughts. I learned to live in the living present.

It is the past that weighs us down with longing. It is the future that unsettles us with its uncertainties. But the present—if embraced fully—never disappoints.

Of late, no one had called me. Perhaps they no longer had the time—or the space in their hearts.

Only Sony Apa, Biny Apa, and Gouri Bhauja occasionally checked in. But their words often felt like barbed needles. They spoke to me like I was still a child, as though I would return home just because they asked.

But they didn't know—I had walked a long, blistering road under a burning sun to reach this shelter. This peace. This roof. What more could I possibly want?

Still, their words hurt. I hadn't expected Akash Bhai—

my own brother—to ask, "Are you Rista's caretaker?" the moment he saw me.

"What do you gain from all this?" he asked. "Doctors say he'll never recover. What relation do you have with this family?"

I answered softly, "I feel my connection with them goes back many lifetimes."

He looked at me, concerned. "And will you live like this forever? No one knows what the future holds, Jhara."

I had no answer. Only one wish: that Rista hadn't overheard.

Thankfully, she didn't understand Odia yet. But she was eager to learn. She'd asked me several times.

Yet sometimes, language isn't necessary. Feelings find their own way.

Later that day, I found Rista asleep, her head resting gently on her father's chest. She often did that—studied beside him, fed him with her own hands, watched him with tearful eyes. What thoughts flickered through her mind? What questions stayed unanswered?

I looked at Suren. His face looked so innocent—like a sleeping child. I pulled the sheet over him gently.

How helpless, how dependent, we humans truly are.

Suren opened his eyes, staring blankly at the ceiling. Those eyes, once full of dreams with me at their centre, now held only emptiness.

Once, he had painted dreams in this very house. We had planned a future—tiny, colourful dreams gathered like seashells.

How cruel fate is. This tragedy had struck while he was hanging my photograph.

In all my life, I had never met a man like Suren. His

gentleness had drawn me toward him. Those few days we shared—I would cradle them forever in my heart.

The next morning, I prepared breakfast for Akash Bhai. He was getting ready to leave. He tried to decline, but I insisted.

Rista looked thrilled. The love in her eyes for him bloomed visibly. She had woken up early just to help me—an unusual joy lighting up her holiday morning.

I couldn't understand why my sisters didn't offer even a word of kindness for her. Why couldn't they say, *"Jhara, you've done the right thing. At least this innocent girl will have a chance at happiness, because of your love. You're raising her like a mother."*

But no one said that.

Instead, it was the same questions, the same old doubts.

Akash Bhai said, "I'll return, but not without worrying about you. I can't be at peace."

Rista heard our voices, grew quiet, and slipped away. Her face was downcast. I felt a wave of pain wash over me.

I couldn't hold it in. My voice trembled as I folded my hands before him. "Please," I said, "don't speak about this anymore."

He stood frozen, stunned into silence.

I turned and walked into Suren's room.

There, I found Rista, silently weeping, her face pressed against her father's hands. Perhaps she thought I would leave with Akash Bhai.

I knelt beside her.

"No, Rista. I will not leave. I will never leave you. You are my dear one—my life. I will be with you always. You and Suren are the only truth I know. Everything else… everything else is an illusion."

My voice broke, and my scream seemed to tear through Bhai's imagination.

He came in quietly.

Placing his hand gently on Rista's head, he drew her into his lap and wiped her tears.

"From today," he said softly, "you're not just Jhara's daughter. You are ours too—our Rista. Our own."

I turned back to Suren. Two tears had rolled from his eyes. I wiped them away, smoothed his dishevelled hair, and looked at Bhai.

"See, Bhai… how helpless Suren is. How could I possibly leave him? Forgive me. I know you all have suffered because of me. But please… please forgive me."

I broke down, sobbing.

Akash Bhai stood there, wordless. His voice, his judgment, all lost in the wilderness of that moment.

Rista, still holding her father's hand, reached out with her other hand—and held mine.

That single clasp was enough. It spoke of trust, of love, of quiet strength.

And in that tender triangle of joined hands—mine, Suren's, and Rista's—I found the only truth I needed. The only family I would ever want.

Black Eagle Books

www.blackeaglebooks.org
info@blackeaglebooks.org

Black Eagle Books, an independent publisher, was founded
as a nonprofit organization in April, 2019. It is our mission
to connect and engage the Indian diaspora and the world at
large with the best of works of world literature published
on a collaborative platform, with special emphasis on
foregrounding Contemporary Classics and New Writing.

www.ingramcontent.com/pod-product-compliance
Lightning Source LLC
Chambersburg PA
CBHW020417110726
47899CB00006B/2024